LOST WITHOUT TRACE

"Linda, I've heard stories about ships being found at sea, in perfect condition, but with everyone who was aboard"—he hesitated over the word—"vanished." He started to laugh, but the look on Linda Colee's face stopped the first sign of that amusement.

"The stories are true. I know, because I was involved with several of them." She shuddered with memories. "It was summer—the last two weeks of July. The weather through the whole area was perfect. The satellite pictures—we went back to study those later—confirmed everything."

He saw her stiffen slightly. "And in those two weeks, we found four ships—all of them within a hundred miles of the Florida coast—drifting. Without a soul on board."

"You mean abandoned?"

"I do *not* mean abandoned," she said with anger. "I mean that we found the ships—I personally boarded two of them—and not a single living thing was aboard. Not a human being, not a dog or a cat or a bird. Nothing that was alive. And there had been no weather at any time. . . ."

MARTIN CAIDIN

THREE CORNERS TO NOWHERE

THREE CORNERS TO NOWHERE

A Baen Book

Baen Publishing Enterprises
260 Fifth Avenue
New York, N.Y. 10001

First Baen printing, April 1988

ISBN: 0-671-65401-2

Cover art by Miro

Printed in the United States of America

Distributed by
SIMON & SCHUSTER
1230 Avenue of the Americas
New York, N.Y. 10020

This book is for
Frank Quentin Ray,
who's cut a few corners himself.

Chapter 1

She was that kind of woman. Stunning. Long-haired slenderness complimented a high, thrusting bustline. Flashing green eyes above a wicked smile. Twenty-six years old and a knockout. And Rena Kim Maynard had other things going for her. An oceanographer, a skilled diver, an accomplished pilot. An unshakable self-confidence whetted by those looks, brains . . . and money. Some people call that power. Whatever, Rena Kim had it all. Her body made her athletics all the more fascinating.

As she wheeled her Corvette around the circled drive of Fort Lauderdale Executive Airport that March morning, she saw through the fence the gleaming executive jet of Positronics, Inc., her father's computer firm. She parked in the reserved slot before the offices of Solar Aviation and walked, tanned and lithe, into the executive pilots' lounge.

Margo Jackson threw her arms about Rena Kim. The black model was joining Rena Kim for a two-week flying vacation through the Bahamas and the Caribbean. If the urge reached them, they might continue on down to South America. Or wing it across the Atlantic to the Riviera. Or Majorca. At their disposal was the Gulfstream II, a jet that cruised the lower stratosphere at well over five hundred miles an hour. Any whimsy lay within easy grasp.

James "Rocky" Lavagetti emerged from the flight-operations room and threw them a casual salute. "Morning, Miss Maynard. Your guests are waiting for you in the airplane. I'll have your bags brought aboard."

Lavagetti had come to Positronics as chief pilot after a full career in the Air Force. He had nine thousand hours logged in his books, of which seven thousand were in jets. He was too old for the airlines as a new career, and he'd looked to civilian life with misgivings. Then the personnel office of Positronics tagged the tall, neat, intelligent man as perfect for their needs and made an offer he couldn't resist. Lavagetti was married, with three children; he preferred not to rock any boats. He saved his passion for flight machinery rather than for the president's daughter or her equally compelling friends.

Rena Kim and Margo crossed the flight line, oblivious of the admiring looks of mechanics and pilots. They waved to copilot Art Younger, who was giving the Grumman its customary painstaking preflight check. Younger had come to Positronics from the Navy, with more than two thousand hours in a variety of jet aircraft. Stocky, sandy-haired, with a grin that sliced age from his twenty-eight years, Younger too was married, but he never let it bother his life with the company. Still, so far he'd managed to keep his lusting to himself. He knew a wrong move would gain him Lavagetti's boot into the ranks of the unemployed. So he played it cool.

The two women climbed the stairs into the cabin and greeted the two guests already there: Nikki Stephenson and her date for the flying vacation, Dr. Harold Mazurski. They both satisfied Rena Kim's appetite for the unusual. Nikki was not just an outstanding attorney; she was pure genius. No shortage of looks or build, either, but her physical attributes ran a poor second to her commanding personality. Few men could keep up with Nikki. Damned few even tried. Some men have instinctive recognition of the barracuda.

A man with that recognition, but also a casual contempt for its existence, was Nikki's companion for the two weeks. Dr. Harold Mazurski notched several levels higher than Nikki in the genius category. The battle between them assumed a more equal level through Nikki's speed in sizing up, meeting, or even creating situations to her liking. Dr. Mazurski was the intellectual heavyweight, but Nikki was much faster with the infighting.

Harold Mazurski remained blissfully unaware of the tension generated by his presence aboard the Gulfstream II. Not among those at the Florida airfield, but those within the executive offices of Positronics, Inc., in Maryland. The Positronics laboratories, where Dr. Mazurski had spent years developing a revolutionary type of electronic computer based on the operating principles of the human mind. Not the brain; the *mind*. The tension was shared in a special-projects office buried deep within the Pentagon, which had financed the biocybernetics program and shouldered the responsibility for its success. The man who had nursed to life a computer that thought it was God was cavorting off to sunny islands in a hot jet aircraft filled with beautiful women and a well-stocked bar.

Dr. Harold Mazurski didn't *look* all that important. He could have posed for an *Esquire* ad for new shoes. The scientist showed prematurely thinning light hair. He weighed in at just above flyweight; 152 pounds on a frame nearly six feet tall is dangerously akin to cadaverous. Yet he was supple and in excellent physical condition.

And he *was* a bloody genius. His mind moved through the ether of physics as easily as an accomplished pianist runs his fingers along a keyboard. He had mastered algebra, geometry, calculus, cybernetics, differential equations, probability, heuristics, the topological sciences, biochemistry, neuronite systems, and God knew how many related and intertwined disciplines. And he was the master of the new biocybernetics system, his intellectual awareness linked with that of the electronic mind coming to life under his direction. If anything happened to him, the whole damned computer effort could well disappear down the nearest drain. Yet, the man had earned (*needed*, said the staff psychologist) his time away from the electronic mind. The Positronics company and the Pentagon had cursed the psychologist soundly, but had no choice.

If there had to be a vacation trip, Charles Maynard of Positronics would control it. He discussed the matter with his daughter, promised her the company's Grumman jet and all expenses, received assurance of the female company selected for the scientist, and then reminded Dr. Mazurski that the staggering insurance policy on his life imposed certain severe restrictions on his travel, among them the requirement that any air travel be done only with aircraft and crew at or above commercial-airline standards. Which were met by the Gulfstream II owned by Positronics.

The passenger list, for the moment, was complete. Three others would be picked up at two other stops in Florida before the jet winged to the southeast and the vacation islands.

Lavagetti and Younger were still firing up the powerful jets when the steward made ready the first round of drinks. Wilfredo Pérez stood high on the list of prized possessions of Charles Maynard. His paycheck reflected the fact that the steward spoke five languages fluently and was quite expert in handling customs and government details in the Bahamas and the Caribbean. Much more to the point, he stood ready at any time to meet the extremely personal needs of Charles Maynard. Pérez had escaped when a young man from the clutches of Castro, and Maynard had befriended him.

Nancy Jameson could not, except for her stewardess uniform, be told from any member of Rena Kim's select crowd. Twenty-four years old, five feet five inches tall, and a splendidly distributed 122 pounds, the young blond woman had flown for three years as stewardess with Trans World Airlines. Not quite one year before this moment, she had caught the eye of Charles Maynard, who had offered her the job on the Gulfstream II at three times her TWA salary. It wasn't all peaches and cream, for she had to put up with Rena Kim, and a millionaire's daughter, especially one with long nails, can be very trying.

Lavagetti wheeled the thirty-ton airplane smartly onto the active runway, lined up, and braked gently to a halt. Far ahead he watched a Baron ease from the active. He was ready when the tower gave him the word. "Gulfstream Triple-Six Delta, cleared for immediate takeoff." To his right, Art Younger acknowledged the call. "Triple-Six rolling." Lavagetti brought the twin throttles forward in a steady motion, and when the iron bird trembled to rush forward from the howling jets, released the brakes. The Gulfstream II took the runway smoothly, and Lavagetti rotated the nose-wheel off the macadam barely four thousand feet from first motion. They went into the air in textbook fashion, and Younger cleaned up the bird, calling off gear and flaps retraction. "Triple-Six Delta right climbout," Lavagetti said into the mike. "Cleared right turn, Triple-Six. Have a nice day. Exec out." It would be a short flight, a fast slice across the peninsula to Tampa to pick up a passenger.

Lavagetti eased to the right of an early-morning cumulus, the yoke barely moving beneath his fingers. This low, he preferred to fly the Grumman himself rather than dump into the autopilot. He listened idly as Younger confirmed their clearance to Tampa International and gave him the active runway and winds. Everything was neatly in the groove, and the morning air was pleasantly calm. Lavagetti flicked off the seatbelt sign in the cabin behind them. Time enough for another drink, anyway.

The cabin was certainly made for drinking. Or whatever. Thirty-four feet long from the cockpit door to the lavatory, it seated no more than thirteen passengers. So they could relax in comfort. The Gulfstream was a flat-floor, high-ceiling, posh bird with deeply cushioned seats, two divans, a fully stocked wet bar, stereo, movies, lavatory, vanity, walk-in baggage compartment, a marvel of foldaway tables, and, when called for, two privately enclosed bed compartments. Queen-size, thank you.

When Lavagetti considered the marvel beneath his hands, it seemed almost too much to believe. The best piston fighter he'd ever flown, the great P-51 Mustang, couldn't hold a candle to this twin-jet flying carpet. It had more power than twenty of the great P-51 fighters! Lavagetti could arrow the Gulfstream away from the ground at nearly a mile every minute. In splendid air-conditioned and pressurized comfort, the sleek Grumman could soar to 43,000 feet, there to rush with silken smoothness through rarefied air at 590 miles an hour. And if he lost an engine, his passengers wouldn't even know it. The iron bird had power to spare, to handle any emergency they might anticipate. *You're one hell of a machine, baby*, Lavagetti said in silent admiration.

Art Younger was on the radio working radar and then the tower, with no bidding from the pilot to his left. Lavagetti brought her around in the gentlest of wide turns and locked her onto the invisible rail leading along the final onto the runway. It was another of his usual "paint-'em-on" landings. Wilfredo Pérez often boasted of his pilot that Lavagetti was the only man he knew who could touch down a thirty-ton jet without clinking the ice cubes in the highball glasses. They rolled from the active to the executive terminal, and Younger climbed from his seat to extend the sliding stairway.

Through his side window Lavagetti watched their passenger approach the airplane and with an athletic bound start up the steps. Tall, rangy, ruggedly good-looking, Greg Harrison was one of the better professional tennis players in the country. Lavagetti understood that Harrison could have been *the* best, except for his willingness to spend as much time with certain spectators as he did breaking his ass on the courts. Lavagetti thought of Rena Kim and Margo in the cabin behind him and grinned.

Art Younger retracted the steps, checked the locking mechanism, and returned to the cockpit. With everything still running and ground control alerted, they moved back to the active, waited out an Eastern 727, and eased smoothly back into the Florida skies. Another short hop, angling east-northeast this time, to Daytona Beach. Lavagetti had scheduled topping off their tanks at Daytona Beach, which meant shutting down the bird.

The newcomers came aboard with plenty of time to spare. Lavagetti recognized Jacques DuFour, the French news photographer who'd been in a dozen wars, his camera recording astonishing and impossible scenes that had made him world-famous. DuFour was the kind of man who never sounded real. He was handsome to the point of being dazzling; broad-shouldered, cleft-chinned, wavy blond hair, flat-bellied, brave, and intelligent. Epitome of the lady-killer.

Behind DuFour walked Albert Deutsch. And with his coming, Lavagetti sensed a wrong note, a discord in the otherwise generally harmonious structure of the group. Deutsch was the sales manager and partner in a West German electronics firm that did heavy business with Positronics. He was horribly predictable in his looks—square-jawed, cropped hair, a promise of growing girth. But brilliant, and no fool. He was too much like a water buffalo to suit Lavagetti. Placid enough until cornered, then known to gore to death even a full-sized and hungry tiger. Lavagetti shrugged to himself. None of his business.

Yet, it could become his business. He'd had more than one party aboard this aircraft that had gotten out of hand. A slap in the face or squeezed nails in the groin to quiet down someone was fine if the passengers kept their affair to themselves. But a knock-down brawl was something else again, and not even old man Maynard would ever fault Lavagetti for taking whatever steps he deemed necessary to control his passengers. And saving their lives in the bargain.

Lavagetti received the nod from Art Younger. They'd been fueled, the passengers were aboard with drinks in their hands, the baggage was loaded, and Younger had sealed the cabin door. Lavagetti went through the motions by rote *and* his inevitable checklist. One part of his mind clicked in machinelike fashion to bring the Grumman to life. Another part thought of Rena Kim and the way she had once again set up an unstable condition among her guests: the "odd man out." Three women and four men, and that was *it*. The unbreakable rule aboard this aircraft was that no member of the crew would ever mix socially, in the air or on the ground, with any guests of hers. So the odd man out could only frustrate himself with the presence of Nancy Jameson, a stewardess who could easily grace the centerpiece fold of *Playboy*.

They were rolling along the taxiway when Lavagetti recalled the surprise Rena Kim had set up for her guests. He thumbed the transmit button. "Ground, Triple-Six. You people have a hot line to Patrick? Over."

"Affirmative, Triple-Six. What you need?"

"Ah, Ground from Triple-Six. The Cape has a shot scheduled for, ah, sixteen minutes from now. Can you check with them on the count for us?"

"Triple-Six, wilco. Stand by one." They came back just as Lavagetti turned from the taxiway to hold up before rolling onto the active. "Triple-Six from Daytona Beach Ground. Roger the count. Fourteen minutes to go."

"Thank you, Ground. Triple-Six Delta going to tower frequency. Good day, sir." Lavagetti thumbed the tower frequency and was told to hold position. A DC-9 and a 727 rumbled ponderously down from the sky, and the tower told them to roll onto the active and hold. When they received the nod to take off, Lavagetti held the Grumman down until they were well past the point where the huge Boeing touched the ground. The wake turbulence from those monsters could throw them about like a cork in Colorado rapids. No sweat; he held her down to well beyond the danger point and rotated, letting the wings grab air. He took her up in a steep-climbing turn over the Atlantic, easing to the northern edge of the restricted area of the Kennedy Space Center.

Younger tuned in to a local radio station with a newsman chanting the final minutes of the count-down for the Titan IIIC rocket on its pad. They fed the broadcast into the cabin speakers, and Lavagetti picked up the cabin mike. "Ladies and gentlemen, at thirty seconds we will fly directly to the east. So you can see the rocket from the windows along the right side of the aircraft." He switched off and brought binoculars to his eyes. There it was, a slab-sided toy on its pedestal more than two miles below them and off to the side. At forty seconds he rolled onto a heading of ninety degrees and held the Grumman steady. The count rolled away, and the launch pad disappeared in a brilliant gout of flame.

A thick pillar of white smoke from the solid boosters rose steadily, bending away from the vertical, led by a lengthening sheet of dazzling fire. Those aboard the Gulfstream II watched wide-eyed as the monster ripped past them, a mindless howl of naked energy. It tore away, higher and higher. They watched the big solids wink out, saw the shock wave of small explosives jettisoning the wasted cylinders, the stabbing light of the main stage coming to life. Several more seconds of looking into a bright sky, and it was gone, leaving behind the twisting rope of the smoke trail.

Lavagetti turned back to what lay before him. "In a couple minutes that thing will be in orbit at eighteen thousand miles an hour." He shook his head. "Around the world in ninety minutes flat."

"And you get good gas mileage, too," Younger quipped with a straight face.

Lavagetti laughed with him, told his copilot to get to work to clear them through the Air Defense Identification Zone on their way out from the coastline. Patrick Air Force Base took their flight plan and cleared them through the ADIZ, and they were on their way. Now it was time to let Grumman's pride and joy do its job. Lavagetti set up the iron bird for the long climb to altitude and brought in the autopilot. The Gulfstream seemed to quiver a fraction of a second as control passed from human to electronic brain. Only that fleeting sense of change. The jet settled down and locked into the groove, climbing steadily, eating up the miles below. A beautiful morning. Lavagetti stretched slowly, cracking his knuckles for sheer pleasure. The sky directly above them deepened slowly, the dark-blue and purple shades gaining in clarity as they left the greater mass of the atmosphere below. Air Traffic Control changed their planned cruising altitude to 33,000 feet, but up here this morning it was no nevermind. A solid sky, unquivering, unbothered with clouds. Lavagetti leveled off at thirty-three grand, scanned the panel to be certain everything was in the slot, and eased his seat back from the yoke. "Next stop Puerto Rico," he murmured, and Younger, still busy with paperwork, nodded.

Lavagetti waited twenty minutes, figured that was enough time for Nancy to attend to the needs of the passengers, and buzzed her for coffee. He got back a single short response, their signal that she'd be along within a few minutes. Six by the clock, Lavagetti noticed as the door into the cockpit opened, and Nancy handed them coffee and doughnuts.

It began then.

Nancy leaned forward between the two seats, looking ahead of the airplane. She never missed the opportunity to study the world from this remarkable vantage, as it seemed to unroll slowly toward them. At their height it was possible sometimes to see the first signs of the curvature of the earth; she tried to imagine what it was like another hundred miles above her, as the astronauts saw a planet from which all straight lines had vanished.

Then she frowned. Before her stretched a world unlike any she'd ever seen before. She had flown this same route before; she was familiar with the broad sweep of the south Atlantic, the emerald island shapes spreading forward, the clouds hugging the low distant horizon. But none of it was there.

It felt as though they were flying within some enormous milk bottle. A creamy, yellow-tinged hue, faintly frightening to the eye. She had flown in fog and rain and clouds, even at night over the oceans, when nothing could be discerned through any window. But nothing like *this*. She turned to the pilot. "Rocky"—she gestured—"what is it?"

Lavagetti let his eyes sweep what should have been the horizon. A smudge showed along the edge of the earth, and the only features worthy of the name were high cloud buildups at some indeterminate distance.

Art Younger stirred from his paperwork, glancing through the windshield. "It happens," he murmured. "High-altitude haze, that sort of thing. Sometimes you get sand blown from the Sahara. That drought has been going on for years now. Things like that, Nancy."

She shook her head. "But there's no horizon," she protested.

And there wasn't. The last vestiges of a visible planet had faded from sight. It was as if . . . It *was* being cut off from all the world they knew. There was no distant horizon, no ocean below, no clouds visible anywhere, no islands. Only that creamy-yellow glow in every direction.

Lavagetti drew up short within himself. In *every* direction? That was impossible. Ridiculous. . . . The thought died stirring in his brain, for he had looked upward, confident of that deep-blue-purple sky marking the beginning of space. *It wasn't there.* Just that incredible and now-frightening creamy—*what?*—in the world above, below, to the sides, ahead, and behind them.

Instinctively Lavagetti moved his seat forward so that he would be within instant reach of the controls. *All* the controls. He didn't bother even to glance at Art Younger to his right. "Art, put away your papers." He said it as casually as the words could come to his lips, but he was on the edge of a mental seat, and he didn't like it. Still, he didn't want Nancy going back to the passengers with her face showing signs of distress.

"No sweat," Lavagetti said easily, throwing a quick smile in Nancy's direction. "We'll break away from this stuff, whatever it is, when we start down."

He didn't fool her, and they both knew it. Those small signs of his: coming back to the controls, scanning the gauges, telling Younger in a voice unmistakable with its command to get rid of his goddamned papers and pay attention. . . .

Nancy felt a shudder sweep through her body. She rested a hand lightly on Lavagetti's shoulder. "I . . . I'd better be getting back to the cabin."

The pilot nodded.

Nancy turned, then stopped. Her voice was quiet against the hiss of air rushing past the Gulfstream. "This would happen," she said slowly, just a touch of strain coming through, "right when we're in the middle of the Devil's Triangle." Lavagetti turned sharply, but she was already on her way through the door.

Several moments later he forced himself to relax. That incredible all-enveloping yellow glow, or haze, or whatever the hell it was, still surrounded them, still banished the visible world. But Lavagetti refused to be rattled. He'd been flying long enough, had been in enough damned emergencies, not to be spooked by something crazy like this. Crazy didn't mean dangerous, and keeping his wits about him was more important than any rash action. The iron bird checked out perfectly. Everything was in the green, right where it belonged. Lavagetti leaned forward to take a doughnut from the tray. He bit deeply and sipped coffee. He glanced at his copilot and chuckled.

"I've been through what they call the Devil's Triangle, or the Bermuda Triangle, or whatever name they give it," he said easily, "for years. Must have flown through here a hundred times, maybe three times that much. And you hear more damned stories. . ." He swallowed coffee, attacked the doughnut, shaking his head slightly. "You hang around the local airports long enough, and you'll hear anything and everything before you're through. . . ."

Art Younger laughed with him, but he didn't believe the sounds his own throat made. He didn't care how many times Rocky had flown through this place. He did *not* like the sky about them. Things didn't go that screwy without some explanation, and nothing he could bring to mind fit even remotely.

"Maybe so," he said finally, frowning, "but you got to admit we've never seen anything like this before." He squinted and leaned closer to the windshield. "Goddamnit, Rocky, all you can see is the wingtip. There's *nothing* out there."

"I've seen this sort of thing before," Lavagetti replied. He didn't avert the sudden stare from his copilot. "You get a lot of this stuff in the Arctic," Lavagetti went on. "It's a whiteout. Or like one. You'd swear there wasn't any world anymore. You can't see *anything*. The whole world's white."

Younger grunted. "There's only one problem," he

said slowly, looking outside and frowning. "This isn't the Arctic."

"Drink your coffee," Lavagetti said with a laugh. But Art Younger's body had frozen where he sat, the coffeecup poised in his hand. "Now what the hell's the matter?" Lavagetti asked brusquely.

"The mag compass," Younger said with a hoarse whisper. "Jesus, Rocky, *look* at it!"

Lavagetti turned to look. The magnetic compass was spinning, whirling around so fast the numbers were blurred. And that wasn't possible. It . . .

The jet seemed to wallow. There wasn't much to it, really, but the strange sinking sensation was so out of place . . .

Something wrong with the autopilot, figured Lavagetti. He had his hands and feet on the controls. He locked his eyes on the flight instruments.

"Okay," he said, his tone brisk, no-nonsense. "Autopilot off." Younger repeated the command for confirmation, switched off the system, to return control directly to the pilot. Lavagetti now flew manually. He resisted the impulse to grip the yoke, kept the controls lightly, caressingly in his hands. But Art Younger, watching him from the right seat, knew instantly that something was wrong. Very wrong. . . .

Lavagetti sensed the question. He moved the yoke ever so carefully, lightly. "It's . . . it's the feel," Lavagetti said finally, his voice flat. "The controls feel like . . . mush."

He moved the yoke gently, cautiously, to start a left turn. But there was no familiar response. The Grumman wallowed in a sickening slide. "Jesus," swore the pilot, "it's like there's no air out there . . . like we're twice as high as we are. . . . She's not responding. . . . We'd better get the hell out of here, start down now." He was totally involved, every fiber committed to his moves with the aircraft.

"Punch in the RNAV," he said, his voice crisp again. "Get us lined up to the nearest field. We'll take anything . . ."

As he talked he eased forward on the yoke to lower the nose, to start the Gulfstream on its descent to a more familiar world. Younger's voice hit him like a sandbag full in the face.

"No readout. Mag compass is spinning, the gyro is wandering and won't lock. Omni needles—they're . . . floating. Damnit, the ADF has no response . . . no signal, no voice. . . . DME has no pickup. I'm squawking emergency on the transponder, but nothing . . . it's like nothing can get through to us. . . ."

They turned, stared at each other. It was as if the airplane had been thrust into some impossible place in sky and time, where electronic devices suddenly became so much junk. The RNAV system provided them an electronic pathway in the sky. Signals flashed between the Gulfstream and ground stations gave them headings to fly, told them their speed over the earth, announced to them their exact position in time and space over the earth's surface. Now it was junk. The magnetic compass had become a spinning dervish. Even the gyroscopic compass, about as reliable an instrument as could be devised by man, drifted aimlessly, as though it had been built by idiots. Their ADF, the radio direction finder, worked on a wavelength different from other radios; it responded to the same sort of signals sent out by AM radio-broadcasting stations. It was so reliable it had been known for years to pilots as the "old bird dog" for finding the way home. Now it refused to respond to signals, was as useless as if it had rusted solid in its container. Even their DME system, the device that measured distance between the airplane and a ground station, had gone electronically mute. The transponder, which flashed a powerful radio signal to be picked up by ground radar stations, had lost strength and effectiveness; whatever, it was also so much junk. The omni needles, another standby system for determining position in flight, had failed utterly.

If ever there was an electronic vacuum, this was it. All their expensive and elaborate devices had no more strength to them than a human voice speaking in the vacuum on the moon.

And at the moment, in complete silence, each saw the golden reflections on the face of the other. The golden light that reflected and washed over them and metal and glass and . . .

They looked ahead, disbelieving, yet knowing it was real. All about them, in a cloudless sky, huge sheets of lightning blazed from as high as they could see, disappearing far down into the impossible yellow world far, far below.

Chapter 2

"Man, she's right on the money. They had a perfect count. She's climbing good, a real clean bird. We should get first indication any moment. . . ." Sergeant Charles Hewitt of the 3199th Range Tracking Squadron, Air Force Eastern Test Range, hunched closer to his plotting board, adjusting a display brightness control. As he studied the display, a small light blip appeared suddenly along the lower-left corner of the board. "There she is," he called out to the other technicians in the remote-tracking station. Hewitt nodded to himself with satisfaction. The Titan was bending sharply along its line of flight, and the digital readout flashed with constantly changing numerals the increasing velocity and height of the rocket. Hewitt enjoyed working the tracking site when one of the big birds tore down the slot. And this one was headed way out. A big weather satellite lifting to synchronous orbit 22,300 miles above the equator. He listened to the calm chanting of time and performance readouts and . . .

"*We have a warning light.*" The voice repeated itself at once. "We have a warning light. We've lost one of the ARIA's."

"Ben, take my board," Hewitt barked to a technician. He spun away from the tracking plot to Smitty, who'd called out the warning. Smitty handled the tracking and communications of the Boeing C-135 jets, the Apollo Range and Instrumentation Aircraft that took over the telemetering of the climbing rocket when it was out of range of the ground station.

"It's not the rocket," Smitty confirmed unnecessarily.

"I can see that," Hewitt said, impatient. "What happened with the ARIA?"

Smitty shrugged. "It's crazy. See for yourself."

Hewitt was studying the grid plot in front of Smitty. And it was crazy.

"See?" Smitty went on. The radarscopes were a mess of sparkling, glittering notes. Bright streaks flashed across the dull glowing plastic. Hewitt tapped Smitty's shoulder and pointed. "What the hell is that?"

"Hewitt!" Another man called from across the room. "We're getting telemetry from the Titan, but no tracking with the target." Hewitt turned, puzzled. He was accustomed to minor glitches, the small problems that always attended the operation of complex electronic gear. But what the hell was happening now? First an ARIA just fell into some electronic hole, and now they couldn't track the rocket. "Johnson, how's the cable down the line?" Hewitt called to his communications man.

"We're on," came the reply.

"Pass the word," Hewitt ordered. "Ask them what they're getting on the rocket and the ARIA's. Soon as you finish that, sound the alert on the ARIA we lost." Hewitt turned back to Smitty. "Anything on skin track with that aircraft?"

Smitty shook his head. "Double negative on that, Sarge. No transponder, and no skin track. It's like she vanished."

Hewitt really didn't have much confidence in skin tracking. With all that crap fouling Smitty's scope, they weren't going to get a thing by following the big Boeing with radar bounced off the metal surface. Hewitt picked up the red phone to the Range Safety Office on Cape Canaveral and passed on the word. "Can you people pick up that ARIA on the military satellite net?"

"Hewitt, this is Captain Larkin. Did you get any sign of a Mayday signal before or since you lost the ARIA?"

"Negative," Hewitt answered. "All we got is a snowstorm on the scopes. From the way I see it, Captain, the problem is somewhere between this station and the ARIA. Let us know if you hear anything, will you, sir? We'll do the same from this end. . . . Right. Thanks."

A sergeant came in through the door with a blast of midday heat and handed Hewitt a message slip. "We've got a priority request from the FAA. Anybody pick up a call or transponder signal from a civilian aircraft?" The sergeant glanced about the room, received no confirmation. "They're on the lookout for a Gulfstream II, call sign Triple-Six Delta."

A technician made a sour face. "We can't follow our target, we got an ARIA wandering around the ocean, and you come in pissin' about a civilian bird. For chrissakes, ain't they on a flight plan?"

"Course they're on a flight plan. But the automatic report failed to come in from their last checkpoint. They're at angels three-three, so this station should have had an indication of some kind." He looked around the room again; nothing. He turned back to Hewitt. "Hey, they're really riding our ass on this one. Give that bird a call on their flight-plan freqs, will you, Sarge?"

Hewitt nodded, set it up. They made six attempts to contact the civilian aircraft by voice radio. Nothing. Hewitt shared the other man's uncertainty. "It is kinda crazy," he said after a long pause. "If their track is right, I mean, if they're holding to their flight plan, then they should be within sixty miles of us right now. And we ain't gettin' a thing." He pointed to the radarscopes, a sneer on his face. "And all that fancy crawdad stuff ain't worth a tinker's damn right now. You better tell the FAA we got nothing coming in on auto report, we can't get transponder pickup, we got no skin track, and we can't raise them on voice. Anything else I can do for you?"

The other man made a face. "What's your next offer, Hewitt? Cancer?"

"We've got a target!"

They went immediately to Smitty's console. "I'm getting skin track," Smitty said quickly. "Nothing on transponder. There. Got him good now." They studied the blip coming in sharp and clear. "Big bird," Smitty said. "From the looks of the report, it should be the ARIA." They watched for several minutes. "Okay, we've got a solid track now. It looks like he's descending. Right on, man, he's heading straight for Nassau if I've got him pegged." Smitty turned to Hewitt. "From all the signs, they had trouble, Sarge, and they're under Mayday condition. It might be a good idea to sound the alarm."

Hewitt clapped Smitty's shoulder. "Good move." He went to his emergency line and patched in along the military cable system to the control tower for Nassau on New Providence Island. He explained they had a Boeing that apparently had lost all radio and was coming in mute. Nassau took down the course as tracked and started hunting with radar, at the same time notifying all aircraft in the area to be on the alert for the big airplane coming down without contact.

Nassau Control called back within twenty minutes to tell them the big ARIA had landed safely. "Nassau, did you people get a handle on what their problem was?" Hewitt asked.

Nassau Control hesitated. "The, ah, pilot says they were hit by lightning," came the answer. It was a reply obviously tinged with disbelief.

"Lightning?" The word echoed in Hewitt's mind. "But that's impossible! We've been on these scopes since early this morning, and there hasn't been any weather for five hundred miles in any direction!"

"We know that," Nassau came back. "But something happened to that aircraft. My own feeling is that they had a failure of their electronic equipment. Secret, that sort of stuff, and they aren't talking about it. Lightning seemed to be a good answer. If you'll stand by there, Hewitt, I'll have your pilot ring you up as soon as we can reach him again."

The call came through within ten minutes. Hewitt ended his conversation with the pilot, shaking his head. "Lightning," he told the others in the tracking station. "He insists it's lightning. He says they all saw the bolt. Couldn't miss it. They were blind for a while from it. He says the ARIA's got burn marks all along the fuselage. All the antenna was blown off. You know the big radar in the nose? It's gone, he told me. Just blown right off the airplane. They lost every radio and electronic system they had."

Smitty couldn't buy it. "But did he say how they got a lightning strike without any clouds?"

"All he said," Hewitt announced, "was that he was very glad to be alive, he was going somewhere to get drunk, and he didn't want to talk about lightning no more with no one." Hewitt stuck a cigarette in his mouth and lit up. "Forget him. He's down safe, and he ain't our business no more. What about that Gulfstream? Anybody pick him up yet? You guys check again with the FAA?" Hewitt studied his watch. "He's seventy-four minutes overdue on his call. Okay, troops, that's it. Send out the alert. Full emergency procedures. Smitty, you notify air-sea rescue. I'll call Larkin at the Cape to notify all stations down the line. And, Matthews, get the word out to all ships inside our contact, okay?" He paused, voicing aloud what they all thought. "It sure don't look good."

But one man shrugged his indifference. "Hell, Sarge, what's to worry? Like you said yourself, there's no weather out there. Not a sign of trouble. At his altitude, there ain't even a chance of a midair. Besides, everyone else is accounted for." He laughed. "They probably put the thing on autopilot and they're gettin' laid. They—"

"Knock it off," Hewitt said brusquely. He stared down the technician. "You know sumpin'? For a guy whose ass is safe on the ground, you got a big mouth. Now shaddup and get to work."

Within another hour, ships at sea were taking up a search pattern along the recorded and still-anticipated flight path the missing Gulfstream was to fly. The experienced teams in air-sea rescue tried to figure every possible course that could have been taken. Queries were made to every station in the island chain, including military, civilian, and private installations. No results. Nothing. Not a sign or a hint of the airplane.

Sixteen Air Force, Navy, and Coast Guard planes took to the air to slide into grid search patterns. Airliners flying routes crossing the possible flight path of the Gulfstream were requested to "keep your eyes open." All private aircraft received the same word. A plane is missing and presumed down.

At Fort Lauderdale International Airport, a flying boat taxied away from the Coast Guard station while the copilot read aloud the pertinent details of the missing aircraft.

"That goddamned Devil's Triangle," the pilot said quietly. "It's done it again."

Chapter 3

Thirty-five minutes after the Gulfstream 666D vanished from all contact, a priority call reached the executive offices of Positronics in Maryland. The call went first to Arthur Hayden, the director of research and development. Hayden, panicked, dashed unannounced into the office of the company president.

Charles Maynard took the news in stony silence. That was his way. Listen. Absorb. Let reaction be controlled. It was during this wicked, unblinking silence that Arthur Hayden comprehended what he had done, and came unglued. Hayden had thought only about the fact that Dr. Harold Mazurski was aboard the missing airplane. He had not considered the other people aboard the Gulfstream, including, of course, Rena Kim Maynard.

Arthur Hayden's hand-wringing contrition had a salutary effect upon Maynard. "Shut up," he snarled, gesturing impatiently. "Just shut up and sit down over there." Maynard kneaded his forehead with his knuckles. He had to *think*.

All he really knew at this moment was what this numbskull had shouted hysterically. He wasn't going to begin weeping in the face of a blurted message that could have been screwed up . . . He stopped himself short and glared at Hayden. "Who called you about the airplane?" he demanded.

Hayden blinked his eyes rapidly. "Why . . . why, the people at Executive Airport in Florida. They said they had been notified by the FAA that the Gulfstream failed to report."

"Where, damnit!"

"They didn't have that information yet, Mr. Maynard. But they said the airplane had missed a reporting checkpoint and that they were going to get a search under way."

Maynard glowered at the other man. True enough, then, but still a far cry from a confirmed loss or even a missing airplane! So the Grumman was overdue. . . . Maynard thought of Lavagetti and his strict adherence to the rulebook. Missing a checkpoint meant no contact. That would have brought on an interrogation of all stations down the line to Puerto Rico. If things had gone so far as to report the aircraft missing, then there was substance to what Hayden had brought to him. Maynard's hand edged toward the telephone to call the nearest office of the Federal Aviation Administration. But if the Grumman were really missing, he couldn't learn that much with a single call. And word would reach the Pentagon fast enough. No matter his feelings about his daughter; he'd have to be on top of *that* situation when the balloon went up. Maynard rang for his secretary. "Get me Matt Sims at the field," he ordered. Sims was facility chief for all aircraft operated by Positronics. If anyone had the contacts to find out what the hell was going on, he . . .

Sims had already heard. "All right, then," Maynard said carefully into the phone. "You find out what the situation is now. Get me every scrap of information you can. Stay right on top of it. Find out about the search under way, and . . . Oh, hell, you know what to do, Matt."

"Yes, sir. I'll get right with it. Will you keep your private line open, Mr. Maynard?"

Maynard breathed a sigh of relief. The man was already thinking. Of course, in the hours to come the main lines would be jammed. "Yes, Matt. I'll keep it open strictly for your call. Thank you." He hung up, buzzed again for his secretary.

She came into the office. One look at her face and he realized she knew. The news must be spreading through the building like a prairie fire. He saw the tears, and he took a tighter grip on himself. "None of that now," he said gruffly. "I need you with a clear head, understand?" She nodded. "All right. Call Helen Rush right away. Put the call straight through to me."

Moments later he was talking with his wife's closest friend. He explained what he had heard, and that he still hoped the information was bungled. "But in any case," he concluded, "I've got to have someone with Alice, and I would be grateful if you—" He had no chance to finish.

"Of course," Helen broke in. "I'll leave right away."

She hung up, and Maynard felt some of the pressure ease. His wife wouldn't be alone, *if*. But there was another call to be made. No use waiting for the ax to come whistling out of the north. He sighed and gave instructions to his secretary.

Major General William R. Scott was not calm. Not as soon as Charles Maynard passed on to the general what had happened up until the moment of their conversation. Maynard heard the general suck in his breath, mixing the shock of sudden inhalation with a stream of murmured invective. The general knew that Harold Mazurski was a passenger on the Gulfstream. The general kept close track of everything Mazurski did. Mazurski was General Scott's greatest pride, as well as an albatross dangling awesomely about his neck. The general ran the computer project from the Department of Defense. The general would find the albatross swiftly gaining mass as it hung ever more obscenely about him. General Scott, of course, didn't offer more than cursory solace about Rena Kim, but then, Maynard expected nothing more in that vein. But the words Scott chose for his consolation astonished even Maynard: "They tell me you and your daughter were not especially close," the general flustered. "Maybe that will make her loss less."

Then, undismayed by Maynard's silence, Scott returned to his own problems.

"Goddamnit, stand by one," Scott snapped. Maynard heard him barking orders into another phone. Good; Scott was ringing in all the facilities of the military to update every detail on the missing Gulfstream. That would be the fastest and most accurate. Several minutes went by, and Scott breathed heavily into the phone. "You still there, Maynard?"

"Still here, General."

"Well, hang on. We'll be getting something in a minute or two. I'll feed it into this phone as soon as we get the report."

Maynard listened. Except for minor details, and confirmation through both the FAA and the military tracking range extending southeast from Cape Canaveral, it was tragically real. There was final confirmation of several vital points. There had been no emergency signal. No one had reported any sign of a downed aircraft. The weather was excellent and promised to remain that way for at least several days. A vast air-sea search effort had already been launched, abetted by the Pentagon's throwing top priority to the need to find Dr. Harold Mazurski.

It was all said and done. There was nothing left for General Scott to pass on from other authority. But he had bile to expend. "How the hell could you have let Mazurski go off on some goddamned drunken . . ." Scott drew himself up short. "The responsibility," he said in a tone suddenly ominous, "doesn't rest with this office for carelessness where Mazurski is concerned."

The general's words were received in silence by Charles Maynard. But silence was a thin coverlet for the father who had held his emotions in check. Now there was nothing else to learn. Now there was only waiting and quiet frenzy. But there was no need to be the iron man any longer. Maynard had a twisting vision of his daughter and the shattering explosion of the Gulfstream slamming into the sea. As if his body reacted physically to the nightmare in his mind, he slammed down the telephone.

Maynard waved Arthur Hayden from his office. He needed badly to be alone at this moment. He took a deep breath and opened his lower-right drawer, pulled out the Scotch, and poured a full glass. He downed it neat, knowing it was poor recompense for what was happening. But there wasn't anything *he* could *do*. He had to keep everything in its context. Goddamnit, he couldn't even blame the general.

A far-reaching critical project—critical in the sense that so many other actions and events hung on its failure or success—was now in jeopardy. An electronic brain that could function on the basis of scientifically drawn "hunches," using a far vaster supply of data than could any human brain, offered a quantum jump in thought mechanics. Expand the scope of that capability, and you were functioning on the international scale. The computer didn't care, of course. It was like the airplane that never knows how high it is above the surface. Laboratory test problems or the actuality of thermonuclear confrontation was immaterial. It didn't choke up in the clutch of nuclear poker, but played its hand based on consideration of all possible odds, *including the human factor*.

Even in its test phases the computer project had assured the United States an unpublicized but unquestioned gaming advantage in the "ultimate weight of pressure" between the United States and the Soviet Union. Considering *and anticipating* cybernetics growth in any other part of the world, the heuristics system created by Mazurski appeared to guarantee the United States a lead of not less than ten months in any strategic arms situation with the USSR.

And the government made certain the Russians were aware of the cybernetics system, for it was powerful medicine for making the Russians abstain from precipitous military conduct.

It was the best of all possible standoffs in a situation where the "throw weight" of Soviet missile systems had placed the United States second-best in computer-run war games, and both powers were acutely aware of that salient fact.

But Dr. Harold Mazurski was the irreplaceable key to continued development of the computer project, and he was aboard the missing Gulfstream.

Chapter 4

"I don't care where he is! Get him!" The president of Sierra Insurance, Inc., stared through a picture window at Colorado mountains as he shouted into his telephone. Herbert Carruthers stood so rigidly that his leg muscles trembled. He shouted anew into the phone. The hapless woman at the other end of the line in Orlando, Florida, held the receiver well extended from her ear, bringing it closer only to speak.

Miss Johnson explained for the third time that Dale Fenton was out of town and his whereabouts were unknown. "Even if I knew, Mr. Carruthers, there's no way I could possibly reach him. He said that if . . ." She tried to swallow the words even as she recognized the tactical error. She was aware that Carruthers also recognized the slip. His end of the phone had gone ominously quiet.

In his Denver office Carruthers took a deep breath, then began to speak in precise tones.

"Miss Johnson, listen to me carefully. *Very* carefully. Do you understand me, Miss Johnson?"

"Yes, sir."

"Miss Johnson, we are in the middle of a bonafide, grade-A, triple-damned priority. Unless you reach Dale Fenton for me, and get his overrated ass out here to my office, there is every good reason to believe that not only you, but Fenton as well, and perhaps even I, will discover that the nameplates on our desks belong to people of names yet unknown. Do I make myself clear, Miss Johnson?"

"Yes, sir."

"You will, in your own secret way, get these words to Mr. Fenton?"

"Yes, sir."

"Then get with it!" The telephone went dead.

It took Miss Johnson nearly twenty minutes of cursing and concentration to rid herself of hiccups. Only then could she begin the steps to reach her boss.

Dale Fenton kept to an almost religious belief in his privacy. Vacations came to him rarely, and he afforded those he had the protective instinct of a lioness toward her cubs. At that moment, with Miss Johnson curing her hiccups and Herbert Carruthers still breathing deeply, Dale Fenton and an especially well-endowed brunette were isolated from the rest of the world. The point of isolation was a cabin in remote Maine, to which there was no road large enough for a vehicle. The cabin was the creation of a millionaire friend of Fenton's: every piece of its structure, its amenities and luxuries, and all its supplies had been ferried in by large cargo helicopters. It nestled within thick pines, was surrounded with marvelous skiing and hunting. For critical emergency, the cabin had a powerful shortwave radio to be used for calling out; the equipment was shut off against incoming calls. Dale Fenton believed implicitly that if things were really *that* bad, an enterprising man would always find him out, and that the difficulty of the search existed in direct proportion to the urgency of the moment.

On that crisp, wonderfully clear morning in March, Fenton was enjoying the eighth day of a long-delayed vacation. He removed snowshoes from his boots and carried the carcass of the still-warm deer he had just killed. He slung the animal within a heavily screened enclosure; it would be their dinner. The thrill of the kill, executed with a bow and arrow, was still on him, as was the fresh scent of blood from the animal, when he entered the cabin door.

Joyce Manors' nostrils flared. Emotion swept through, and with the cabin door still open, she clawed at his clothes. He recognized the sudden glaze of her eyes, and took her as she wanted, as an animal ruts in total passion with its mate. Then he continued to make love, slower and more tenderly now, bringing them with superb touch to a second mutual climax, just as the entire cabin shook heavily. Even as he cursed furiously and rolled away from the woman, Fenton recognized the sound of a powerful engine immediately overhead.

For a long moment he crouched on the floor, head tilted back, listening, judging the sound, the ebb of thunder telling him the machine was climbing steeply. Then the sound slipped through its pitch change and began to rise, and he knew it was coming back again. No mistake; this was no idle pass, no coincidental flyover of the aircraft. A deliberate visit. *Here?* Rage galvanized his limbs to sudden movement. He spun away from the astonished woman, snatched a repeating rifle from its wall rack by the open door, and dashed outside into the snow, stark naked, rushing through a clump of trees to an open area where he could see the sky. The rifle was at his shoulder, and he was aiming, first holding the target in the sights and then leading expertly, when he realized the insanity of the moment. But that drop back into time, as if he'd been a caveman wanting only to destroy, had been so intense, so utterly fulfilling . . . He shook away the feeling and lowered the weapon.

He knew he had perhaps five minutes more in the cold before skin damage would begin. But five minutes was more than enough. He watched the plane circle, and he knew what would happen even as he watched. The aircraft flew to a position downwind of the cabin, rolled out to and held a steady course, and when it was upwind, just so, a black shape tumbled away. He watched the chute open and went back, still cursing, into the cabin. He jerked a thumb behind him. "Company."

He tossed the rifle onto the couch, turned, and slammed the door, dropping a heavy wooden bolt into place. He slipped back to the thick rug, pulling Joyce down with him, his hand moving to her belly and then to where she was still wet, still so inviting to him. "We're going to finish," he grunted, "what we started . . ." and he entered her, grinning at the delight on her face. Moments later there came a hammering at the door. Joyce lifted her eyebrows as he paused between sliding into her.

"Let the bastard wait," he chuckled. "It's our party, nd nobody invited him."

"Well, just don't stand there, damnit. You're letting in the cold. Move!"

The chutist stared in disbelief at the two naked figures before him. Dale Fenton closed the door quickly behind the stumbling entry of the man who'd dropped in from the sky.

"You got a name?" Fenton demanded.

"Uh, yessir. Todd. Bill Todd, sir." He tried frantically to keep his eyes from the sweat-glistening body of the woman.

"What's your pleasure, Bill?"

Todd jerked his head aside to concentrate on

Fenton's face. "Pleasure, sir?" He was stricken. "I, uh, I don't understand, sir."

"A drink, man. What do you want to drink? Scotch?"

"Oh. Uh, sure, yessir, Scotch will do fine." Todd shifted from one foot to the other. Joyce Manors swayed from the bar, drinks extended, breasts provoking.

"All right, Todd." Fenton leaned back against the couch. "What's the story?"

"Story, sir?"

Fenton nodded. "Todd, what the hell are you doing here?"

Todd took a long swallow, choked, and fought for air. "Uh, it's an emergency, Mr. Fenton. I was told to get word to you, uh, no matter what." Joyce Manors moved within his vision, walking slowly, and the sight of her brought on more clubfooted shifting by Todd.

"What kind of emergency?"

"I don't know, sir. My instructions were to tell you that all hell was breaking loose. In, uh, just a moment, sir." He groped in a jacket pocket, dragged out a folded sheet of paper. "Back in Mr. Carruthers' office, sir. In Colorado."

"I know where it is," Fenton said dryly. "What kind of emergency?"

Todd shook his head. "I don't know, sir. I'm suppose to tell you to get back there just as fast as you can."

"How?"

"Oh. Well, as soon as I've talked with you, Mr. Fenton, I'm supposed to call my plane. I've got, uh, a radio outside, and I'm supposed to tell them you're here, and you're ready to go, and they've got a jet helicopter standing by to pick you up and take you to the nearest airport, and—"

"Shit." Fenton took a long swallow of his drink and

stared at Joyce. "If Herbie is going to all this trouble, luv, it's got to be heavy." Fenton turned back to Todd. "Call your iron bird and tell 'em to send the chopper." He turned away and took Joyce by the elbow. "At least there's time for one last shower. Let's go, doll."

Bill Todd beat a hasty retreat as the two naked bodies moved across the living room. Outside, he called the circling plane and received confirmation of the helicopter starting on its way. He stared at the door to the cabin, shook his head, finished his drink, and knocked loudly. He waited, then pushed the door open slowly. Muted screams came from the direction of the bathroom. Todd collapsed in a chair to wait. Twenty minutes later he leaped to his feet as Fenton and the woman—fully clothed this time—came into the room.

"Joyce, make our guest a drink," Fenton said with a gesture. "Son, how long before that whirlybird makes it here?"

Todd glanced at his watch. "Ten minutes or so, Mr. Fenton. Uh, it really won't give you much time, sir." Fenton showed the question in his face. "What I mean, sir, is that there's a real mean front moving in. It's only about an hour or two away. If I hadn't gotten to you the way I did, we wouldn't have been able to reach you for a couple of days."

"That's *swell*, Todd."

The chutist turned crimson. "Oh. Well, I'm sorry it had to work out this way, Mr. Fenton. Jeez, I didn't . . ."

"Forget it." Fenton took his drink in silence, thinking. At the sound of a turbine whining its way across the trees, the helicopter coming in, he grinned. He gestured for Todd to join him across the room. "Joyce, you too. I want the both of you here. Todd, hold her hand. Take her hand, damnit!"

He chuckled at their expressions. "Now, listen to me. I've got a gift for each of you." He laughed. "My gift is each of you to the other. You two stay here and wait out the storm. I'm sure you'll, um, find something to do to amuse each other. No use breaking up vacation time for everyone."

They waved at him wildly as the chopper carried him off into a darkening sky.

The chopper was a fast turbine Alouette, and the pilot chewed his way through low clouds to make it safely into Portland, Maine. He settled to ground with the rotors whipping away the first early messengers of the heavy snow rolling closer to the field. Fenton had just time enough for a surprisingly good steak before climbing into the chartered Lear jet waiting for him.

Someone had been busy. On the seat next to his in the small jet was a stack of late newspapers from several cities. There was also a telegram, three pages of it, and he knew without looking that it would be from Dottie, his secretary in Orlando, giving him the reasons for hauling him away from broad, booze, and bed.

He settled in his seat, his brain still cruising easily. The details could wait just a bit longer. He strapped in and lit up a long thin cigar and lifted his feet to the cushioned seat directly across from him.

The two pilots looked back from the front office, questioning silently the safety breach of smoking before takeoff. Fenton lifted a thick eyebrow at their stares and waited. The pilot, in the left seat, shrugged and motioned for his copilot to start earning his keep. The sleek iron bird came alive with pressures and temperatures and flow and rolled away from the parking ramp. Fenton flew mentally all the way down the strip, his muscles making the involuntary pull as the pilot rotated the nose, and he was still chewing on his cigar and flying inside his head when they were several thousand feet up and boring through thick clouds. At some unknown point high above the earth, he knew that all mountains and other rocks in the clouds were well below.

He eased off the seatbelt pressure, flicked an ash from the cigar, and weighed the telegram in his hands. The first few lines told him what and why, and he scratched his planned monumental chewing-out of Herbie Carruthers. He understood now why Herbie would have dragged him back from a seal-hunting expedition in the Arctic.

He read on. Jesus. It was a rough one. Adding up all the numbers, the people and the missing airplane, and that special policy on the body of one Dr. Harold Mazurski, the insurance company stood to take a bath of forty to sixty million dollars. That could break a lot of financial backs.

Fenton followed his own time-honored routine. He read through every newspaper story, reread the telegram, again scanned the newspapers, and marked off certain passages. He glanced at his watch. He was still in form. Ninety-two minutes for the whole job, and he considered one hundred minutes his point of saturation for soaking up raw data. He tossed the papers onto the other seat, inserted the cigar stub into the ashtray, and fell asleep.

Chapter 5

"I'm calling to confirm our aircraft off the ground at 1320 hours local time. Yes, sir, your party is aboard. The telegram and the newspapers requested were waiting for him on his arrival."

Herbert Carruthers let out a long sigh. "Thanks for the call. It was good of you. Good-bye." He hung up, leaned back in his chair, and let the pressure begin to slide away. For the first time since this disaster he felt he could breathe without forcing the air past paralyzed muscles. He'd be here soon. Dale Fenton. The best in the business. The man who'd brought unheralded scientific and human techniques to the always intricate business of insurance investigation. Dale Fenton's name was synonymous with the company name of "Heracles." The silent division of Sierra Insurance, Inc. It had come into being when Dale Fenton came into his life. How long ago? he wondered. Four years, give or take a few months.

At that time Herbert Carruthers had occupied the president's chair of Sierra Insurance for just about two years. When he'd inherited it from his father, it was one of the older, well-established insurance firms dealing heavily in family trade. Sierra Insurance did very well indeed, but Herbert Carruthers was out to make changes.

There were two ways to be big in the insurance business. One was to be patron and father-host, as Sierra Insurance already was, to hundreds of thousands of people. The second way was to be viable, interesting, exciting. It gave you appeal.

Herbert Carruthers had thought long about Lloyds of London and their manner of operation. Handling the insurance on a single special project could bring in more dollar return than baby-sitting 150,000 people eking out their living. The cost of things in the world was soaring. People wanted things, objects, projects, and other people insured heavily. Depending upon the circumstances, they were willing to pay exorbitant prices. After all, exorbitant was a relative term. What was exorbitant to the Outsider looking in didn't have the same meaning if you were the Insider; then the only game in town was High Risk.

It worked both ways. One of the best means of making a financial killing was to have your pet project come apart at the seams. *After* it had been insured to the hilt. Why break your ass closing a hundred-million-dollar deal from which you might clear two or maybe five mill when with a little extra effort you could arrange for a "disaster" and collect many more millions through an insurance payoff? That was the real risk in the seat occupied by Herbert Carruthers. But life without some risk would always be tepid.

Still, it had turned out to be more gamble than he'd ever dreamed, for in very quick order the company suffered a string of financial body blows.

The worst came when they insured a charter flight. One of those big damn stretched DC-8's. One hundred and ninety people, the liquor flowing freely, from Miami to Bermuda to Paris and then down to South Africa. Crazy kind of a trip. Everyone aboard loaded to the ears. Hell, three million dollars' worth of insurance on the jewelry alone. Plus all those people, *and* the airplane, which was on the blocks for a hefty nine million dollars more.

It disappeared over the Mediterranean. The crew had taken the big jet in a night flight to 36,000 feet. For a while everything was right in the groove. About a million dollars' worth of complicated electronics handling everything. The pilot's position report was ticked off by the computer monitoring the flight. Then, several minutes later, there was an unexpected, blood-chilling transmission from the DC-8. Sounds of coughing and choking from the pilot. A frantic message about control problems, shouted voices in the cockpit, and . . . silence. That was it. The boats were moving before daybreak, and planes scoured the area, but Herbert Carruthers knew it was the end, the far and freaking end, and he'd be chopped to pieces by the board of directors, because there was no way out of their paying off something more than sixteen million dollars in cash.

Then somewhere in the middle of his private life's destruction he had had a telephone call. From Lisbon. From a man named Dale Fenton. It wasn't a long conversation, but it started turning the world right-side-up again.

"Whatever you do, *don't* pay off any claims on that machine. Understand, Carruthers?" Fenton's voice wouldn't be denied. "You can't lose anything by waiting. Don't let anyone panic you. It will take me a few more days to wrap up the details. I'll be in your office before the week is out." The man hung up.

Five days later Dale Fenton stood before him. He studied the man. Six feet two inches, about 190 pounds, rawboned, and lean-muscled. Dark hair, slightly tousled. He moved . . . like a big cat. Dark eyes, fairly dark complexion. A scar along the side of his neck. Carruthers would learn later it came from a knife intended to go through the neck. Carruthers didn't miss the heavy wrists and slight discoloration. This man was a long-time user of the martial arts.

They met, and Fenton jumped in with both feet. "That airplane," he started, "was blown up."

Carruthers stared at him, unblinking. "Go on," he urged.

"It was a bomb placed aboard before takeoff," Fenton said. "Detonation was by radio signal. I was in Europe at the time. The more I heard about the incident, the more suspicious I became. I—"

"Why would you become suspicious?" Carruthers broke in.

Fenton held his gaze, then nodded slightly. The question had its place. "Accidents have been my business for years, Mr. Carruthers. You can have the personal details later." Carruthers agreed, and Fenton went on.

"First, there was too much jewelry aboard. Most of it had to be fake. People who own that sort of jewelry don't carry it along on a trip of this sort. Which meant there was every chance the jewels were never on board in the first place. It's the double payoff. They collect for the insurance, and then they break up the jewels and fence them out for a completely profitable deal." Fenton interrupted himself to light a cigar. He gestured with it like a wand. "We'll let the lesser details go for the moment, Carruthers. All I needed at the time was to find just one item, anything, that didn't fit.

"I made use of certain contacts I have and learned that another jet—Falcon, executive type—took off from a field near Paris about the same time the DC-8 left. I spoke with some people who flew that same run that night. One of them recalled something unusual. A double contrail. Not the split contrail of a ship like a DC-8, but double in the vertical sense.

Two separate vapor trails, maintaining position, one directly above the other."

Carruthers bit his tongue and waited.

"That Falcon I mentioned filed its flight plan from southern France to South Africa. The times coincided. I worked out the possible rendezvous points. I then tried to figure things on the assumption that there was a bomb aboard the DC-8, that the people in the Falcon were responsible for its presence, and that they had the means to set it off by radio signal. That they monitored the DC-8 calls to the traffic-control centers. And after the last checkpoint transmission from the DC-8, they went to that same frequency and passed themselves off as the DC-8 crew."

Carruthers' eyes widened. "You mean . . ."

"That's right. The sounds of choking, gasping, the voices heard from the pilot and copilot in the DC-8, were faked. They were intended to sound as if the crew were exposed suddenly to smoke, or gas, or even to explosive decompression. The people in the Falcon did an excellent job. Everyone on the ground who heard their transmission assumed that the crew in the DC-8 was struggling for their lives. But they forgot one thing. On any charter flight of this kind, even on many scheduled flights for that matter, one pilot must always wear his oxygen mask. *Always.* The requirement was established to keep one pilot ready to take over the controls in the case of explosive decompression. The mask goes to full oxygen flow automatically if cabin pressure ever blows. The system is separate from the rest of the aircraft.

"So whatever happened in the cockpit of that DC-8, whatever broke loose or affected the respiratory system of the flight crew, *would not have affected that man with the mask on his face.* Yet the tapes—and I have a copy of them—make it clear that both the captain and the first officer were coughing, choking, and shouting about a disaster in the cockpit. And both voices come over too clearly for one man to be wearing a mask."

Fenton flicked an ash from the cigar. "I began putting together the many pieces, and it all began to fit. The pattern, I mean. The timing of the Falcon flight with the DC-8. The possible rendezvous points. The vertical separation of contrails. The strange amount of jewelry and the insurance involved. The strangest part of all this, Carruthers, is that the people who engineered this caper have nothing to do with the insurance on the people, or even the airplane itself. They were in this strictly for their payoff."

Herbert Carruthers sat quietly, stunned, staring at this incredible stranger before him. He let out a long sigh. "I hesitate to use the word brilliant, Mr. Fenton, but nothing else I know will do." He stirred uncomfortably in his seat. "But where does it take us? The insurance company, I mean. It seems to come to a dead end."

Fenton showed a thin smile. "Not quite. One man, a passenger on that DC-8, was taken ill just before the airplane left France. Convenient for, uh, you, I might add. He ate in the same restaurant as three other people associated with him—his wife, sister, and brother-in-law. His name is Stewart; Chester Stewart. I checked him out. Got the full medical report. Four people sat at the same table in that restaurant. I checked out the waiter's order. Three of them, including Stewart, ate the same meal. The same food. *No one else became ill.* Stewart insisted the three go on the flight, and he said he'd join them in a day or two.

"Stewart's your man, Carruthers. His wife had with her over one and a quarter million dollars' worth of jewelry. His story is that she was taking it to South Africa for appraisal and sale. Stewart's in some kind of financial trouble. I haven't had the time to root out the details, but I'm sure your own investigation will establish that he's up against the wall for some heavy debts no one else knows about. The money in his family comes from his wife. He's safe from motive on that point, because in the event of her death, her estate—business-wise, anyway—goes to a holding corporation. It never reaches his hands. But he shares ownership in the jewelry, from which an insurance payoff would bring him almost one million dollars clear. As well as her life insurance, which comes to another three hundred thousand."

Carruthers' voice had fallen to a hoarse whipser. "What . . . what do we do now?"

Fenton laughed. His hand opened wide, then closed deliberately, into a powerful fist. "You move fast, hard, like a steel trap closing. You don't let *anyone* know what you know now. Not even the authorities, because you haven't any way of knowing who's been bought and paid for. You wait until this man gets home, until he goes through his mockery of bereavement. You make no waves about there being any trouble with the insurance payoff. You even announce, in a legal document of some sort, that you *are* paying off. And then, when he's relaxed, you walk in and you arrest him. You nail his ass to the wall and hit him with the evidence and—"

"You said not to bring in the authorities," Carruthers protested.

Fenton smiled coldly. "You have a properly designated law officer with you as a witness to make it legal. You bounce this Stewart so hard he breaks. He'll be brittle. They always are in a case like this. Before he knows what's happening, he'll crack wide open. Oh, one more thing. He went as a representative for his company, I believe. I'm not sure . . ."

Carruthers buzzed for his secretary. He told her to

check out the status of the passenger known as Charles Stewart and to get back to him immediately. He turned back to Fenton. "Obviously you attach importance to that representation."

Fenton nodded. "If Stewart were aboard that aircraft as a company representative, then the matter of liability may well pass on to the company, which could take your outfit completely off the hook. Or, at the very least, tie it up so badly in the courts you'll get settlements for a fraction of what you'd be paying otherwise."

Carruthers' secretary came into the office and handed him a note. When she left, Carruthers gestured with the slip of paper. "You were right, Mr. Fenton. The Stewarts were booked on company business all the way."

Fenton laughed. "See? You're already starting to close the trap."

Carruthers studied him. "How . . . what role will you, uh, play in all this, Mr. Fenton?"

The man handed Carruthers a business card. "That's my home office in Orlando, Florida. My initial fee, Mr. Carruthers, will be a check for fifty thousand dollars mailed to me there. I'll be available when you're ready for court. At the successful conclusion of this affair, please send another check for two hundred thousand. To the same address." Fenton rose to his feet and picked up his attaché case.

Carruthers blinked. "That's all? Nothing else? No, uh, papers to sign between us?"

Fenton laughed again. "Why? You're not going to cheat me, Mr. Carruthers. When you send that second check, you're going to do everything in your power to hire me. We'll talk then. Good day to you, sir." And he left.

It worked out exactly. Sierra Insurance stood firm

in court. Liability was conferred upon the company for whom Charles Stewart was an executive. Carruthers was out from under.

He had sent to Dale Fenton the check for fifty thousand dollars within an hour of the man's leaving his office.

He didn't send the second check for two hundred thousand; he delivered it personally. Because by that time he wanted desperately to hire Fenton.

He had never encountered, in real life or fiction, another human being like this man. No term more ludicrous than "insurance investigator'" could have been applied to Dale Fenton. At least, not as the general public envisaged such an individual: a flabby or a cadaverous milquetoast with clipboard and pen in hand asking about automobile accidents, or a fire in the kitchen, or an ass-over-teakettle tumble from a ladder! Penny-ante shit.

A man of Fenton's style, thought Carruthers, outdid in every respect that cinematic buffoon called James Bond. He has far greater freedom, an expense account virtually without limit, and the choice, once he's on a case, of deciding just how he'll do whatever *he* feels must be done. Here was a sleuth—or a crime scientist—who was also a pilot, engineer, technician, and God knew what else. Carruthers had learned much of the man but knew there was still more to be unearthed.

What incited Carruthers' interest was that Fenton had worked the business for years as a free-lance investigator. Obviously he preferred absolution from organizational shackles. The insurance business hewed to rigidity, but in the case of Dale Fenton, Carruthers was quite prepared to throw to the winds even a faint suspicion of same.

Fenton would work only the tough ones. The jobs he preferred to tackle. The big ones that ran into the millions of dollars. Missing ships and missing planes with staggering insurance riding on the hardware, the cargo, the people. Multiples of millions was the name of the game. A few faked claims could gut the cash reserves of an outfit as big as Sierra. Yet Carruthers had to carry his risk policy. It was the old saw of no guts, no glory. But, goddamnit, you needed somebody to ride shotgun on those policies. The prosaic tasks would be handled by the prosaic people in their well-defined orbits.

Getting Fenton to accept the freedom Carruthers was prepared to offer within the establishment of Sierra Insurance was the big question mark. Selling the job on the basis of money was a dead end. Handling the business free-lance, without any of the huge risks, Fenton could knock off a hundred thousand dollars a year without working up much of a sweat. Carruthers was prepared to guarantee that amount—after taxes, he reminded himself—over and above expenses. Jesus, Fenton'd earned a quarter of a million on this DC-8 mess alone. Of course, there weren't many cases of that particular ilk, but a man like Fenton, if he kept moving in the highest risk circles, could pick up that kind of bread every year.

There were other thing going for the tall, muscular man who'd come so explosively into Carruthers' life. It wasn't enough to have the technical expertise. To operate, a man had to be just as much at home in the cellar as he was amidst the clouds. Fenton, if Carruthers was coming to know his man, was eternally suspicious. He had to be, of course. His world crawled with hints, clues, shadows and whispers, and he had to encourage such things into shadows with somewhat more substance to them. There was another problem in solidifying phantoms. They're hard to reassemble when proof—or what remains of it—lies thousands of feet beneath the ocean surface. Somewhere.

And not all his obstacles were so passive. There were some very capable professionals doing their best to confound people like Dale Fenton.

Carruthers went back in his mind to comparing the real Dale Fenton to the cinematic spectacle of James Bond. Agent 007 was a great comic strip character. Any living being who operated in that fashion would long ago have been fed to the hogs.

Dale Fenton, on the other hand (Carruthers thought with a sense of gratitude) was starkly real, but his dossier was as incredible as fiction. He was a graduate engineer—essential to his work—a skilled accountant, and had had some hefty legal training. He had, in short, the requisites to begin an FBI career. And he had studied—and practiced—geology, banking, insurance, chemistry, trade, political structure, and diplomacy. He had mastered the legal structure of different nations as they applied to those areas in which he worked.

Furthermore, the man was experienced in just about everything that flew, from the smallest light planes to helicopters to airliners to seaplanes and flying boats. As such, he was also an expert navigator and meteorologist. He had taken this solid capability from the air to the sea, where he appeared to be equally adept in the handling of surface craft. Not too difficult an exchange: both environments demanded their knowledge of nature and an intrinsic appreciation of mechanical movement under whatever conditions might be encountered.

Fenton had spent four years in the Air Force, but he didn't waste time in uniform. He had served in the AIG—the Air Inspector General, Flight Safety Division—and that meant a full-time career of investigating accidents and what seemed to be accidents (because at times the cargo was worth, literally, hundreds of millions of dollars, in the form of such esoteric goodies as hydrogen bombs). Finding out why this guy or that pranged and bent this much metal, and how, and why, was the meat of his labor. After Fenton's blue-suit tour, he worked for a while with the Federal Aviation Administration and the Civil Aeronautics Board. Those years with the FAA and CAB had polished off the edges of technical, engineering, and practical sides of his detective stripes. And Fenton had spent his own money—a lot of it—to go through a very special and very expensive school for private investigators in which he learned particular brands of governmental mayhem, including how to keep from being killed and, when necessary, how to do the maiming and killing himself. Those thick, slightly discolored wrists of Fenton's came from heavy practice in the martial arts. When he emerged from the school, he had completed a cram course in sabotage, espionage, and murder.

As much as Carruthers had learned of Fenton, he realized that there was still every chance he was missing the totality of the person. And he was right, for Fenton had long ago learned that survival lay in his flexibility. He could be as difficult to see as a flea, could adapt with the natural instincts of the chameleon, or hurl himself into trouble with the explosive fury of a leopard. He was at home in a crummy grass airfield or at an international airport, as comfortable in the finest nightclub as in the shabbiest waterfront dive.

Carruthers suspected that Fenton probably packed hardware, but he would have been surprised at the nature of that heat, for what he did have was small and flat and unexpected: a special case-hardened weapon with a very high-velocity .270 barrel in a .32-automatic frame. He got 3,600 feet-per-second *flat* trajectory from this little killer with its nine rounds.

But then, Carruthers ruminated, there would be some things about Dale Fenton he'd just as soon *not* know.

Carruthers spent a mind-twisting two hours with Fenton after they met in Orlando, two hours in which Fenton refused discussion. Instead, they drove to Cocoa Beach, on the east coast, where Fenton had just purchased a top-floor condominium, close enough to the ocean to lean over the balcony and look down to watch the surf breaking. "A world away from the world," Fenton explained as he ushered Carruthers into his hideaway.

Carruthers made his pitch. Fenton bought it. It was no more complicated than that. What remained were certain details and touches demanded by Fenton, and they were no problem, since Carruthers had come prepared to deal by yielding.

Before the week was out, Carruthers' legal staff had created the organization known as Heracles. Carruthers himself picked the name. "Any investigation team, any group in this business, has almost the same problems as were faced by Hercules. I just like the 'Heracles' spelling better. An idiosyncracy I offer up to myself." He laughed at the expression on Fenton's face. "Heracles had to face a multitude of problems. Twelve deadly tasks, any one of which should have killed him, and all for a sin *he* didn't commit. His 'impossible' deeds were actually in atonement for a crime committed by his father."

Carruthers grinned self-consciously. "Sometimes we'll be in the same boat. Our greatest risk is having to pay for a crime *we* don't commit, but that's really the way the world turns, and we go into this whole thing with our eyes wide open."

Fenton gestured idly. "I could get the idea that you're a Heracles—you do pronounce it 'Hercules,' don't you?—freak."

"That I am." Carruthers sighed. "It's a permanent hangover from facing impossible situations. So I tend to establish challenges in this way. Heracles had some beauts, didn't he? Choking to death the invulnerable lion of Nemea. Killing the nine-headed Hydra. Things like the golden-horned stag, the great boar, the savage bull of Minos . . ." He tossed off the drink in his hand. "Like I said, in the modern sense we're in the same boat." Suddenly he looked sharply at Fenton. "No. Change that. *You're* in the same boat. I don't run much risk behind a mahogany desk. You're the one who will dare the trials of Heracles, and sometimes I think the risks today are a bit worse. Especially where you're concerned. Heracles at least had magic working for him. He had to deal with the judgment of the gods. You, on the other hand, have to deal with the deadliest killer of them all. Your fellow man."

So they set it up. The organization within the organization. Fenton would have the option of working alone or with men or women he selected according to his own standards. Most research and investigation was like police work. You had to be penetrating, studious, meticulous, and above all, patient. But along with patience went that need to move swiftly when occasion demanded. Carruthers made available a variety of aircraft kept on standby basis from a leasing firm. Fenton took what he wanted as his needs became known.

He hired two pilots. Each man was a fully qualified mechanic and radio-electronics specialist, and at least one was always on call, an availability for which they were both paid handsomely. Fenton carried with him on any flight a packaged communications system allowing him to patch in by direct radio or radiophone to the computer system established for Heracles. He was able, even when airborne, to interrogate the memory banks of the computer, either through a manned programmer, or directly by digital readout on a small cathode-receiving screen within his equipment. He had open access at any time of day or night to the enormous memory system.

Fenton took special pains within the new Heracles structure to set up what he called Group One and Group Two. The first team was made up of three people who functioned, in the physical sense, entirely within the organizational structure. They did no work outside the office complex in Orlando, and their task was to handle the computers and to coordinate all detailed research efforts, especially for the memory banks and cross-referencing.

Group One functioned as an information fount, a living data bank, an organic system constantly updating itself. It kept Dale Fenton in constant touch with the always changing, ever-shifting fog of the statistical and legal world. The Group One team was his eternal light burning in the dark of unknowing.

Group Two, on the other hand, was his far-ranging scouts and agents. Investigators, sleuths, hatchet men; they fitted a battery of categories.

If there existed a man perfectly suited to the worn adage of the "dour Scotsman," then Harry McManus filled the bill. Trained as an accountant, and with a bloodhound's nasal sensitivity for ledger records, he was an unerring despoiler of false books intended to deceive any observer. He was as brilliant as any man Carruthers had ever known in his line of work, and he tempered incisiveness with the plodding determination of a camel. Just past fifty years old, immaculate in appearance and dress, he was the perfect chameleon to operate for Fenton.

But of all the people Fenton had placed at his disposal in his new operation with Heracles, none could match the brightness and the swift appraisal of Jill Peck, a beautiful black girl twenty-four years old. "Razor discernment" was the way Fenton would have described her. She had worked for three years as an undercover narc for the police department of San Francisco and would take no nonsense, no crap from *anyone*. She was, obviously, the perfect operative for getting into sensitive areas beyond the reach of male agents. Fenton ordered one immediate change for her field operations: he insisted that when Jill ventured into particularly rough country she would be accompanied by a male, black.

Ernie Wilson, on tap from a detective agency, had learned to expect his summons at any hour of the day or night. He was simple, tough, and reliable, and that was all that was needed of him.

Thirty-one-year-old Ben Davis was more than chameleonlike. He was a master at personal disguise, and equally adept in assuming the nuances of changing ethnic, social, or other situations. Davis was unmarried and a swinger, with the sexual propensity of a three-legged goat trying frantically for balance on a slippery hillside. He had spent nine years with military criminal intelligence in Europe, South America, and the Far East. The same man who could hang around with a group strung out on drugs, and mix with them in superb loose-lipped and eye-glazed fashion, could also speak nearly a dozen languages.

Dale Fenton's "final gun," as he thought of the man, was grossly unthinkable as an insurance investigator. Thirty-four-year-old Mick Satterly never seemed to stand anywhere. He loomed or hulked. He had a massive chest and neck, and his limbs seemed to have been hewn cordwood and grafted onto his tree trunk of a torso.

Buried deep in Satterly, however, lay swift and incisive intelligence, and as far as Fenton was concerned, the deeper the concealment, the better. Also with his keen intelligence and massive musculature lay experience as a steelworker, deep-sea diver, paratrooper, lumberjack, and a half-dozen other demanding and hazardous occupations. Satterly's ugly visage and his hulking frame and thickly haired arms permitted him access to and survival within areas no insurance investigator could have survived. And that, specifically, was his task when not accompanying Dale Fenton: to probe the most unsavory places where information might be found. And to get that information. Quick and dirty, or slow and dirtier—just so long as he got it.

Chapter 6

"Damnit, Herb, first things first. Has everything gone to the computers in Orlando?"

Carruthers stopped in mid-stride. He'd been pacing back and forth in his office like a big cat freshly thrown into a zoo cage. From the moment Dale Fenton had entered his office he'd been hyper. Carruthers couldn't calm himself down. He'd been baby-sitting the fifth of Scotch in his desk drawer too long, waiting too long, anticipating a hundred situations, and racing mentally through every one. And now Fenton was here, and so damned, infuriatingly calm. . . .

"Yes, yes, *yes*," Carruthers snapped. "Everything. It's all gone. They're programming the systems now. But it's all been sent. I—"

Fenton gestured to stem the word flow. "Easy, Herb."

Carruthers looked blankly at him. "Easy? How the hell do you expect me to take it easy!"

Fenton tapped his cigar against the ashtray. "Because I need a shave," he said.

"You need a *what?*"

A shave. I'll use your bathroom here."

"Why in God's name—?"

Fenton held up two fingers. "One, because my

face itches. Two, because it'll give you time to slow down. Full gallop in a circle never wins."

Fenton was slapping after-shave on his face when he saw Carruthers in the mirror, a mixture of a grimace and smile on his face. Fenton turned around slowly, rubbing his hands dry. "We've got company," he said.

"How the hell did you know that?"

Fenton laughed. "The look on your face, Herbie. Whoever he is, he's bugging you. So you left him cooling his heels and came to fetch your favorite watchdog."

"Sometimes," Carruthers growled, "you're too damned smart for your own good."

"That's why you pay me so well. Who is he?"

"He's a surprise, that's who," Carruthers said with some distaste. "Major John Walton. He's Army, from the special-projects office that runs the computer program with Positronics. And he's acting like someone dropped a bagful of red ants in his jockstrap."

"Understandable."

"But I didn't want him to talk without your being there. He could tell me something I'd miss. You know, it might have meaning for you but go right over my head."

Fenton nodded. "Fair enough. By the way, before I forget, I want your office bugged."

"Bugged?"

"Sometimes, Herbie, you can maneuver someone into a fight and get people to say things they might otherwise keep to themselves." Fenton stared directly at the other man. "This is going to get a lot worse before it gets better, my friend, and we're going to need everything we can get for our side."

"Thanks a heap. You're real encouraging."

Fenton ignored the remark. "Tell me more about the major."

Carruthers shrugged. "Not that much I know to tell you. He worked with Dr. Mazurski. Inside—and I mean *all* the way inside—their top-secret computer program."

"Then he should know Mazurski as well as anybody does. From the working end of things, anyway."

"I think," Carruthers reflected, "he was more baby-sitter than scientist."

"That could help. Did he say what he wanted?"

Carruthers shook his head. "Dale, I don't think *he* knows what he's after. He's . . . um, well, 'confused' would be a good word for it. The Pentagon's probably rubbing all sorts of salt up his ass. It sounds like a fishing expedition to me."

Fenton slipped on his jacket. For several moments he kept his silence. Carruthers made no move to break into his thoughts until he was ready. "Let's not go right back to your office," Fenton said finally. "Something stinks here, baby. The Army doesn't have any business coming to see *us* on this deal, Herb." Fenton let the thought sink in. "There's no reason, no obvious reason, anyway, for them to see you, me, anyone in this company. Later, maybe. But at this stage of the game?" Fenton shook his head. "Uh-uh. We . . . you . . . your company—you insure people, machines, events, things. We're not baby-sitters."

"Tell that to the major," Carruthers said glumly.

"Oh, never fear. I intend to tell him that, and a great deal more. After I get from him what I want, of course."

"Well, he's only for starters."

"What does that mean?"

Carruthers sighed. "They're *all* coming down on us, Dale. It's like they're springing from the woodwork." Fenton looked sharply at him. "In the last twenty minutes I've had calls from the National Security Agency. Okay, I can see the NSA tie-in, because the computers are involved. But then the CIA called, for Christ's sake, and—"

"Herb, how much do you know about this Mazurski?"

"What's there to know? A genius, working on one of their secret computer programs. . . ."

"*How* secret?"

"I hear it goes all the way to Q level."

"That's as high as you can go."

"Don't I know it," Carruthers murmured.

"Do you know anything about the program?"

"Very little, but I can surmise some."

"And?"

Carruthers shrugged. "It goes all the way to the White House. The Joint Chiefs of Staff. The National Security Council. NSA and CIA are tied in. God knows who else. I've heard rumors that the whole damned project involved manipulation of national policy. I *think* it's true."

"And Mazurski is the kingpin in all this?"

"That's the way it shapes up, Dale."

"From where you sit, Herb, what happens to this program if someone removes Mazurski?"

"Damned if I know. From all the fire and smoke, I'd say everybody would be getting upset as all hell."

"Lets' go talk to the Army."

Major John Walton, USA, was cut from standard cloth. Strictly government-issue. But a product of ROTC and special schools. Not like the old Army at all. Walton was a mixture of that new breed of engineer-specialist-soldier. Well, that's the way they fought their wars today. He stood nearly six feet, slim, neat; the walking slide rule. And just about as brittle, if you applied pressure at the right point: *Snap*.

The major was already raw nerves, and a man in

that condition was likely to spill more information than he got. "Major, let's cut the mustard without screwing around," Fenton told him after a cool greeting. "We're all here for the same reason. Except that we don't understand your coming to see us in particular."

Walton rubbed his hands nervously. He was under the gun, Fenton judged. "Mr. Fenton, I hope you won't mind my being blunt, sir?"

Fenton waved him on. Carruthers had moved behind his desk, waiting out the opening moves.

"May I ask, uh, why you insured Dr. Mazurski?" The words came in staccato fashion, groping.

"You're not serious?" The best response was a retort to continue the unbalancing.

"Yes, sir, I'm serious." Walton pressed his lips tightly, holding to his point.

"Then I don't understand you," Fenton said smoothly, picking a piece of imaginary lint from his trousers. "This *is* an insurance company, Major. Insuring people, among other things, is our business."

"But a policy on *one man* for twenty million dollars?" The words blurted from Walton.

Fenton flicked a glance at Carruthers, who picked it up. "Wrong, Major. The total insurance on Dr. Harold Mazurski, including accidental death, is twenty-two million." He let it hang. Good for old Herbie, thought Fenton. He was carrying it along.

"I . . . I don't understand. I thought when you had that much insurance on one person, you . . . well, you'd farm it out to several companies, you know?"

"You don't understand the size of Sierra Insurance," Carruthers told him. "We've handled individual policies for greater amounts before this."

Walton looked at him dumbfounded, unbelieving.

"Major." Carruthers was his old self again. "I don't

understand what you're getting at, Major. Our coverage on Mazurski is hardly any secret. We've carried it now for over two years. I find it surprising that you trouble to even bring up the subject."

"He's missing."

"I know damned well he's missing," Carruthers snapped.

"But how could you let him just fly off the way he did? I mean, you've got to protect your investment, don't you?"

Fenton and Carruthers exchanged glances. Fenton almost smiled. The Pentagon must have descended on Walton like a brick wall. Fenton nodded to Carruthers.

"Major, let me explain something to you," Carruthers said, his voice brisk. "Any coverage we write depends upon many mitigating circumstances. It depends upon the individual, his manner of work, his private life, the restrictions we place upon the policies, the conditions under which the individual may encounter disabling injury or death. There's no cut-and-dried rule. We've written coverage when, at least on the surface, the risks seemed unduly high. But every one of them was considered down to the last detail. We don't take unnecessary chances. And this affair with Mazurski, well . . ."

Carruthers swung his chair about, took the time to light a cigarette, gesturing at the Army man sitting ramrod-straight in his chair. "Are you aware that Mazurski is only a part of the problem we face, Major? Did you know that this company carries the coverage for the entire Maynard family? His daughter was aboard that missing Gulfstream, if you weren't aware of it. *And* we also wrote the coverage on the airplane itself."

Suddenly Carruthers was hot under the collar. Here he was knee-deep in financial disaster, and some uniformed popinjay was dumping silly-assed questions on his desk. Carruthers' hand slapped the desk top like a pistol shot. "Goddamnit, Major, I think you're forgetting your place! You were Mazurski's baby-sitter, weren't you? Then what were you doing letting the man out of *your* sight? It seems to me that if anyone screwed up, then I'm looking at him."

"Hold on, Mr. Carruthers!" Walton gestured like an old schoolteacher. "I wouldn't say I was his baby-sitter. I—"

"I don't give a shit what you say," Carruthers ground at him. "You show up here with egg all over your face, and you start asking questions that are completely out of line. Damn you, man, you aren't the only one with problems! We stand to take a beating of more than sixty million dollars on this whole caper! We're a hell of a lot more interested in finding out what's happened to that airplane, and *all* the people on board, than you are. Jesus! If you fuck up, someone slaps your wrist and you get a new job somewhere. You're not out a nickel. Not one blessed goddamned cent. Don't point any fingers at us." Carruthers smiled coldly. "As far as I'm concerned, Major, you can just—"

Reprieve came with the door to the office opening. Carruthers looked up, the anger unquenched as his secretary stood in the doorway. "What the hell is it?" he barked. "And why didn't you buzz me, goddamnit, instead of just busting in here like this!"

Pamela Self had worked for Herbert Carruthers for thirteen years. She waited out the verbal explosion before she spoke, and when she replied, her tone was modulated carefully. "You probably didn't hear me buzz, Mr. Carruthers. Mr. Schechter and Mr. Conway are here. They said you were expecting them."

Carruthers' expression was blank.

"Mr. Schechter is"—she hesitated a split-second—"from the NSA, Mr. Carruthers." She saw the recognition in his face. No need to add that Dick Conway was CIA.

Herb was hesitating too long, losing his momentum. Fenton nodded to the secretary. "Show them in, Miss Self."

She returned moments later. Irving Schechter was all high-dome. He was stocky, his clothes comfortably rumpled, but the whole college-campus presentation was so much window dressing. It took Fenton no time to recognize the brain behind his piercing eyes. And Dick Conway wouldn't be any easier, judged Fenton. Tall, well-built, thick dark hair, a man so sure of himself he was disarmingly relaxed. Fenton studied the sudden quiet relief on the face of Major Walton, and what he saw only confirmed his first impressions.

These two cats were cool, *very* capable, and they packed a lot of authority. He gave Carruthers the high sign to cool it, to pass the ball back to him. He didn't want Herb passing off to these people the drubbing he had been handing out to the major. When you got into the range of this kind of heavy artillery, you took your steps slowly and carefully to find out just what *was* happening. For the moment, Fenton had no idea as to why the big guns of government were zeroing in on the insurance company. But suspicion began to grow swiftly.

Irving Schechter turned to the Army officer. "Major Walton, how long have you been here?" It wasn't a question, but a demand, and Walton came close to jumping from his seat.

"Uh, just about ten or fifteen minutes, sir," he blurted.

"Who sent you?"

"Well, it seemed the only thing to do, sir. I mean, someone had to start picking up the pieces, and—"

"That's enough, Major," the NSA man broke in, his annoyance clear. "If you have no objections, we'll take it from here."

With those few words the major's presence was ignored as effectively as if he'd left the room. But Walton was far from unhappy. Higher authority had displaced him from whatever interrogation was going on between government and Sierra Insurance. And that meant that the major was off the hook. It was the old Peter Principle in government. If someone with bigger clout moved in, you were free.

Fenton didn't want Schechter or Conway picking up the ball and running with it through their office. Once they gained the edge, he knew he might not get it back, and he still wasn't privy to what the hell was going on.

"Schechter, why don't you tell us what's been going on with the search." Fenton had chosen his words carefully. No "Mr." in his address to the man. A statement instead of a question. The grudging look of respect from the NSA man told him he'd scored. Just those few words had brought them back to eyeball diplomacy.

"Just what you'd expect, Fenton." Okay; now they had the rules laid out. Conway's eyes had narrowed. Assessment of the situation was his bag. That told Fenton those two worked as a team, and between National Security Agency and Central Intelligence Agency they had a lot of muscle going for them. But Fenton had no intention of letting this become a push-pull contest. "We've got every available ship, submarine, and airplane involved. Full military reconnaissance satellites as well."

Fenton recalled something he'd heard on the radio that day. Just an incidental item, but now was when you put two and two together and added a few ingredients of extrapolation. "It must be important," he said quietly, "for you people to send up a Big Bird."

The sharp looks from both men told him he'd scored.

"I, ah, didn't know you were that well informed, Fenton." Schechter said it smoothly, but he was probing.

Fenton shrugged. "If Mazurski is as important as the flap being generated over his disappearance," he said easily, "the most natural thing would be to get one of the big camera satellites into position for a close look through the . . ." He hesitated only a moment. He'd come to a sudden decision, and he played the card that had dropped so unexpectedly in his lap. "Through the Devil's Triangle," he added. "You people always keep one of those Titan IIIB boosters on the pad with a Big Bird ready to go. If you've got a camera system that can read a license plate from a hundred miles, it seems the only logical thing to do." He smiled. "And I imagine you've tuned in the Ferret satellites for any electronic pickup."

"Where the hell do you get your information?" The CIA man was fairly growling the words.

Fenton locked eyes with Conway. "That's not really the issue," he said coldly. "You people didn't come here to banter." He turned back to Schechter. "We're in the same boat. Play your cards."

Schechter shifted his weight in his chair. Before he could talk, Fenton gestured with a finger. "Careful. You may crimp that wire, and your recording will be screwed up."

Schechter didn't blink an eye. "How much do you know about Dr. Mazurski?"

"Mr. Carruthers," Fenton drawled, "would be quite willing to show you our complete file. Provided, of course, that you'll sign a document swearing whatever privileged information you obtain from that file will never be repeated out of this room."

"Neatly done," Schechter parried. "Like you said, Fenton, cards on the table. Shall we deal?"

Fenton couldn't help it. The absurdity of the thrusting demanded a sudden laugh. He kept Schechter waiting as he lit a cigar. "All right. We don't *know*—and by 'know' I mean to the point where we could swear under oath that our information is certain—that much about Mazurski's situation with your computer complex. With Positronics. We know more than we should. Or more than you'd like us to know."

"Such as?"

"It's really not that difficult to surmise. The very nature of the policy this company has written on Mazurski speaks for itself. The extraordinary security in that part of the Positronics complex. The case of severe acne Major Walton brought into this office. Your own presence. All of it. Bits and pieces. General knowledge. It all adds up to Mazurski being something like a catalyst, a firing pin for some enormously vital program. It has international implications. According to what Mr. Carruthers has pieced together, the fact that one Dr. Harold Mazurski is missing has already been laid on the desk of the president himself."

Dick Conway rubbed a heavy chin. "That's a hell of a lot of surmising," he said coldly.

"Stuff it," Fenton snapped back to him. His voice was suddenly as short as his fading patience. "And don't lean on us, man. I don't like it. You can surmise without violating a single tenet of security. So cut the veiled threats, Conway."

The CIA man came slowly from his chair, his face twisted.

"*Sit down.*" That from Schechter. Conway retreated slowly to his seat.

Fenton couldn't resist the moment. He gave a glance of contempt at the CIA man and turned his attention back to Irving Schechter. "All right. Now we know who's boss here. Whom to talk with. Let's have it, Schechter. Why are you here?"

Schechter examined his fingernails. "It should have been obvious that we didn't want Mazurski to do any flying."

Fenton's laugh was harsh, humorless. "I don't believe I heard you really say that. Even the president of the United States flies. Who the hell doesn't?"

Schechter nodded his agreement. "Sure he does, Fenton. But he *has* to fly. No way out of it. Mazurski, on the other hand, did *not* have to fly. He was off on a pleasure trip, and—"

"What did you do? Write out your lines before you came here? What kind of crap is that?" Fenton shook his head. "You're working overtime to *seem* stupid. It doesn't fit, Schechter."

"Let's assume," Schechter said, leaning forward and making a steeple of his fingers, "that Mazurski is everything you people have, ah, surmised. On that basis it's clear that everything possible would be done to minimize the risks to his person. Of course we didn't want him to fly. We would have preferred he lived in an apartment right within the computer complex." He held up a hand to ward off any interruptions. "I'm aware we couldn't keep Mazurski in a cage. I'm also fully cognizant of all the details behind your people writing the coverage, the insurance, on this man. We went into this company more thoroughly than you'd ever guess before you received the nod, and—"

"And I bloody well wish we hadn't," growled Carruthers. It was the first time Herb had made a sound in many long minutes, and he didn't seem to be disturbed in any way by the look of annoyance on Schechter's face.

Schechter, for his part, seemed to recall suddenly in whose office he was sitting. He acknowledged the complaint with an easy gesture. "Well, Mr. Carruthers, even if it seems a side-handed compliment, we figured your company was the best-equipped to handle the arrangements. You've handled the odds in high risks before in a way that was eminently satisfying. This policy was so stiff, we knew how badly you could get hurt, and—" He paused at the grunt from Carruthers, then went on: ". . . and we thoroughly approved of your requirement that any flying that Mazurski did must be according to the minimum standards of a scheduled commercial carrier."

Carruthers glanced at Fenton, who stared back without expression. "Mr. Schechter," Carruthers said with open sarcasm, "you've just explained to me exactly what I have done to write this policy. But since you're so interested in reviewing details, then let that little recorder you're carrying take down the fact that the Gulfstream II flown by Positronics meets, absolutely, every air-transport standard, and even goes them some better in many ways. Did you ever find out how we computed our odds on Mazurski and any air travel he might do? No? I didn't think so. We used government standards."

Carruthers didn't hide his pleasure at the surprise his remark brought forth. "We simply followed the procedures used for the Air Force Eastern Test Range. A computer runs the range-safety operations for any shot from Cape Canaveral. If there's a ship at sea anywhere along the planned track of a shot and the odds are greater than—or perhaps I should say less than—one chance in a million of the ship being struck in the event anything goes wrong, then they hold the launch until things improve.

"We worked out our coverage for Mazurski the same way. The Gulfstream II is the finest airplane of its kind in the world. That's for starters. That machine is as strong as, if not stronger than, a 707, and *that's* good enough for the president. The Gulfstream could lose an engine at the worst possible point of a transatlantic flight—smack over the point of no return—and make it all the rest of the way on one engine, without straining. We even did an exhaustive computer study of the Gulfstream with its two engines as against the safety record of a bigger jet with four engines going for it. Strangely enough, the two engines had a slight margin in safety. And everything else, *everything*—electronics, emergency systems, crew standards—met not only the requirements of the FAA and the Positronics company, but also *our* standards, and they're as tough as anything you'll find anywhere. We even run a spy system to check out the customer."

He leaned forward, wrapping it up for the NSA man. "The policy reads that if we find any deviation, any failure, any laxity, of *any* kind, the policy is canceled automatically. And we'd make it stick in court." He leaned back in his chair. "Mr. Schechter, I wish we *had* found some flaw, somewhere. We'd be out from under so fast, all you'd see would be a blur. But there's never been so much as a hint of deviation from standards. And we're stuck."

Schechter didn't answer. But Dick Conway had been holding back, and now he let all kinds of expressions cross his face. Fenton knew the CIA man to be too good an actor to splash his emotions across his sleeve like some spilled drink. Conway was about to drop his verbal grenade.

"It's convenient, though," said the CIA man.

Carruthers fairly clawed at the remark. "What the hell do you mean, convenient? *What's* convenient?"

Conway's expression was that of a hunting animal. "The fact that the airplane, with Dr. Mazurski aboard, disappeared in the area known as the Devil's Triangle."

"What in the hell is so convenient about *that*?"

"It's the only area in which the airplane's disappearance could be laid to other than natural or mechanical causes."

Fenton studied the CIA man with great caution. Carruthers was half out of his seat when he caught Fenton's open gesture to sit and be quiet.

"That is what I call an asinine remark," Fenton said carefully. "May I remind you that this company, at least at this moment, is *still* stuck for the tab? But before we go on with that, I think you'd better spell out just what you call the Devil's Triangle." Fenton managed a thin smile. "After all, it's something like religion, which may or may not lie within the province of the CIA. Nothing would surprise me at this point. So, for the record, Conway, just what *is* the Devil's Triangle?"

"I think you already know," Conway said, acid creeping into his tone.

"Jesus Christ," Fenton said, to no one in particular.

"It's also called the Bermuda Triangle," Conway said suddenly. "*For the record,* then. It is more than a half-million square miles of ocean, with many islands and part of the Florida coastline thrown in. It runs from Bermuda in mid-Atlantic in what's generally a southwest or west-southwest line to about Saint Augustine on the northeastern coast of Florida. Then, almost due south, through the Miami area, to the Keys. The line then extends southeast to Puerto Rico, and from there back up, generally northeast, to Bermuda."

"That's not a triangle, Conway." Fenton enjoyed being a stickler for detail. "What you just described is a trapezium. That's basically a rectangle in which no two sides or angles are the same."

"Call it whatever you want, Fenton. Triangle, rectangle or trapezium. It's all the same." Conway was as cool as ice; the man with wounded ego had vanished into thin air. "Like I said, having the airplane disappear while in that area is peculiarly convenient. No matter how extensive our search—and by God, it will be extensive—if we don't turn up anything, then the Gulfstream is simply added to the list. Several hundred planes and ships have disappeared within the Triangle in the last thirty or forty years, without a single trace ever being found, and—"

Fenton turned his attention suddenly from Conway to Irving Schechter. "He's off, and running with his speech," he broke into Conway's monologue, "so maybe you'll answer the prize question for me."

Schechter shrugged, as if expecting the interruption and the query.

"You're NSA. You've got a direct stake in all this." Fenton jerked a thumb in Conway's direction. "But him? He's CIA. And according to the rulebooks I know, CIA gets into the act only when there's involvement with a foreign agency, or government, *and* when it's outside of the United States. Otherwise the FBI has jurisdiction. So who wrote him into the act? What the hell is he doing here?"

Schechter didn't respond. He just watched the CIA man as Conway leaned forward in his seat, eyes boring into Fenton.

Well, it comes finally. . . .

"Part one, *Mister* Fenton. That airplane *was* out of the country when it disappeared. Or whatever happened to it."

"I guess you've got a part two."

"By all means. The aircraft was last reported in an area where there's heavy activity by Soviet fishing fleets, Soviet oceanographic vessels, and Soviet submarines."

Fenton digested the words. "It's a big ocean. You've got more to say, Conway. Say it."

"Part three is that we do *not* know what happened to that Gulfstream. We don't know what happened to Dr. Mazurski or even where he might be. But we recognize several very clear and distinct possibilities." He glanced at Carruthers and returned his gaze to Fenton.

"You people," he said slowly, the words coming across the room with a metronome beat, "*could* be involved in some crazy scheme to deliver Dr. Harold Mazurski into the hands of the Russians."

Silence filled the room like freezing mist.

"*Get—the—fuck—out—of—my—office!*"

Herbert Carruthers stood like stone behind his desk, his finger stabbing at Conway, his anger so great that he trembled visibly.

"You rotten piece of shit. . . ." He had to force the words through clenched teeth. "I flew in two wars for my country, you miserable bastard," he swore. "And not you, not *anybody*, is ever going to say to me what you just did and get away with it. Now, you get the hell out of here or I'll—"

"I apologize."

Carruthers swallowed air. He fought desperately to find his voice. Mingled rage and shock trapped the words in his throat.

"I don't think that will be enough," Fenton answered for him.

The CIA man nodded, utterly sure of himself. He turned from Fenton back to the nearly apoplectic Carruthers. "I *meant* what I said. About the apology."

Herb looked at Fenton, who nodded. "I believe him," Fenton said slowly. "He may be a bit of a shit, but I think it's only his job."

He got a wry smile for that from Conway, and a chuckle from Schechter. Conway rose to his feet, still not sure of Carruthers. "Sir, I'm well aware of your combat record. B-24's over Germany for nineteen months. Then you volunteered for B-29's. You made it all the way to light colonel. Wing navigator. I know about every day you flew, with whom you flew, what missions, what decorations you were awarded, what . . . There's no question about your loyalty, Mr. Carruthers."

"Then what the hell was that all about?" Fenton relaxed as Carruthers slowly resumed his seat.

They were looking at a different Conway now. Someone who was ready to come out of the woodwork without any more games.

"I said what I did, Mr. Carruthers"—Conway glanced to the side for a moment as he talked—"and this goes for Mr. Fenton as well, of course, because what I said had more than a grain of truth in it."

Carruthers appealed to Fenton. "I swear I think I'll kill him."

"I wouldn't blame you," Fenton said smoothly.

"When you sit in our position," Conway went on, unruffled by the exchange, "you consider all possibilities. Not just the human angle, but those the NSA computers give us. We're not exactly new to heuristics. We touch every cornerstone possible. And there *is* that chance that this company, through you two gentlemen, *could* have engineered passing Dr. Mazurski on to the Russians. *If* that's what you wanted to do, of course."

He gestured to gain time. "If it helps, put yourselves in our position. Personal feelings aren't involved here." Conway continued to impress Fenton with every passing moment. He was building his case slowly, but with a solid foundation, and if Fenton knew psychology and semantics, at the precise moment, Schechter would step in with the clincher.

"Imagine, if you will," Conway went on, now pacing the room slowly, his hands animated, "the enormous payoff involved to get Mazurski into Russian hands. Just getting Mazurski out of the way, removing him from the program—always assuming the Russians were fully informed of it—"

"And you're assuming that, of course," Fenton broke in.

Conway favored him with a blank look. "Of course. Wouldn't you? Now, if they've cottoned on to the program at Positronics, then getting Mazurski out of the way could reap enormous benefits for the Soviets. All they have to do is put him on ice for a while. That brings up the biggest can of worms you ever saw." He stabbed a finger in Fenton's direction. "The pilot of that airplane. Lavagetti. Could he have been bought? By the Russians, by anyone representing them? There *are* international groups for hire. We use them, the Russians use them, and—"

"Are you really suggesting Lavagetti was *bought?*"

Conway shook his head as he turned to Carruthers. "I'm not *suggesting* anything. I'm examining. There's the steward, Wilfredo Pérez. That one is wide open for possibilities. He had communist connections in Cuba. Solid connections, I might add."

"But he—"

Conway didn't let Carruthers finish. "I know, I know," he said quickly, holding up both hands. "He got disenchanted with Castro, and he split."

"He did more than that," Carruthers told him quietly. "His family was killed. Pérez got three of the people who did it before he broke out and made it to this country."

"It's a nice story," Conway said, and let it hang.

"Damnit, we checked him out coming and going," Carruthers protested.

"So did we," Conway said. "He checked out clean. But we've been taken for a snowride before. Maybe the whole thing was a setup from the beginning.

These people plan for years amd years ahead, just on the possibilities. They don't leave out a thing. They have their people in place, and they keep them on ice until they need them."

He stopped pacing, serious enough for his words not to be taken lightly. "Listen to me, both of you. We know the Russians would easily pay a hundred million dollars, or even more, to pull Mazurski from his computer program, because the price is cheap when you consider what this man has been doing. Mazurski has had the Russians tongue-tied and baffled ever since we started using his answers and recommendations in both the diplomatic and the military fields. Sure, sure, I know the Russians could have made a direct move to kill the man. But in the long run, that would have cost them badly. Both of us—their side and ours—despite what the world may think, operate within certain unwritten rules. Breaking them means a breakdown in what we like to think of as détente, or whatever the favored term is nowadays."

He slammed a fist into his palm. "They could accomplish what they need just by getting Mazurski out of circulation. That's enough. He could be in one of the Arab countries. He could be in Europe. Hell, everybody aboard that plane could be aboard a Russian sub or a trawler right now. The airplane could have been ditched at sea. We're pretty well convinced it wasn't forced down. Too much radar and electronic coverage the day the Gulfstream vanished. Because of that shot from the Cape, the whole missile range was alive and especially alert. So it wasn't anything that blatant."

They took it in silence. Fenton relit a cold cigar. He blew away a cloud of smoke and looked at Conway. "You're in the wrong business. Hollywood's in the market for good suspense stories. You'd make a killing."

"Damnit, Fenton, stop sparring with—"

"Do you want a signed and sworn statement from us that we didn't kidnap, hijack, sell, dispatch, kill, or otherwise become involved in any way with Mazurski or anyone else aboard that airplane?"

Carruthers jumped in with both feet behind Fenton. "We'd even throw in polygraph tests for free," he said.

Conway had stopped where he stood. He didn't attempt an answer to the sarcasm.

Irving Schechter stirred in his seat. "No, of course not," he said quietly. "Conway's explained the sort of possibilities we have to consider." He gestured to Fenton. "You, more than anyone else we know outside our group, understand the need for such suspicions, for considering anything and everything." He pursed his lips, then resumed. "And you know that if we believed, even for an instant, that there was any chance you *were* involved in any way, we'd hardly be here openly telling you of our suspicions."

"Maybe yes, maybe no," Fenton threw back at him.

"Which means?"

Fenton laughed. "It's about time you got to the obvious instead of the unlikely. What's your pitch, Mr. Schechter?"

The NSA man didn't share his seeming good humor. "*You* are, Mr. Fenton." He paused. "Shall I go on?"

"Right now, you're the only game in town," Fenton said with an easy wave of his hand.

"We're moving rapidly into a dead end. We've explained the extent of our search. If the president of this country were missing, we couldn't be doing more than we are right now."

"And the answer is still zero," Fenton prompted.

"Precisely. Obviously, we'll continue the search

under maximum effort for some time. But no one really has any strong hopes at this point."

Fenton's gesture showed impatience. "Spill it out, Mr. Schechter. The hard nut. Or don't you want to admit—at least, not yet—that the real reason you came here, as did Major Walton and your vaudeville buddy from the CIA, is that we represent what may be your last hope?"

Irving Schechter nodded calmly in agreement to Fenton's words.

"It seems, Mr. Fenton, that you're the best. You've got to carry on an investigation of a nature we're not equipped to handle. We deal in hard realities. The strange phenomena of the Devil's Triangle are hard for us to square with higher-ups."

He waited for Fenton to reply, but no words came. "There's always the chance that the aircraft was lost from causes unknown but still perfectly natural," Schechter said after his pause. "If that's the case, we might yet track down those causes and any subsequent events. Then again, we may not. Given the conditions at the time the aircraft was lost, the odds for that happening are less than one in a million."

Herbert Carruthers had visions of sixty-two million dollars going down a hole. "Would you mind telling me," he said directly to the NSA agent, "just what it is you're getting at?"

"Simply that, as I said, we need your help."

"Ah." that's all he got from Fenton.

"Dale Fenton," Schechter went on, "just happens to be the only man of his kind in the insurance-investigation business. His particular background as a pilot is important. The time he spent with the air inspector general in the Air Force. His work with FAA and CAB. His own . . . well, special pursuits in engineering and other fields." For the first time in many minutes Schechter permitted himself the luxury of a smile. "There is also that, ah, very special training he received in our school in that remote area of New Jersey, where—"

Fenton was straight up in his chair. "What the hell do you mean, *your* school?"

By way of answer Schechter opened his attaché case and removed a thick file. He held it up. "Here's your complete record, Fenton. Do you think we'd really permit a special training facility to exist, staffed with what you believed were ex-members of NSA, CIA, OSS, FBI, and other agencies, without full control of what went on? Do you really think we'd allow people of your caliber to learn what you did if we didn't consider you useful, in an emergency, to this government?" He tapped the file with his forefinger.

After a pause Schechter returned to his message. "We're betting sixty-two million dollars—*your* sixty-two million, Mr. Carruthers—that Fenton will come up with the answers. If he doesn't"—Schechter presented what was a shrug of monumental indifference to financial problems—"then you've got to pay out. To repeat, we do not believe this airplane simply . . . vanished. So we can't do otherwise than to lean to the likelihood that some direct involvement figures in here, that *someone* made the attempt, and successfully, either through hijack or prearrangement, to control the movement of that aircraft so that Mazurski came under their hand."

Schechter was as businesslike as an accountant as he ran through his summation, the end result of all the sparring up to this moment. "If the aircraft isn't found, or if you don't produce the kind of evidence we believe is there, then you people, within the time limit written into your coverage, must pay through the nose. You can't even hold off payment for seven years, working that old legal angle, because there are certain elements involved, elements considered obvious, in the dangers of flight. So you've *got* to pay.

"We're interested, desperately so, in what you uncover. We must know what happened to Mazurski. Whether he's lost, kidnapped, dead, or on ice somewhere—whatever. Until we have a trace of something specific, our government is mired in the quicksand of this whole situation. The balance of power between this country and the Soviet Union is involved, and you can't go much higher than *that*." He occupied himself with putting away Fenton's file as he talked. "So we're both in the same ball game. Our government, and your company. And I will state now"—he looked first at Fenton and then at Carruthers—"for the record, that we offer any and all assistance in whatever you may—"

"Hold it right there," Carruthers broke in. "Not so very long ago, you, or Conway, here, it doesn't matter, were making unhappy noises about what you called impossible causes. I think you'd better spell that out some more. You were talking about the Devil's Triangle. And you had a look on your face that said you wished you'd never heard about it. So how does *that* fit into our investigation?"

Conway came back into the exchange. "Ask your computers in Orlando, Mr. Carruthers," he said, his words lacking assurance. "I'll give you the basic numbers. In the last thirty years, and we're going back no further than that, but I'm including certain military and government aircraft that aren't in the public records . . ." He took a deep breath. "In the last thirty years, a total of sixty-seven ships and boats of all sizes and types, *and* no less than 192 aircraft of all types, involving approximately seventeen hundred people, without any known explanation, or justification, or whatever, have disappeared in the Devil's

Triangle. I'm *not* including those that have been lost for identifiable reasons."

"You mean total blanks?" Fenton queried.

"I mean total blanks, Mr. Fenton. The cases I've cited—and we'll make available to you whatever details we've gathered—are, on the basis of all facts known, and I stress the word 'facts,' both inexplicable and impossible."

Carruthers tapped a pencil on his desk. "I still don't understand why you people don't carry out your own investigation. I know you say you deal in hard reality, but you've had a bunch of UFO-project teams for years. Hedgehog, Blue Book, that whole bunch. It seems to me that—"

"Mr. Carruthers," Conway said with distaste in his expression, "we plan for many, uh, contingencies, but we, ah, don't—"

"What he's trying to say, Herb," Fenton interrupted the uncomfortable CIA man, "is that despite their reputation, they don't have a spook division."

"Neatly said, Mr. Fenton," Schechter quipped.

"And," Fenton added, "what all this boils down to is that they'd like us to chase their ghosts for them." He stood up and motioned to the door. "Don't call us, gentlemen. We'll call you."

Chapter 7

He studied his stopwatch. "We fire up in exactly three minutes," Dale Fenton told his copilot.

Neil Walker nodded. "Right. Three minutes it is."

Fenton glanced through the pilot's window of the Grumman Gulfstream II. He had gone to great lengths to prepare for this flight. Gulfstream 679D was as close to duplicating the missing airplane, Gulfstream 666D, as memory, logbooks, and technicians could accomplish. The electronic equipment *was* exactly the same, including the placement of instruments within the panel, in the overhead, and through the console between the two pilots' seats. Behind the flight deck the airplane was configured to the same specifications as the still mysteriously vanished airplane. The same lounge arrangement of seats and couches, the bar, stereo, the supplies. They'd even figured the most likely baggage loading and the possibilities of baggage being thrown about wildly in event of encountering the clear-air turbulence. Fenton had researched the individuals aboard 666D, and the passengers he had aboard now, and would pick up later, were almost physical duplicates in weight of those from the missing Gulfstream.

He accumulated the information in meticulous records and then ran a computer simulation of the flight, studying fuel depletion at different points of the flight, considering every factor of weather, air traffic . . . the works. The computer gave him the exact performance of Gulfstream 666D right up to that moment when the airplane stopped reporting its enroute positions.

Fenton arranged a meeting with the crew of the big Boeing that had been struck by lightning the day the Gulfstream II disappeared. The ARIA pilot and his crew all hewed to the same story, with the minor variations resulting from different viewing points and subjective reaction to lightning. But the crew was completely in agreement that the area had been free of any cumulus-cloud structuring, and even of noteworthy stratus. Master Sergeant Al Engle, crew chief, broke it down a bit further. "We had some strong Saint Elmo's fire that day," he told Fenton. "You know, buildup of static electricity, that sort of thing. Interference in certain electronics, but nothing to jar our teeth."

"Is that rare?" Fenton pressed.

"Uncommon for that day, for the weather conditions," Engle said, "but not rare."

"Would that kind of condition alarm you at all?"

Engle laughed. "It never did before, but it sure as hell would have me on my toes—in sneakers—now. Hey, man, we made it back okay. The iron bird got chewed up a bit, and we blew about two million worth of electronic gear, but no one was hurt. Can't complain about that."

Dead end. First, the concept of a lightning strike—a major opposite-charge bolt—just did not jibe with the conditions known to produce lightning. That, thought Fenton, should have brought on some sharp questioning. It didn't, and he saw why. There are areas of high static electricity, and the ARIA itself was a powerhouse of energy within and without. It *could* have built up so much static electricity that it discharged its own bolt. That was common enough. So though no one knew for certain that this in fact had happened, since there wasn't any need to check it out further, no one did more than shrug it off. The big ARIA aircraft had flown through the same area thousands of times, in weather conditions far worse in terms of electrically saturated air, and they'd never lost one.

As a pilot, Fenton understood the attitude of the crew. *They* weren't weather scientists. They flew with the intrinsic attitude of most military or airline crews. It was a takeoff from Ernie Gann in *Fate Is the Hunter*. That no matter what the science or engineering, no matter how thorough the planning, how skilled the crews, how exhaustive the preparations, airplanes go down from causes unknown. Somewhere in the heavens, wrote Gann, there is a great invisible genie who every so often lets down his pants and pisses all over the pillars of science.

"Time to light up." Fenton emerged from his introspection and nodded to Neil Walker. They called off each item on the checklist and brought Gulfstream 697D to life. The engines came in smoothly, and the intricate systems and subsystems of the jet flowed and purred. Fenton called ground control and got the nod to roll. He let Walker handle the taxiing to the active runway. It gave him that last-moment time to review the other soldiers he'd lined up in a row for the flight.

Fenton had called Irving Schechter, and the NSA man had seen to it that every man in ground control, radar, the towers and in air-traffic control who had been on duty when the Positronics jet took off with Mazurski aboard was on duty right now. The federal aviation administrator had balked at first, but a call from the White House had laid to rest any objections—or questions. Then came setting up the Air Force along the Eastern Test Range. Fenton wanted a duplication, or as close to it as possible, of what was happening on the range when Triple-Six Delta arrowed away from its grandstand seat of the Titan IIIC launch. The range was fully alive. Every facility of the Cape was running through a mock countdown and launch. All downrange stations were alive and tracking a simulated launch day. The same people were at their stations.

The weather couldn't be so handily arranged, but the variations present in the heavens could be ironed out through computer comparison.

At exactly the same moment that Gulfstream 666D had left the ground with Rocky Lavagetti at the controls, Dale Fenton came back on the yoke as he raced along the runway of Fort Lauderdale Executive Airport. Neil Walker had filed the exact flight plan activated by the missing airplane. They arced into the sky in the same right turnout from takeoff. They went into Tampa International, and every move was again a textbook repeat of the airplane whose shadow they pursued. On the ground Fenton kept the engines running. Neil Walker extended the stairway, and their passenger bounded into the cabin—a man of the same build and weight as the tennis player Rena Kim had invited to join their group. Then it was another long, smooth lunge down the runway, and they were slicing across the Florida peninsula to Daytona Beach. They taxied to the executive terminal and opened up the bird. Two more passengers to fill the list. They took on exactly the same quantity of fuel as had been loaded by 666D, buttoned up, and again, following the ghost trail, eased into the sky.

Fenton held the airplane on what he believed was the closest approximation of the path flown by Lavagetti when he set up the aerial view of the Titan launch. He waited the appropriate time and then eased the Gulfstream into a steady climb. Since 666D had followed a specific flight plan under air-traffic control and had crossed the Air Defense Identification Zone at a time and altitude identified in traffic for that day, he had no problem in duplicating that portion of the flight.

His notes told him that Lavagetti had filed for a cruising altitude of 30,000 feet but that air-traffic control had edged them higher, to 33,000 feet. Fenton let the autopilot ride her up, as he assumed the other man would have done. At flight level 330 he nosed the Gulfstream into level flight, checked everything three times over, and settled back in his seat, some unknown anticipation preventing him from being comfortable.

Everything was perfect. They were on their way to Puerto Rico in a machine that made you try to feel even the slightest tremble.

The minutes passed slowly. Fenton felt a strange sensation—strictly visceral, he reminded himself—as they neared the point of the last position report sent back from Triple-Six Delta. He found himself holding his breath, searching for a sign, *any* sign, damnit!

Nothing. They were suspended, seemingly without movement, in a world of air as steady as a sheet of glass. Oh, sure, there was a change. So obvious it couldn't be missed. Lavagetti had flown 666D on a day of perfect visibility. They'd lost that, in terms of having the ground visible to them. The winds aloft had been predicted to boost them along their flight path, but that was the kind of variable the computer digested easily enough. The only visible change was the solid cloud deck blanketing the world. No sign of an ocean or islands; no indication that this entire planet wasn't a twin of Venus, covered by impenetrable clouds stretching from horizon to horizon. The sun tore at them through a deep-blue sky.

It wasn't a problem. Anything but, for they were more than ten thousand feet above the cloud tops, turbulence was only a memory, and flying conditions at their height were perfect. Before takeoff Fenton had personally checked the weather from half a dozen sources, including the Air Force, for the entire range. He'd gone so far as to study thirty-minute readouts from weather-satellite photos. The ARIA planes along the range had radioed in real-time weather reports as well. There wasn't a single flaw in the information flow to Fenton.

Hold one; sure, one change requiring a power reduction. By the time they reached cruising altitude and gave the Gulfstream her head, they'd be riding an invisible river of air, a jetstream carrying them along at 33,000 feet with a free bonus of just about seventy-five miles an hour.

How many times, Fenton thought unhappily, had thousands of other planes of all types flown this same route at this same altitude without even a hint of difficulty and . . . ?

He locked his eyes on the navigation instruments.

Something *was* amiss. . . .

He sat quietly, scanning, studying. He glanced to the flight instruments, the engine gauges. Everything perfect. Then . . . ? Back to the navigation systems. He recognized what had snatched at his attention. An inconsistency. Slight. Easily missed.

He studied one gauge in particular. At a certain point in time, to correspond to a predicted position over the earth, two needles were to cross. That moment would register his position over an electronic checkpoint, specify a distance between two stations, read out the real time and constantly changing distance between the aircraft and each station.

Yet . . . there it was. They were several minutes beyond that point in time when they had been predicted to cross the checkpoint. But they hadn't yet reached that position. That was wrong. So wrong that it began to set off alarm bells in his head. He checked the DME, the instrument that read out distance between the Gulfstream and the station to which it was tuned. It provided an instantaneous digital readout of distance from the station as well as their speed across the earth, so invisible below.

"This thing is crazy," he murmured to Neil Walker. And the likelihood was that the DME *was* wrong. Except that they had two such instruments on the panel, and both gave the same readings. "We're twice the distance to the station we should be," he said to his copilot.

Walker hesitated before answering. He leaned forward, flicking the DME control from one setting to another, then back to the original. "It can't be," he said quietly, "but it is."

Again silence between them as they studied and considered. By now every instinct was alive in Fenton, his senses razor-keen, and he knew Walker was going through the same mental exercises that raced through his brain. Fenton leaned forward to adjust his DME for a ground-speed readout. He stared at the instrument. "Give me a ground-speed readout from your DME," he instructed Walker.

The Gulfstream II at their altitude and weight had a true air speed at long-range cruise of 438 knots—just about 505 miles an hour. They had a tailwind of 65 knots, or 75 miles an hour, which should have given them a speed over the earth's surface of some 580 miles an hour. The DME digital readout was in knots. If the world hadn't gone crazy, then the readout from each instrument should have been 505 knots.

It wasn't. It showed a ground speed of 339 knots.

That was only 390 miles an hour, and it was also flatly impossible. They went through a meticulous check of every instrument available to them. Everything was right on the money. Altitude, true air speed, expected temperature, course—everything except position and ground speed.

If the instruments were true, then the Gulfstream was racing into *a direct headwind of 190 miles an hour.*

But that was patently ridiculous.

Under conditions the meterologists described as "light and variable," there could be, along the route from Florida to Puerto Rico, some winds from east to west. But it was rare, for the prevailing atmospheric flow moved from west to east. The jetstreams flowed in that same pattern. And the weather satellites, as well as all other sources, were positive in a wind flow of west to east for this very moment.

But according to the instruments, all that had been thrown into the nearest trash can. If the instruments were correct, and certainly they seemed to be, they were flying into a headwind of 190 miles an hour.

Fenton radioed one of the range-tracking stations that also provided a daily weather feedback to headquarters of the Eastern Test Range. He made no comment as to what was happening, but asked for a winds-aloft report from 20,000 to 40,000 feet. He found himself staring at Walker as the station report came in. They were still "showing" a sixty-knot wind flowing from west to east, and that included the band from 30,000 to 35,000 feet. And they were at 33,000 feet.

"How the hell," Fenton said quietly, "do we reconcile an error in wind speed of 265 miles an hour?" When you expect, and have confirmed, a westerly wind of 75 miles an hour, and get instead an easterly flow of 190 miles an hour—*unknown* to the men operating the most sophisticated weather-surveillance equipment in existence—it's time to pay close attention to the hackles rising on the back of your neck.

Neil Walker motioned to the DME instruments and then to other navigation and course dials. They were flying with an automatic pilot using a heading lock, tracking several VOR (very high frequency) navigation stations, and also using a highly sophisticated RNAV (area navigation) computer. Everything reading information to the pilots could be cross-checked by their directional gyro and other instruments, and these were now showing a new effect on the aircraft. "We're picking up a crosswind now," Walker said. The Gulfstream was no longer pointing in the direction of its flight. With the wind force now partially from one side, blowing the airplane off course, the autopilot had detected the change and was compensating. It turned the nose of the airplane more into the wind, to offset its effect, so that the Grumman was—in terms of its track over the ground—flying at an angle to its course. It was like a man looking over his shoulder as he runs—his eyes pointed in one direction but his body moving in another. The autopilot was trying to keep the airplane steady on its course no matter in what direction the airplane was pointing its nose.

"Do you want to hold the correction?" Walker asked.

Fenton shook his head. "No. Let's say we're sitting up here fat, dumb, and happy. We let the electronics do our work for us. Okay; the autopilot's got the course lock engaged. Let's turn that little goodie off."

The autopilot had been holding a heading of 120 degrees, no matter what effect the winds might have on the airplane. By turning off the course lock, Fenton had placed the machine at the whim of the winds.

He sat back and held a conversation with himself. You're up here, he mentally reviewed, and everything's in the green. It's all working like a charm. You've got everything going for you except a course lock. But why worry? The wind's moving along your course. No variations. All the forecasts gave you that prediction. The updates haven't changed. So. You've got a cloud deck below, but that doesn't affect a thing. It doesn't even matter. Everythings perfect.

He leaned forward, his eyes moving slowly about the instrument panel. You've been told you've got a tailwind, he continued in his mental review. You can always get a change in wind velocity, but the effect will be minimal. No sweat. The last thing you'll ever expect, especially because of those weather-report updates, is a change that adds up to 265 miles an hour. . . . It's so ridiculous that you don't even consider it . . . especially if the change means a headwind that violates all of nature's rules. So you relax. No visual checkpoints on the ground. The flight isn't so long that a change in sun position is noticeable. Time for another cup of coffee. Light up a cigarette. Pleasant up here. . . .

And before you know it, that invisible, impossibly crazy river of air that's come out of nowhere is throwing you far off course. . . . Even as he chewed slowly on his own thoughts, Fenton watched the deviations appearing on the navigation instruments. Silent, slow, but representing an enormous change in what was happening to them. No way for human senses, up this high and over the cloud deck, to tell a thing. You had to scan the gauges, monitor constantly the messages proclaimed so silently by those small, thin needles.

And the message was clear. The Gulfstream was taking that impossible wind now at an angle of forty degrees. Now that the autopilot wasn't slaved to get them to the next navigation homing station down the line, they were being blown far off course.

With the tremendous speed of that wind, it wouldn't take long for an aircraft to be far from where any crew thought it might be. Once you're within a moving river of air, you're part and parcel of it. It's like being in a balloon. The air may be carrying you over the ground at a hundred miles an hour, but up there you don't even feel a breeze. Very quickly you could be in the middle of nowhere.

Could this same thing have happened to the missing Gulfstream? But there were ways to know what was happening. Fenton couldn't accept that Lavagetti or his copilot in Triple-Six Delta would have been so lax as not to have observed just what he and Walker had seen for themselves. That is, *if* they had run into this same sort of impossible wind.

And even *had* they been blown far off course before coming aware of that thoroughly unlikely event, so what? Triple-Six Delta at takeoff from Daytona Beach had a still-air cruising range of some 3,800 miles. Getting back to Florida, or landing anywhere in the South Atlantic or the Caribbean, or flying to South or Central America, or . . . hell, it had no end of possible places to fly in complete safety.

Smart-ass, Fenton growled to himself. If you know so much, then where the hell is the missing airplane?

And, perhaps more important, why hasn't anyone—*anyone*—ever mentioned these bloody impossible winds at this altitude? Could it be that no one ever encountered them before? Fenton didn't believe that. The answer was simply too convenient. But the winds, impossible as they seemed, *were real*—as he was seeing this very instant.

So how many planes in the past, of all those that had vanished, lacking modern electronics, were blown far off course, and disappeared, out of fuel, hundreds of miles from where other planes and ships searched for them?

Hold it, *hold it*, Fenton berated himself. That's history. The missing Gulfstream *did* have the finest electronic aids in the world.

Could there have been some mechanical failure of disastrous proportion aboard the airplane? Could there have been a fire or shorting out of electrical gear? And could that have coincided with this same type of tremendous wind?

If those few *ifs* came together at a single point in time, as was wont to happen in this business, then there *was* a remote, albeit definite possibility, that 666D *might* have gone down into the sea, or even somewhere deep within South America, or anywhere else a thousand miles or more from where everyone had been looking for the airplane.

Great, Fenton thought darkly. Just great.

Chapter 8

"Okay. Let's take it right from the top. Triple-Six Delta disappeared under conditions largely known to us. We have known quantities, where the crew, the passengers, the aircraft, and other things are involved. Anything of which we're *not* aware is a complete X factor." Fenton slouched in a huge easy chair as though the chair embraced his body. He held up one finger and continued. "Is the incident unique unto itself?" He grimaced at his choice of words. "Do we have a precedent? Something that could provide some hint or clue . . ."

Fenton sat alone in the dark living room of his penthouse. Through the balcony windows across the room glittered the lights of downtown Orlando. When he faced a particularly thorny situation, he often retreated to his own form of solitude, voicing aloud his thoughts, whipping himself into self-argument. He dropped his hand to the side of the chair, pressed several buttons. He sipped slowly from a drink as he listened to his own voice on tape playback.

The only route now was to search out the details of any precedent. Not some aircraft missing in a storm, but a situation in which impossibility far outweighed probability. "No argument there," Fenton murmured aloud. "Flight 19 leads the pack. . . ."

He picked up his telephone, then hesitated, with a glance at his watch. One-fifteen in the morning. Well, that's what they get those bonuses for, he said to placate his conscience as he punched in the numbers for his chief computer programmer. A sleepy voice mumbled into the phone. "Susan? Dale Fenton here. I imagine you're just lying around wishing for something to do."

He heard sheets rustling as Susan Gray came quickly awake. "Of course. It's what I do every night. What's up, Dale?"

"I need you in the madhouse, Susan. I need every lead I can muster on that case of Flight 19."

"I remember it," she said slowly. "We finished the inputs only this afternoon. Meet you there?"

"I'm on my way, Susan. I'll even put up the coffee. Bye."

"Slave driver."

Susan Gray was a remarkable woman, forty-six years old and a genius in cybernetics—computer—systems. She lived with her husband, an executive with a construction firm in Orlando, and without the distraction of children, she could devote extensive time to her work with Heracles. In the event of a flap, when day-or-night availability was everything, she moved into a small apartment alongside the computer system.

Fenton stuffed some papers into his attaché case, reflected for a moment, and punched in the number to the computer center. Calling the security team before his arrival would have the doors open and ready for him by the time he got there.

The enigmatic case of Flight 19 could be the best possible lead, he thought, wheeling his Corvette from the parking slot beneath his building. Of course, 1945 was a long ways back in history when you were looking for details. Fenton wouldn't have paid that much attention to something thirty years in the past, except for one thing. The naval board of inquiry had given up in despair and bafflement, had crawled away from the inexplicable by issuing the lame-duck but nonetheless honest statement that "This unprecedented peacetime loss seems to be a total mystery, the strangest ever investigated in the annals of naval aviation."

That was strong medicine, for Fenton knew that a naval board of inquiry has about as much interest in the enigmatic as a horse has in galloping across the moon. It was so strong that it deserved Fenton's full attention, and more information than was in the published reports on what had happened to the entire flight of bombers—and a huge search plane—under peacetime conditions as near to perfect for search operations as one could ask for. The printed word was too often the result of someone's extrapolation of data collected by someone else: "facts" passed down from one source to another often became so distorted as to be unrecognizable.

The very first reports Fenton had ever studied on Flight 19 had wrinkled his sense of suspicion. Almost every statement referred to the five missing aircraft as Grumman TBM Avengers. Fenton was familiar with the airplane. A husky single-engine torpedo bomber that normally carried a crew of three. The airplane first saw combat in June 1942, making its debut in the Battle of Midway in the Pacific. Six Avengers had flown in concert with four Army bombers in a balls-out torpedo bombing strike against the Japanese fleet. It was anything but an auspicious start, for the Japanese creamed five of the six Avengers. But the Avenger went on to become the best torpedo bomber operating from American carriers through the rest of the war, and it chalked up a grisly and devastating toll of enemy warships.

Now, that was important. The airplane was tough, and it was a well-known quantity, and it was reliable. That evaluation would have to figure in any judgment of what had happened to Flight 19.

But what made Fenton suspicious was that identification of the airplanes as Grumman TBM Avengers: an inaccuracy at the outset of any report must make the remainder of the report clearly suspect.

Grumman built the airplane known as the TBF Avenger. During the war, so pressing was the demand for the sturdy torpedo bombers that the Navy set up another huge production facility run by General Motors. To distinguish the General Motors aircraft from the Grumman, for there were small but vital differences in construction and equipment, those planes manufactured by GM were designated TBM, while TBF remained the code for the Grumman planes.

Yet almost every writer who had prepared lurid copy on the disappearance of Flight 19 had identified the aircraft as Grumman TBM Avengers. If the writers were so ignorant of basic designations, then how could they be relied upon to be any more accurate in the rest of their alleged reports? Well, he had no choice. He'd have to go on what was available and then separate the wheat from the chaff.

The basic facts were simple enough. On the afternoon of December 5, 1945, Flight 19, consisting of five TBM aircraft, departed the U.S. Naval Air Station at Fort Lauderdale from the southeast coast of Florida. The flight was set up as an advanced overwater nagivation exercise and was led by a highly qualified flight instructor. The remaining four aircraft were piloted by what were described as "well-experienced and qualified pilots, all of whom had between 350 and 400 hours of flight time." Right there Fenton found himself drawing up short. Who the hell was "well-experienced and qualified" with something less than four hundred hours in the air? Maybe by grueling wartime standards, but certainly not by any yardstick with which Fenton was familiar. A man needed a thousand hours just to keep from running into himself in the air, and anything less, no matter how crammed with expertise by instructors, denied a pilot much less than what could be afforded him through that invaluable teacher known as experience. You just did not get enough variables in four hundred hours of flight time to be considered "well-experienced and qualified." You were still damned wet behind the ears. Again, Fenton chewed the inconsistency between so-called official statements and what his own experience dictated to him, and found himself forced to lay aside the wisdom of that experience. He had to go with what he hoped were the facts. More important to him than total flying time was the notation in the official naval records that the lowest flight time in the TBM by any pilot was fifty-five hours; that, at least, provided enough room for a man to become familiar with the husky and demanding iron bird.

In any circumstance in which aircraft disappearance was involved, weather was one of the more critical factors. Fenton went to pains to get more than the reports indicated. It was possible to go back, using Susan Gray at the computer, to the exact day and correlate a dozen weather forecasts, reports, and after-the-fact findings. To his surprise, he found an element of consistency running through all the records. The weather covered the entire area assigned for the TBM's a visibility of six to eight miles within the showers. Within precipitation the crews could expect cloud ceilings above the ocean surface of 2,500 feet. Outside any local precipitation, the ceilings were unlimited. Visibility, the forward distance a pilot could see from his plane, was, in Fenton's opinion, a fractious matter. The reports issued to the crews that day gave them a visibility of six to eight miles within the showers, and ten to twelve miles outside of any precipitation. One glance at those numbers, and Fenton was muttering curses to himself.

The writer who waxed enthusiastic about the stunning mystery of Flight 19's disappearance, who used those numbers without comment, was a fool. Scattered showers could produce, when you were caught in the rain itself, a visibility down to less than a mile. Not being able to see half that distance wasn't uncommon. The variables were simply too great to commit to a definite visibility factor without actually being in the rain. So such numbers were drastically suspect, so much so that they were next to worthless. Disgruntled, Fenton went on to the rest of the predicted weather. Ships at sea in the area assigned for the training flight were reporting twenty knots and gusting to thirty knots. That, at least, could be accepted as reliable, because it was a matter of real-time direct observation.

Fenton didn't need to scan the notes he'd gathered to recall the essential details of the mission. Flight 19 took off several minutes past two P.M. and headed over the ocean. For nearly two hours nothing was heard from the flight of five bombers. Standard procedure. Everyone assumed they were hard at work. Then, at approximately four P.M., things started coming unglued, and fast. A ground station picked up a radio message. No question but that Flight 19 had, suddenly and unexpectedly, encountered trouble on the mission. The records indicated that the radio transmission was between the flight leader and another pilot. From what the ground stations picked up, the entire flight was lost, the weather was going through obscure but dangerous changes, and the compass systems of every aircraft had gone haywire. They were in serious trouble, and it was getting worse.

The official records confirmed what had been presented in newspaper and magazine articles. Attempts made instantly by ground stations to contact any of the TBM aircraft met with failure. Again and again the tower at Fort Lauderdale and the other radio sites tried to contact the airplanes. Nothing. No one could pick up any more tramsmissions from or between the five bombers. The people on the ground couldn't determine the exact nature of the trouble, nor even identify the area in which the bombers were flying when that first radio sign of difficulty was picked up.

The entire flight of five bombers and fourteen men just . . . vanished. That was the only word for it. They flew into oblivion. By eight o'clock that night, the last pint of gasoline would have been gone from the tanks. No airplane could still be in the air. The Navy contacted every ground station.

Nothing.

At 7:30 that same evening, the Navy dispatched a Martin PBM Mariner flying boat, with at least twenty hours' flying time in its tanks, from the Banana River Naval Air Station, just south of Cape Canaveral, on a search mission for the missing bombers.

Sometime that night—without ever having been heard from or ever seen again—the flying boat and its entire crew vanished!

Those were the essential facts—"hold one," Fenton said, to draw himself up short. Those are the "facts" as they were known. He met Susan Gray in his office, and she began to prepare for him obscure items relating to Flight 19.

They began to paint a different picture from what the world understood about what had happened.

First, the weather was much *better* than had been indicated. Early on the morning of Decembr 5, 1945, a heavy cloud cover moved from the Gulf of Mexico eastward across the Florida peninsula. By noon the wide overcast darkened the skies from Daytona Beach south to Melbourne. But it was thin cloud, and the sun had been doing its work. By one o'clock that afternoon, flying conditions along the southeast coast of Florida were just about perfect. A few scattered clouds showed up randomly in what was otherwise an absolutely clear day. The cloud conditions over the Atlantic were down to one-tenth cover; more than ninety percent of the sky was clear.

At 1:30 P.M. the six Navy and eight Marine pilots and crewmen were at the flight line preparing for their mission. One man, scheduled to fly in the lead aircraft, was adamant about not flying anywhere, in anything, that day, a strange premonition that bore fatal fruit for the men who did take off. According to the tower records Fenton scanned, the lead TBM left the runway precisely at 2:02 P.M. The other four planes were right behind. At 2:08 P.M., according to the tower records, the five bombers were in tight formation and heading out over the Atlantic under perfect, sunny conditions.

Fenton studied a copy of the flight charts used by the pilots of Flight 19 that day. Each chart had been plotted to show a navigational triangle. One leg extended for 160 miles to the east. According to the available records, the TBM's at the end of this line would be near several of the Bahama Islands. They would then swing to the north for forty miles, then ease into a turn to the southwest to return to Fort Lauderdale.

Watch it. Every single source but one repeated that basic plan for the navigational exercise. But this was *not* the flight plan flown—or intended to be flown.

Buried deep in the interrogation of ground personnel by the naval board of inquiry was that one dissenting voice; and without the computer searching for anything "untoward," Fenton would have missed it completely. The five bombers did *not* simply fly eastward for 160 miles. Instead, they flew to the east until they reached a wrecked ship in the water just south of Bimini Island off the Florida coast. There they aimed the planes at the concrete hulk—a target ship—and ran through mock torpedo attacks. *Then* they resumed their flight eastward to their first navigational checkpoint, 160 miles from takeoff.

Unimportant? Uh-uh. First, the time spent in the torpedo runs would have to be added to the entire mission time. Second, maneuvering in this fashion grinds up fuel at a prodigious rate, which meant that the anticipated endurance of the TBM's would be overgenerous. It might *not* have an effect on the final outcome that day, but it couldn't be ignored.

Fenton shook his head in dismay as he ran into the next drastic conflict between the reports officially released to the public and what actually had taken place in terms of radio transmissions. Virtually every source insisted that after the brief radio conversation intercepted by a ground station, obstensibly between two aircraft in the formation, no one ever contacted the planes once they seemed to be in trouble.

Fenton swore to himself as he scanned a transcript of conversations buried in the voluminous investigation records. If you believed the face-value stories, you'd . . . He stopped himself from pursuing that line of thought.

At 4:45 P.M. the five-plane formation, if all had gone normally would have been inbound to Fort Lauderdale Naval Air Station, only fifteen minutes from sight of the field. Instead, at that time the tower operator received a distress call *directed to* the tower:

"Flight 19 to Lauderdale Naval Air Station, this is an emergency. We appear to be off our course . . . cannot see land . . . repeat . . . cannot see land."

The tower snapped back its response with: "What is your position?"

The voice coming into the tower was that of USN Lieutenant Charles C. Taylor; his aircraft carried the identification FT-28. Taylor could not offer much help: "We are not sure of our position. We can't be sure just where we are. We seem to be lost."

Fenton held off on further reading for the moment. The bombers at that point were supposed to have been only fifteen minutes' flight time from the Florida coastline. If they were in trouble then, the problem had actually begun well before that moment. Certain questions leaped to mind. Why the delay in reporting their difficulty? And why was Taylor, instead of the flight leader, Marine First Lieutenant Forrest J. Gerber, in FT-81, making the radio call? Fenton put the questions to the back of his mind and returned to the transcript. After the plaintive radio call of "We seem to be lost," the tower operator said the only thing he *could* say:

"Assume bearing due west."

Then came the words that sent chills down the spine of every man involved. Taylor's voice came through with unmistakable signs of desperation. Fenton tried to imagine what was going on in that cockpit, and down through the thirty years of time, he could feel an empathy for the hapless pilot:

"We don't know which way is west! Everything is wrong . . . strange. We can't be sure of any direction. Even the ocean doesn't look as it should!"

Fenton forced himself not to read on. The very sensation of alarm was *wrong*. Could the weather have become violent *that* quickly? With such swiftness as to render five pilots and their crews inept and helpless? That was so hard to believe that Fenton had no choice but to reject the possibility, as had the board of inquiry many years before.

But this business of not knowing what direction was west—that was as confusing as it was mysterious. What had happened to the magnetic compass in each plane? In all five planes? Could the flight have drifted into an area of wild compass variation never before encountered by ships, aircraft, or submarines? It was a big pill to swallow, but something had screwed up the compasses in those aircraft. Either the damned things give a heading or they don't.

Okay, Fenton thought. Let's assume a local but severe magnetic storm. Out go the compasses in the planes. But each TBM was equipped with radio navigation gear. They could have obtained . . . Hold it, Fenton told himself. They *should* have obtained a radio fix on Lauderdale. It was common enough practice. Fenton read on.

Again surprise. For an hour and forty-five minutes the radio transmissions between the bomber formation and the Naval Air Station were hectic and intermittent. On the ground, radiomen could hear the pilots talking between themselves, men who ranged from frantic to hysterical. The same sort of men who were cool under enemy fire were suddenly coming apart at the seams, and *that* didn't fit. It didn't fit no matter what way Fenton studied the possibilities.

Shortly after five P.M., the flight leader unexpectedly gave up all command of the mission, turning responsibility over to FT-117, flown by Marine Captain George W. Stivers. Stivers' voice came in unmistakably in Fort Lauderdale:

"We are not sure where we are. We think we must be 225 miles northeast of base." That was crazy. There was absolutely no logical explanation for the aircraft to be that far at sea, because . . . Fenton's thoughts trailed away. No logical explanation? Only the day before, he had encountered a 190-mile-an-hour headwind, when he believed, and had been told by skilled weather specialists, that he had a 75-mile-an-hour tailwind. A difference of 265 miles an hour.

Now, if that TBM flight had run into the same sort of thing, it would explain, absolutely, their surprising distance to sea. Would such winds, at the lower altitudes flown by the TBM aircraft, have been accompanied by such turbulence that the pilots would know that something drastically wrong was going on? It didn't seem as if they would ever get the answer to that question. Fenton returned to the report.

The notes indicated sudden, heavy static. Then: "*It looks like we are entering white water.*" A period of silence. Then Stivers' voice, with (noted the writer of the official report) an unmistakable sense of finality: "We're completely lost."

Silence followed.

Some of the time elements in the report were confused, but one thing seemed clear. The Mariner flying boat was already on its way out to sea, rushing toward the last reported position of the missing bombers. Fenton put aside the report from the Fort Lauderdale Naval Air Station and picked up a separate document that had been prepared by the Banana River Naval Air Station. Contrary to public stories, the PBM Mariner had more fuel than was needed to fly for twenty hours. Furthermore, her crew of thirteen men were skilled specialists in search-and-rescue missions, and just about every type of apparatus useful to such missions was aboard. The life rafts would self-inflate when they hit water. There were sealed and waterproof radio transmitters that would start sending a powerful signal the moment they struck saltwater. So even if the Mariner crashed at sea, there would—there *should*—have been activation of radio equipment.

Then, there was the matter of radio messages from the big Mariner, The Banana River Naval Air Station noted that the flying-boat pilot, Lieutenant W. G. Jeffrey, had established radio contact, while still taxiing, with Lauderdale. Thirty minutes after takeoff, the Mariner sent a routine message back to base stating it was almost to the point where they would begin searching for Flight 19. So far, they had seen nothing.

One more position report was made.

Nothing else was ever heard from the crew of the flying boat. It disappeared completely. No sign of bodies or wreckage was ever found.

Fenton laid down the report on the rescue aircraft. He'd have to come back to that later.

He picked up the naval-board-of-inquiry report on Flight 19 and noted an insertion in one page. According to one report, the last transmission from Stivers was "We're completely lost." But another radio operator had written down another transmission that threw a strange new light on the event.

According to this radioman at Lauderdale, Stivers' last message was made at 5:25 P.M. and read: "We're still not certain of our position . . . have gas for seventy-five minutes more . . . can't tell whether we're over the Atlantic or the Gulf of Mexico . . . we think we must be about seventy-five miles northeast of Banana River and about 225 miles north of base. . . . It looks like we are . . ." That was all that radioman picked up. He missed completely the messages about "entering white water" and "we're completely lost."

That took some chewing. All through the reports, Fenton had wondered why the TBM pilots didn't just turn toward the sun on the western horizon. God, easy enough to do. The weather had remained good to excellent. *Or so it seemed.*

Stivers had mentioned "entering white water." What the hell could *that* be? One explanation was a squall line that "came out of nowhere," a localized but violent front of howling winds, turbulence, and heavy sheets of rainfall. Sometimes they were associated with severe lightning and even waterspouts. Could such a storm have blown up without any notice, without the first sign of warning?

The pilots hadn't said a thing about severe weather. The repeated references to being lost, the apparent "stumbling through the sky"—none of this could be construed to mean severe weather. The only reference to a sky completely out of whack was that "entering white water." A localized storm, low to the ocean, *could,* with very high winds whipping the ocean surface, present a scene that *could* be construed by a pilot as a wall of white.

But that was stretching the hell out of things. It was searching for explanations amd answers against what little clues were at hand. The "entering white water" would simply have to go down on the books as "unexplained."

Even more baffling was that at 7:04 P.M. that same day the tower operator at Opa Locka Naval Air Station, just outside Miami, received a message so faint that it seemed almost to be whispered along on radio waves. Someone was calling "FT . . . FT . . ." That was all he could make out, but the letters were unmistakably the call signs of the aircraft from Flight 19. No other planes in the entire area would have been using them. Fenton read the brief interrogation of the tower operator, who had stuck by his report.

But the last Avenger would have crashed into the sea from fuel exhaustion long before 7:04 P.M.

No answer to that one.

The missing Martin PBM Mariner was creating its own ghastly effect. When the minutes began to stretch into alarm, without the flying boat sending back any radio reports—especially on an alarm of its own—the crash button was pushed for *that* aircraft. A search aircraft took off from the Coast Guard station at Miami, flew along—retracing—the flight path of the missing PBM, searched the area of last report, well into darkness. Nothing. The Coast Guard plane returned to base without having seen a thing.

It began to get wilder. At 7:50 that same night the captain of the merchant vessel *Gaines Mills* was well out to sea from the Florida coastline, due east of New Smyrna Beach. According to a frantic radio report from the merchant ship, its crew had seen an explosion in the air, and in near-darkness had watched *what appeared to be* an aircraft spinning into the ocean.

There was speculation that two of the TBM's might still have been in the air and then collided and exploded. No one accepted the explanation. Nothing flies that long on fumes, and even those would have been gone from the TBM tanks.

Well, could it have been the missing Martin PBM Mariner? The big flying boat was not the most reassuring aircraft in the world when it came to temperament. There had been several cases of the big airplanes exploding from difficulties with the fuel systems. But the same could be said about other airplanes. The problem was that last call from the missing PBM; it had been picked up almost two hours before the *Gaines Mills* reported the explosion and spinning object. Would the PBM have suffered complete radio failure and still continued to fly a search mission into darkening skies? No way, no way, judged Fenton, as did the reports before him. Besides, even if the airplane had suffered complete radio failure from loss of its own communications systems, it had at least one and likely two or more self-contained radio transmitters that would have operated in the air or on the surface of the water. That two-hour gap between the last radio report and the message from the merchant steamer was too much to swallow. Most likely the seamen had been witness to a bolide—an exploding meteor. Fenton knew of many cases where the latter had been mistaken, even by skilled witnesses, for an exploding airplane. The *Gaines Mills* report had to be scratched.

The rest of it was statistics. Before darkness had fallen completely, the greatest air-sea search effort up to that time was under way. Every available ship left Florida ports to start the sweep for the six missing airplanes and twenty-seven men—or what remained of them. They kept a full search for lights or flares. Through the dreary night they saw . . . nothing.

By the morning of December 6 the search had become the massive sweep that would continue for the next five days. Twenty-one surface ships, including warships scanning with radar, moved through the search area in an ever-widening pattern. The escort aircraft carrier USS *Solomons* raced under full steam into the search area, launching its thirty aircraft for a methodical search. By noon, more than three hundred airplanes of all types were crisscrossing the ocean, the Bahamas, even lower Florida and mid-Florida, and parts of the Gulf of Mexico. The Royal Air Force at Nassau's Windsor Field sent two large search aircraft to join in. The Navy, the Coast Guard, and the Army kept adding planes to the now frantic search.

By late that day the only feeling was incredulity. It was impossible for six airplanes, all designed and equipped for impact with the water, not to have left even a *trace* of their existence. Airplanes and debris, radio transmitters, men with self-inflating preservers and rafts, automatic radio-transmitting gear, flotation equipment. *Something* had to be out there in the water.

Nothing.

On Friday, December 7, the search directors expanded greatly the areas covered by planes and ships. Long-range bombers and patrol aircraft swung for two hundred miles across the Gulf of Mexico. Other reconnaissance planes sped up and down the Florida coast from the Keys to Jacksonville, scouring the land and the ocean. Below them, twelve veteran search teams made up of dozens of trackers began their sweep of three hundred miles of coastline between Miami Beach and Saint Augustine. Planes and ground teams crisscrossed the Everglades.

Nothing.

What about that radio report from the merchantman *Gaines Mills*? Even though no one accepted the report, a full swarm of planes and ships raked the area where the *Gaines Mills* reported the explosion in the air and the spinning aircraft that smashed into the sea. There should have been an oil slick, bodies, some debris. No one ever saw a damned thing. Then someone began to put pieces together. The crew of that ship had made its report of seeing something in the sky. But the Coast Guard patrol plane that traced the flight path of the missing Mariner had flown directly over the area where the airplane supposedly exploded and crashed, and yet the crew never saw or heard the Coast Guard plane—a powerful machine with bright running lights. The ship's report was crossed off the probability list and consigned to the "unknowns."

An Eastern Airlines pilot caused a flurry of activity on December 8 when he reported red flares and flashing lights "in the middle of a swamp" just to the southwest of Melbourne, Florida. Shortly afterward, he spotted another fire in the bleak and open country about twenty miles to the north of the first flares.

The Banana River Naval Air Station sent a search plane out immediately. At 2:30 A.M. the pilot confirmed sighting a flare—but this one was fifty miles inland, or at least forty-five miles away from the area reported by the airline pilot. By morning the ground was covered with a thick, tree-hugging fog. Nonetheless, a small army ground its way through the dismal countryside in marsh buggies, alligators, jeeps, assault craft, weasels—anything that could make its way across that country. A small fleet of planes crossed the area. A Navy blimp droned in low sweeps over the sites where flares, fires, and men had been reported. Several times the blimp dropped low enough for search teams to comb the undergrowth on foot.

Nothing.

Men who fly throw themselves into such a search. They know what lost or downed pilots must be going through. Sometimes they search so hard they begin to see things that aren't there.

It happens all the time. It happened during this search effort. An Army pilot some three hundred miles due east of Melbourne sent in an excited report: "*Two men aboard life rafts . . .*"

Rescue planes rushed to the area. The Navy planes flew over the exact area where the men in life rafts had been discovered. They found several packing cases bobbing in the sea.

Nothing.

Hope becomes so buoyant that it must also be regarded with suspicion. Nonetheless, the reaction to a radio report from the tanker *Erwin Russell* brought loud cheers at the airfields from which the search planes were flying. The first report stated without question that two survivors from the six missing planes had been rescued and were aboard the ship.

Then a corrected report explained that the tanker had actually sent a radio message that it was lowering lifeboats to pick up several survivors found in rafts. Hell, it was only a matter of time, then.

The survivors aboard a life raft turned out to be an old tow target used for gunnery practice. It had been dropped by a plane and managed to stay afloat instead of sinking. There were no men, no rafts.

Yet the very finding of the tow target raised its own questions. If something of that nature would float for days and nights, how could there be that total absence of wreckage or debris from the six missing planes? No one had any answers.

Shortly after the up-and-down emotional raking of the report from the tanker, hopes soared again. This time the report came from veterans in the business. An Army four-engined B-24 bomber, making its search grid sweep 290 miles east of Melbourne, radioed its sighting of two life rafts, *with two men in one raft*.

Was this another of those unreliable sightings? No way, for the B-24 bomber circled the rafts for four and a half hours, assuring their exact location, until other planes or ships could reach the area. Running low of fuel, the B-24 returned to its base at Boca Raton on the south Florida coast. Ships and planes in great numbers covered the area where the rafts had been located.

They didn't find a thing.

Naval officials queried the B-24 crew. In his official report, the B-24 pilot explained: "At 10:45 A.M. we located rafts and circled over them. While circling, we saw two one-man rafts, apparently tied together. At the beginning, every man in the crew believed there were two men in the rafts."

Dale Fenton sighed and laid the report on his desk. The next line was the inevitable clincher that had characterized this whole insane case: "*However, as the day wore on, we could not be sure.*"

Jesus!

Fenton went through the remainder of sightings that turned out to be false; flares that could be fired only by people who weren't there; life rafts that turned out to be packing cases, tow targets, and seaweed. He shook his head with disbelief at the report of another TBF flight commander, a man who had been in the same area of sky with twelve bombers under his command, who reported he had been talking to Flight 19 by radio even as they were encountering trouble. This incredible man, if he were to be believed, insisted that a combination of sudden bad weather and confusion on the part of the Flight 19 pilots had caused their loss at sea.

Why hadn't he gone to their help? It turns out, so he insisted, he lost his radios. But he had eleven other aircraft in his formation. Why didn't they do something? Why didn't *anyone* do something? No answers came forth. Besides, there were so many inconsistencies in his story that the whole thing had to be relegated to the trash bin.

Another group of men actually *did* talk with one or more pilots of Flight 19, even as they were going through their hellish time at sea. This was through a ground facility on the Florida coast, a naval radio unit that tried desperately to offer help—and made sworn statements to the effect that the naval command at the Lauderdale Naval Air Station *refused* to listen to what they had to say. The charges and countercharges became so confused and vitrolic that they were valueless.

The sum and substance of it all?

For five days and nights the United States Navy, Army Air Force, Coast Guard, Royal Air Force, and civilian units scoured 380,000 miles of sea, coastline, swamps, and isolated land areas. Warships, merchant vessels, private ships, and an aircraft carrier added to the search. More than three hundred planes of all types were involved. Hundreds of veteran search-and-rescue teams, including one airborne by Navy blimp, crawled and struggled through backwater lands in the search.

The odds against not finding *something* were so astronomical as to be ridiculous. Yet the six airplanes and twenty-seven crewmen vanished as effectively as if they'd been sucked completely from the surface of the planet.

Fenton pushed aside the voluminous stack of bound reports and documents. Aside from the hard and thorough examinations of weather, mechanical difficulty, and other "acceptable" causes, he would be forced to wade through an enormous quantity of errant nonsense. For Flight 19 had produced its own army of soothsayers, prophets, a straggling horde of know-it-alls who could explain everything and anything so long as you were willing to accept a vanished Atlantis snatching ships and planes at its own desire. Or, if not Atlantis, you might have to nod soberly to variations on the theories of a hollow earth and the beings inhabiting that bizarre netherworld. There were those who came forth to propose huge vessels gliding silently from space to wreak their havoc on unsuspecting ships and planes. Others glided just as silently and huge from deep within the oceans. And all contributed to calamity. Of course they did.

Fenton chewed on the dead, wet, cold end of his cigar. He looked up as Susan Gray entered his office. She lifted her eyebrows at the disgruntled expression on his face. "That bad?" she asked.

"Worse." He nodded in the direction of the documents. "Want to try something for me with that mechanical idiot of yours?"

"Careful, there," she warned. "My computer is sensitive to insensitive louts."

"Guilty as charged," he murmured. "Look, if we

throw into that electronic maw you call your idiot-savant all the known factors of effectiveness of air and sea search, the grids flown, the conditions under which the planes were lost, and—"

She held up a hand to head him off. "I've anticipated what you'd be asking for," she told him, smiling.

"Smart-ass. Tell me."

Susan pulled up a chair and tapped a cigarette against his desk before answering. "The idea intrigued me, too. The odds, I mean."

"And?" he prodded with impatience.

She wasn't to be hurried. "I plotted the curves on the basis of insurance coverage," she told him. "That way, I would have something specific for the computer to work on, rather than what would be on the order of a mathematical game or puzzle."

"Great, great. What'd you get?"

She looked at him carefully. "You're not going to like it, Dale."

"Woman, come *on.*"

"If we were to write a policy for the loss of the six airplanes and the entire crews, under the conditions prevailing"—she ticked off the points one by one—"and then add the search as it took place, and compute a payoff by this company, predicated on the basis that all six planes and all the men must vanish, without a single trace of any kind, you know . . . ?"

"You're fired," he said with a groan.

She exhaled smoke. "You can't fire me. You need me."

"I need some aspirin. What the hell did you find?"

"On the basis of payout—with no trace ever found of anything, you understand . . . ?"

He waited.

"The odds against those planes and the men vanishing as they did, Dale, are more than a billion to one."

"A billion?"

"Spell it with a *b*. That's right. There isn't one chance in a *billion* that it could have happened the way it did."

"But it did happen," he said hollowly.

"I know," she said, and then there wasn't any more to say.

The goddamned thing was getting away from him. Jesus *Christ*, if he tried to pursue ancient mysteries, he'd end up with his head in a barrel and everybody outside slamming away with their own sticks. Sticks that came in the form of theories, from the wild to the sublime.

Oh, sure, there were those theories—even the hard scientific ones—for the enigma of Flight 19. But the problem with such things as electromagnetic storms, or even the gravitational waves that were propounded, was simply that they might or might not be responsible for what had happened with Flight 19. That was the rub. Suppose, even that there were walls of magnetic tornadoes—literally, whirling funnels of electromagnetic force that could bat airplanes from the sky like some monstrous flyswatter—was there a direct association between them and what had happened with Flight 19? And could this association be extended to explain what had happened to the missing Gulfstream 666D? *That was the only aspect of any theory or investigation that mattered.* Everything else was conjecture, and even *probability* was no more than a parlor trick in his business. He wasn't chasing theories. He wanted the kind of factual material that would stand up in the cold and heartless light of a courtroom.

If the Gulfstream had vanished—he was getting to hate the word—because of unnatural forces, then . . . *Hold it, hold it!* he shouted in his head. How the hell can something like freak weather, an electromagnetic disturbance, or even a tear in gravitational time, if that was the way to describe it, be an *un*natural force? Just because it wasn't in the lexicon of everyday experience didn't make it unnatural. Hell, until Yuri Gagarin tore around the planet back in 1961 at five miles every second and experienced the first real zero gravity, or weightlessness, that was about the most unnatural force any man could have experienced. But only up until that moment.

Until the year 1803 the French Academy of Science, one of the most respected bodies in the world, had been not only aloof but downright vicious in its criticism of those fools and charlatans who insisted that rocks rained down, day and night, on the earth from whatever strange space surrounded the planet. Rocks from the sky? Ridiculous, stupid. And then proof began to come in about things called meteorites, and the French Academy of Science skulked like schoolboys with thumbs burned from too much cerebral sucking.

The point was that any unnatural force was unnatural only in that we lacked experience—yet—with that force. It was God-made, as the courts would mumble down from the bench, and therefore it was just as natural as a hurricane, or a storm of electrons in space, or anything else that constituted the miracles of life.

And he, Fenton, had been chasing such ghosts when their reality, seen or invisible, was everywhere about him all the time.

Which meant that, no matter whose fault or why, he was losing his grip. He *had* to get a handle on what was happening from a specific point of view, from a matter of mechanical force or human action, because the longer of time between *right now* and some rapidly approaching deadline in the future, the more tenuous would become his understanding of the loss of Triple-Six Delta.

Damnit, he had *never* been caught short like this before. It was time for some positive thinking, time for Fenton to start acting like himself, and screw all this mumbling from the past.

The goddamned airplane did not simply *vanish*. Every force in nature demands its payment in an opposite force. *Something* had happened to the Gulfstream. He needed only a single thread to start unraveling the mystery. Just one thread. No more.

He sent Susan Gray back to bed, went home, and stumbled into the shower. When he came out, he turned off his head. Just turned it off. He sprawled on the couch in his living room with some soft music barely discernible in the background and tried to stay awake.

Chapter 9

He was dragged up from deep sleep at eleven-thirty in the morning by a conscience nagging him to remove his ass from the horizontal. He reached for the phone.

"Schechter? Dale Fenton. Look, I need some of that help you so generously offered. . . . What? . . . Oh, yes. Well, it turned out that the weather people have been blowing grass for years and really don't know what the hell they're talking about. Look, there's a full report on my flight in the Gulfstream on its way to you right now. For Christ's sake, man, I didn't call you to discuss the weather! You'll get it in the mail, like I said. Now, you said you'd put together full dossiers on everybody concerned with the flight of Triple-Six Delta. I want all of them." A long pause for the expected crap from officialdom. Then: "Schechter, I don't give a shit about Watergate or whatever new rules you're so worried about. I *need* that material. We can run the personal investigations on our own, but it'll take too much time. And, by the way, I want the works on the ground people associated with that airplane, as well." The second long, expected interruption. Then: "Goddamnit, are you working with or against us? Of course I'm pissed when I hear . . . Okay, we'll drop it. Send the staff down by courier. To hell with the mail. Bye."

Fenton brewed himself the kind of coffee that effectively scrubs squirrel shit from your tongue in the morning. He sat naked by his dining-room table, sucking on the coffee and scribbling ideas and notes on a large pad.

One possibility kept looking back at him from the paper. He'd thought of it before, but all the flak that had surrounded this case from the beginning, especially with the appearance of people from the Army, NSA, and CIA, had thrown him off the track. Now he decided grimly, as he drained the coffeepot into his cup, he might just start winging this thing the way he should have from the start.

What about the pattern that had developed with that DC-8 case, the one that had first brought him to Carruthers? A bomb aboard the airplane.

Question: Was this a possibility where the missing Gulfstream was concerned?

Answer: Does a bear shit in the forest? Of course the possibility was there! What the hell was the matter with him?

Next question: Define the level of possibility.

Answer: Never mind this "define" crap. It was so possible it hovered on the edge of probability.

Fenton, Fenton said to himself, *you've been an absolute dummy. A half-wit. Worse than that, man. At least a half-wit has something he can use to generate thinking. You, on the other hand . . .*

He pushed his chair back from the table and paced the room slowly.

Question: Was there a motive for the deliberate destruction of Gulfstream 666D?

Answer: IT'S AS PLAIN AS THE NOSE ON YOUR FACE, DUMMY!

Motive? Of course there was motive! The insurance coverage was staggering. Any one of a half-dozen payoffs on claims would have been worth the destruction of the aircraft and its passengers—to say nothing of motive as Schechter of NSA had spelled it out.

And there were all sorts of ways to getting a bomb aboard an airplane. You didn't need much of a bomb, either. People envisioned a hulking crate of dynamite or some highly advanced system packaged with an attaché case. That was Hollywood glibness. An entire system, including the plastic explosives, the detonator, and a host of sensing and actuating systems, was smaller than a pack of cigarettes and still big enough to blow a critical piece of an airplane into the kind of wreckage that would guarantee total disaster.

Jesus, he needed more coffee. He didn't want to wait, and threw together a cup of instant.

He was still indicting himself for sloppy thinking. He'd been so uptight with that hovering shadow of impossibility from the nature of the Devil's Triangle that he had sloughed off on his own tried-and-proven procedures. And procedures were the key to this business. If he went by his own rules, then he must follow alternate—parallel—lines of probability and impossibility, and he must afford each such possibility the same intensive interest as any of the others.

What if . . . ?

The thought died even as it struggled to get through the midmorning fumes of his head. Back up, man; take that one again, and go it slow.

What if Mazurski wasn't even involved?

Why hadn't anyone said anything about *that*? Why hadn't *he* even scratched on paper that possibility? Again he wanted to deliver a mighty kick to himself. What if Dr. Harold Mazurski was simply along on a flight where his presence didn't matter one way or the other?

Fenton dressed and drove slowly to his office.

He'd been flailing his arms for survival in a huge tank of soft cotton that denied him a grasp. Well, that was over now. He was starting to move steadily and surely. He enjoyed the feeling of accomplishment.

He spent the day amassing details, making certain the dossiers he wanted were on their way, and sending out his second team to gather information on other people who, as yet, had only a peripheral relationship to his case. He called Grumman in Bethpage, New York, and upset their engineering staff no end by requesting an engineering study of what points of the Gulfstream II were most likely to yield from a localized but sharp blast overpressure.

There was another list of names to be made up. Professionals who either sailed through or flew over the Devil's Triangle as a matter of course and might be counted upon to deliver to Fenton, through personal coversations, the most reliable judgment of the area and its unique problems.

And he started his team working on unusual or even startling natural phenomena not yet recognized or accepted by the world body scientific. Inquiries were started to obtain *reports*, if nothing else, by qualified observers. The inquiries would go to every government agency. They were also sent to private and business flying groups, to the airlines, to the Bahamian government, to charter fishing-boat fleets, to amateur flying and boating organizations, to skin-diving clubs—in short, Fenton was opening wide the door to any information that could prove useful to him. The computer and his teams would keep him from drowning in such detail. He could winnow out the purer essence of the cascade, as it were, and direct his inquiries with a rapier rather than a broadsword.

He finished late that night, and knocked off further work, simply to stave off a walloping headache.

The telephone dragged him from sleep at 3:42 A.M.

"Fenton? This is Ben Philpot." Who the hell . . . ? He heard a soft chuckle. "I know; you're still asleep. I'm with the FAA in Miami. Air Traffic Control. You asked that we call you if anything came up with a bearing on that case of yours."

"Oh, Christ, *yes*. Sorry, Ben. I'm awake now. What's happening?"

"This isn't a direct connection, but it might be. In this business, you never know."

"Go on," Fenton urged.

"We had a complete disappearance tonight," the FAA man said. "About two hours ago. And, Fenton, it's a real beaut. Miami control is half out of its mind. It's another of those impossibles."

"What happened?"

"We lost a chartered airliner. A Convair 440 with thirty-nine passengers. Four in the crew, also. It was coming back from the down islands. It . . . well, the dammed thing just disappeared. It was only forty miles out from Miami International when it vanished. We had it on radar. We were talking with the crew. Everything was perfect. In fact, he was setting up a long approach, when . . ." The voice faltered with its own disbelief. "When it vanished from the scope. Look, do you remember that case some years back when the same thing happened with a DC-3? This is almost the same thing, but with a difference. We were talking with the crew when everything just stopped. Right in the middle of a sentence! They went off radar at the same instant. We checked with other radar units in the area. They were on the transponder, so it was a clean pickup. Everybody lost the ship at the same moment."

"Did the thing go in? I mean, did you get any reports of—"

"Fenton, it didn't crash. It *disappeared*. Look, all

hell is breaking loose down here. I can't stay on the phone right now. Can you get down to Miami right away? I go off duty in an hour, but I'll wait for you. Come into the tower at International Airport. Third floor. I'll see you there."

Fenton hung up slowly. He sat on the edge of his bed for perhaps a minute, thinking. Then he picked up the phone and punched in the number of Space Coast Aviation at McCoy Airport. He told the lineman on the graveyard shift to roll the Baron kept available for him from the hangar and do a complete preflight. He'd need the airplane. Nothing commercial was moving this time of night in the direction of Miami.

Five minutes later he was on his way to his office, There he pulled a folder from a file marked "Incidents/Unexplained," and returned immediately to his car. He drove to McCoy, parked at the office of Space Coast, and walked around the building. The Baron waited for him beneath the flight-line lights, waxed and gleaming. He did a fast preflight check and went up on the wing to enter the cabin. It all went quickly. He fired up the engines and called ground control. They would take his flight plan as he taxied to the active runway. Four minutes later, the runup was complete and he was cleared on his instrument flight plan to Miami International. He'd asked for and was given eight thousand feet.

The Baron raced into the air. He hit the gear button and let her climb quickly to cruising altitude, where he leveled off and brought in the autopilot. He'd be in Miami in less than an hour. He scanned the gauges and took a small penlight from his jacket, playing it on the folder he'd brought with him.

That other incident Ben Philpot had mentioned . . . Here it was. December 28, 1948. Captain Robert Lindquist and his copilot, Ernest Hill, were just completing a thousand-mile charter flight in their DC-3 from San Juan, Puerto Rico, to Miami. The twin-engined piston airplane, the famed Gooney Bird, was owned by Airborne Transport, Inc. They had thirty-two passengers, including two infants. One stewardess. Mary Burks. From the reports, a good flight in the old, reliable airliner.

The records showed that at 4:13 A.M Lindquist called in to Miami tower. He could see the deep glowing bowl of light that was Miami looming into the sky. "Approaching field. Fifty miles out. South. All is well. We'll stand by for landing instructions."

A lazy, quiet time of night. Radar had picked up the DC-3 on its long, shallow descent. The weather was good. Some patchy clouds, gentle winds. Everything was perfect.

Except that several seconds after Lindquist spoke to Miami tower, the airplane vanished.

With Miami dead ahead.

Vanished.

There was a hell of a search. They looked for everything. An oil slick, wreckage, bodies, any small debris, even the telltale signs of converging sharks and barracuda. In the daylight hours the sea was so clear it would have been almost impossible not to have seen the wreckage of the plane on the bottom. There was nothing, Forty-eight ships took up the search. More than two hundred planes scoured an area of 310,000 miles, including the ocean waters, the Keys, the Everglades, the Caribbean, the Gulf of Mexico. Occupants of boats in the area were questioned.

Nothing.

Fenton swore as he closed the folder. He was again facing something that was absolutely impossible, but that had happened.

He brought the Baron down in a long, sweeping

curve to the glowing airport below. Philpot had notified Ground Control that he'd be arriving. An FAA car was waiting for him when he parked and shut down the airplane.

"That him?" Fenton nodded in the direction of a man who sat unnaturally stiff in a straight-backed chair, his eyes staring directly before him. Others in the large radar control room walked quietly about the man.

"Alan Sherwood," confirmed Ben Philpot. "He was working the plane. He's, ah, in a bit of shock."

"It shows."

"Christ, he shouldn't be here," Philpot said. "But he won't leave. These people"—he gestured to take in the air-traffic controllers before their radar consoles—"take their jobs a hell of a lot more seriously than anyone outside this business realizes. He was working the Convair, like I said. Sherwood is taking it personally."

Fenton showed his surprise. "Christ, man, he's not to blame."

"I know that, you know that, everyone else in here knows that," Philpot sighed, "but Alan Sherwood doesn't know it."

"When can I talk with him?"

"Not now," Philpot said with a shake of his head. "Let's get some coffee. You're not even supposed to be in here. I've told everyone you're with some flight-safety outfit. We can come back in here later if you want." He paused to dig in a pocket, and handed Fenton a clip-on badge. "Put that thing on. I've signed it personally, and no one will bother you while you're wearing it. It's a temporary badge to let you move around here. Now, let's get that coffee. I *need* it."

They sat in a private coffee shop for the FAA

crews. "I really can't blame Sherwood, you know. A long time ago I was doing a GCA. The old talk-them-in radar control. Military field." He stared into the coffee, remembering, and Fenton saw him wince. "We never found out if the kid flying the thing didn't listen to what I was telling him, or if he'd lost power, or what. It was pea soup out there. Really blind." Philpot sighed, a tremulous movement through his body. "Anyway, he went in, and he took fourteen people with him. I was a wreck for a week."

Fenton made a show of measuring a teaspoon of sugar and then stirring. He waited for what he thought was a tactful pause. "What happened tonight, Ben?"

Philpot looked up. "You know about that one back in 1949? The Christmas Horror, they still call it here."

Fenton nodded. "I scanned the file on the way down here. DC-3 from Puerto Rico. The last call was fifty miles out, and he was starting a long, shallow descent when . . ." Fenton shrugged.

"It happened again."

Fenton pushed gently. "Would you spell it out?"

Philpot drained the coffee in a single long swallow. "I told you we lost the target forty miles out. Wrong. They were down to twenty-eight miles. Christ, let me take it from the beginning."

The FAA man got a good grip on himself. He began to recite the hard nut of what had happened. "About one-twenty this morning, Fenton. The weather's perfect. There isn't a cloud in the sky for fifty miles in any direction. There's been a high hanging around here for the last two days. At ground level we had a guaranteed visibility of at least fifteen miles, but you could see twice that distance with any height. Anyway. Winds aloft were light and variable. Not a thing was offbeat tonight. All avionics in the green. All radar working perfectly."

He leaned back, fished in a pocket for a crumpled pack of cigarettes, and straightened out one as he continued. "Sherwood was working the Convair. Everything right in the groove. Like I told you, the bird was painting the scope clear as a bell. Transponder squawk clean as you can get 'em." He dragged heavily on the cigarette, blew out a nervous plume of smoke. "We learned later, by the way, that Lauderdale also had the Convair painted. We have a new experimental radar we're working on at New Tamiami, and they had transponder squawk as well as a skin track. And everybody lost the target at the same instant. All four sets—ours, Lauderdale, and the two at Tamiami."

Fenton shifted in his seat. "All *four* at the same moment? No break in the time?"

Philpot laughed, a humorless sound. "Fenton, we correlated down to less than a second. All four radar units lost the target at the same instant."

"What about debris in the air?"

"Fenton, there was *nothing.*"

"And the voice contact?"

"The pilot was talking to center when his voice cut out. At exactly the same moment all the radar lost contact."

"You said no weather?"

"Hell, man, you flew down here yourself. What was it like up there tonight?"

"Perfect," Fenton agreed.

"So there wasn't a thing between the Convair and the radar. The pilot, by the way—we have the tapes; you can listen to them later if you want—was talking about just what a beautiful night it was. Said the lights of boats in the water looked like fireflies floating on velvet. That sort of thing. As he was coming in, there was just a crescent of a moon low over the horizon. The whole thing was set up as if ordered by the Chamber of Commerce."

"What about the boats the pilot talked about. Did they see anything?"

Philpot shook his head. "The Coast Guard has already talked to some of them. One man remembered the airplane because he'd just come on deck for some air, and he heard the piston engines. He glanced up, he said, saw the lights going away. He turned to something on the deck, and when he looked up again, he could no longer see the plane."

"That's all?"

"That's all."

"Did the Convair have an ELT?"

"Yep. It had *two* emergency location transmitters aboard. Both checked as of a week ago. Both working perfectly. Both designed to set off transmission in the event of impact on land *or* water. And before you ask—nothing."

"Choppers go out?"

"Three from the Coast Guard. Six Navy. Two Air Force. Five private. *All* of them with powerful searchlights. And—"

"I know," Fenton broke in sourly. "Nothing."

"You guessed it."

"It's light outside now," Fenton observed.

"And we'll be going over the area. We've already asked the Navy to bring in some MAD equipment. You're familiar with the Magnetic Anomoly Detection gear?"

Fenton nodded. "Antisubmarine."

"Right. They'll have two P3V's out there. At the depth concerned, they'll pick up anything right down to and including the bottom. But I don't count on them finding anything."

Fenton had to press. "Could the Convair have made an abrupt change in course? You know what I'm talking about, Ben. A sharp, diving turn. Down low to the water, so he's beneath radar?"

Philpot shook his head. "First, what the hell for? Second, you forget that skin tracking we were doing out of New Tamiami. That radar didn't get a change in altitude, Fenton. They tracked the shallow descent through every foot of the way, so we know the equipment was working. Then . . . she was gone. There's no way that airplane could have gone off the screen without the track. We've already had another aircraft out there trying to spook the radar, going through rapid altitude changes, sharp turns, the works. The radar works like a charm."

Philpot's hand suddenly smashed against the table. His cup bounced onto the floor and shattered. "Goddamnit, Fenton, I know just how Alan Sherwood feels. An airplane in perfect weather only twenty-eight miles from landing, operating with the most sophisticated air-traffic-control equipment in the world, just vanishes right under our noses? *It can't be!*" His look at Fenton was almost pleading. "Because if we can't handle this when everything is perfect, then what the hell is going on!"

"Christ, Ben, take it—"

"And it's the third time! Right in this area!"

Fenton looked sharply at Philpot. "Third? Another one besides tonight and that DC-3 back in forty-eight?"

Philpot nodded glumly. "The other one didn't get any real attention. It was back during the Cuban missile crisis. In a way, it was even more maddening than tonight or in forty-eight. Because that other ship was a Navy Constellation, and it was absolutely loaded to the gills with electronic gear. Besides, everybody on the ground was tracking it. And"—his voice was a hoarse whisper—"it was in broad daylight! It was coming north, up over the Keys, when . . ." His voice faltered. ". . . just like the others, it vanished."

Fenton stared at him. "Nothing ever showed up?"

"Nothing."

Fenton was getting to hate that word. He was also coming to despise himself for too much time spent unmoving on his ass. He rose abruptly. "I wouldn't be wrong if I said you didn't feel much like sleeping, would I?"

"What? Oh, shit, of course not."

"Then let's get up in that blue sky and see what we can see."

Philpot rose beside him. "Thanks. Maybe it will help."

Fenton took the Baron a hundred miles out, following a radar vector supplied by Philpot through Miami Control. At twelve thousand feet he went into a wide turn and was needled onto a duplicate of the approach flown by the Convair.

They went through seven thousand feet precisely twenty-eight miles out from Miami International. The air was so calm that the Baron never even trembled.

They flew over the area being searched. Planes were above them and below. They watched ships cutting white wakes across the ocean in their systematic grid pattern.

Not a bloody damned thing out of the ordinary. Except that the Convair 440 and forty-three people no longer existed. Not on this world, anyway. Fenton caught himself with a start. Jesus, he'd have to watch that kind of thinking.

He landed at Miami to drop off Philpot. "I'll be back tonight," he told him.

He flew back to McCoy, gave his staff details on what had happened, and went to his apartment, where he passed out. His alarm woke him at ten that night. He went to an all-night restaurant and put away a huge meal of steak and potatoes. From there to McCoy, where he ordered the Baron to the flight line. From the airport office he called Philpot.

"If I fly out again over the water, you know, the same route we flew today," Fenton asked, "can you work me personally on your radar?"

"What's your number?"

"Baron. Two-Seven-Three-Three Alpha."

"Sure can. Just give me a call. I'll have the boys alerted to pass you on to me."

"How about that skin-tracking equipment at New Tamiami, Ben? I'm going to do everything I can to get off your scopes."

He heard a guttural laugh. "Go ahead and try. When are you taking off?"

"Soon as I hang up."

"I'll have everything ready to go."

The flight to Miami from Orlando was a repeat of the previous night. Air as slick as glass, only a few scattered clouds at three thousand feet, winds light and variable. He could see forever down the coastline to Miami. Coming up on the city, he called Center and was passed immediately to Ben Philpot. He went through a rapid and thorough confirmation of his radio frequencies, squawked his transponder for radar confirmation, and received assurance from Philpot that he was being skin-tracked by the New Tamiami radar. He raced directly over Miami International at eleven thousand feet, the city to the north and east of the airport, and beyond to Miami Beach, a glittering wonderland of color. The Baron swept out to sea, Fenton checking his distance from the airport by his DME. Philpot's radar confirmed the changing miles. They checked the encoding altimeter, and the altitude readings on Fenton's panel and in the radar control room matched perfectly.

Eighty miles out, Fenton turned and began the long descent toward Miami International. He could see almost forever as the Baron sped through the night sky, easing away her altitude.

Coming up to a distance of twenty-eight miles, he was ready. He didn't say anything to Philpot. He watched the DME giving him his readout as he talked with the radar controller. Exactly at twenty-eight miles he cut off his own words in the middle of a sentence. In swift movements he shut off the transponder and the encoding altimeter and went hard forward on the yoke, coming back on power as the Baron plunged. Gear down, props to flat pitch, flaps full down, and the airplane fell like a rock in a steep descent.

He kept one eye glued to his radar altimeter, knowing the ocean was leaping up at him. At the last possible moment he brought in the power and came back on the yoke to bring up the nose. Quickly he cleaned up the airplane, tucking in the gear, bringing up flaps. The radar altimeter showed only one hundred feet. He was far below the ability of Miami radar or even that skin-tracking equipment at New Tamiami to pick him up. He would seem to have vanished from all the radar tracking him. For a short while he was even too low for his VHF radio gear, which was direct line-of-sight, to permit voice communication with Philpot. But for good measure Fenton hit the manual switch on his ELT, held it down for ninety seconds, and turned off the set.

"You son-of-a-bitch! You almost gave me and everbody else in Center a heart attack!"

Fenton chuckled. "Well, it worked, didn't it? You all lost me."

"Oh, *we* lost you, but Homestead didn't."

Fenton felt the laugh starting to strangle in his throat. "Homestead?"

Philpot didn't try to hold back the grin that widened across his face. "We had all radar systems on the alert, Fenton. But we didn't need to alert Homestead Air Force Base, since they operate coast-defense radar. And it works right down to the deck. When New Tamiami finally lost you with the skin track, we spoke to Homestead—on the open hot line—and they had you painted on their scopes."

Fenton's face was grim. "How low, damnit?"

Philpot showed grudging respect. "They said they could keep you painted on their scopes down to three hundred. How low were you, by the way?"

"One hundred."

Philpot paled. "At *night*? Jesus, Fenton, that's—"

"Radar altimeter, Ben."

"Even so, man, that's still crazy."

Fenton's patience was thin. "Never mind that. What about the ELT? I was on the deck when I activated it."

"And nearly started a riot," Philpot told him. "Three separate towers amid RAPCON facilities, as well as Homestead and four Coast Guard and Navy stations, picked up your signal. We alerted them that it was a test, but they were pretty damned unhappy with us about it."

Dale Fenton cursed to himself. Even when he *tried*, he couldn't get himself lost.

But that Convair did.

Chapter 10

More and more, and always against his instincts and his judgment, circumstances demanded that he lend credence to the reality of strange, inexplicable, and, yes, even "impossible" forces existing within the area known as the Devil's Triangle.

The admission of possibility to events or forces in the realm of the paranormal was galling to him. He had prided himself on his extensive knowledge of events and forces in the world. He knew intimately the elements with which nature scoured or caressed the planet; he was understanding of radiations and atmospherics and science and engineering and aerodynamics and technology and that there are mechanical laws of life that are *always* obeyed.

Now these laws were being flaunted, and all was not right with the world.

He had been with the air inspector general's office when they were inundated with reports of UFO's, many of them from qualified and seasoned observers. He'd been assigned to help dissect these reports, and he had run into a world he never knew existed. The UFO's included not merely strange objects in the heavens, but many that were strange only to the observers: sun dogs, airplanes, comets, meteors, birds, ice-crystal clouds, balloons, satellites, plasmoids and corona discharges, cloud reflections of searchlights, inversion layer "mirror reflections," flares, fireworks, noctilucent and nacreous clouds, rockets . . . you name it, and they were buried in it. And that was exclusive of hallucinations, delusions, illusions, hoaxes, pranks, misconceptions, and autosuggestions by people who *wanted* to see their strange goodies in the sky.

Using hard and scientific investigation, they were able to break down into identifiable categories, almost as quickly as they were received, at least ninety percent of every report that came in. The not-immediately-identified took longer, but no longer than a few days or weeks for even the hard nuts that needed cracking.

One "UFO" that people insisted was a machine, a disk at high altitude, invariably turned out to be some form of balloon, especially the really high-altitude research balloons, because they looked like anything *but* balloons. Balloons made of highly reflective material soared to heights of 130,000 feet or more. At certain times of the day, especially at dusk, with the sun's rays at a low angle, the balloon became a tremendous disk hurtling through the high stratosphere, some carried by jetstream winds as great as four hundred miles an hour. With a few clouds between the observer on the ground and the balloon at 130,000 feet, the speed relative to the eye became several thousand miles an hour. Already, the ingredients existed for a magnificent sight, and the rest came as the balloon disturbed the tenuous atmosphere behind it, creating a wake of swirling ice crystals and dust. Caught by the sun at a precise angle, the swirl, too thin even to be seen normally, became the blazing exhaust of a huge disk hurtling along the edges of space.

A camera could furnish photographic proof of the event. The problem was that the camera essentially is a stupid bird. It records optical effects—just what the human eye sees. Nothing more and nothing less in normal light.

And the camera also takes perfect film of a mirage. Why? Because a mirage is an everyday, common event, and people encounter the phenomenon just about every day of their lives.

The very word gives it away. *Mirage.*

Mirror image. That's what it means. All that's needed to take a picture of a mirage is to take a picture looking into a mirror. Or to look at a window from inside a lighted room when it's dark outside: one of those good, old-fashioned mirages is waiting.

The sky is a grab bag of visual distortion and mirror-imaging. The air is filled with inversion layers, refraction, reflection—everything in the form known as reflectional dispersion. Haze, ice crystals, industrial smoke particles, clouds, water droplets, sand, dust, chemicals, stir up the potpourri with the wind, layer everything in different atmospheric strata, mix in oddball lighting effects, and you've set the stage for a vast orchestration of eye-twisting visual effects.

Normally, light rays travel in a concave path that intersects the horizon, but "normal" refers to temperature distribution through the air. Sometimes the air just above the ground becomes exceptionally warm, the air expands and becomes less dense, and the convex path shortens. If the air is really hot, the air becomes concave, and *shazam!*—light starts playing tricks because it is everywhere it shouldn't be. And since all the human eye sees is reflected light, things start moving around or ending up where they shouldn't be. Then there was temperature inversion: a layer of warm air over another layer of cold air. That's when the path of light rays lengthens. The light rays parallel the earth's surface at greater distance.

It wasn't nearly as fearsome as it sounded. You get

a mirage because the distortion and the displacement are astonishing, *once you know what's going on.* Under such conditions, the light reflections from a city can bounce wildly and erratically through the air. This had happened to Fenton once when he was flying at six thousand feet over open country in the midwest.

All of a sudden a city floated in the sky before him. He whacked the heel of his hand against his head, but it was still there, towers rising into the air, the full skyline. It was, of course, a mirage. The sun slanted from the sky, and its rays bathed the city, nearly two thousand miles distant. Light rays bounce back up into space. In this case the bouncing rays struck an inversion layer and reflected the light back down again, so that nearly two hundred miles away Fenton saw the reflection. He couldn't see the invisible air that functioned as a reflecting lens, but he sure as hell saw that city floating in the sky.

Castles in the air. They were real. To the human eye and to the camera.

Often the same effect was encountered at sea. There were plenty of reports of ghost ships drifting through clouds. Sometimes the vessel would be of normal size; sometimes, because of distortion effects in the reflectional dispersion, hundreds of feet long. No one was *ever* going to convince the viewers they hadn't seen a ghost vessel trapped in a tunnel of time and condemned forever to wander haplessly as . . . as whatever the hell they supposed it to be doing.

In the computer research they were doing on the Devil's Triangle, the subject of UFO's was inescapable. It was easy enough, especially with Fenton's past experience with the AIG, to weed out the reports that essentially were worthless. A brief sighting of an object, a light or series of lights, something seen dimly—all these were discarded at once, because there was no way to *do* anything with such reports. But as in all studies of reports of unusual phenomena, there were enough to demand further attention.

The lightning strikes against that big ARIA aircraft, on the same day the Gulfstream disappeared, were ample proof of energetic electrical activity. Despite what the textbooks said, you did *not* need clouds to generate lightning, which was simply the discharge of an overloaded situation. And there was a hell of a lot more to this electrical activity than lightning, which was simply one form of discharge. Saint Elmo's fire had scared the hell out of a lot of people.

Plasmoids were a major source of UFO reports, especially near the ground. There were ball lightning and corona discharges and atmospheric plasma, and a great deal more, all of which convinced the smarter scientists that they still had a lot to learn.

A plasma is essentially an electrified gas, inside of which electrons flow freely. But the electrons move in the middle of positively charged molecules without being attached to those molecules. That's important, because it makes them electrically neutral. And a plasma cloud—and it *is* a cloud—also has its own magnetic field. Put all these things together and relate them to other events, and you're boiling a broth of UFO's.

The magnetic field of the plasma, as well as the surrounding magnetic fields that are always in the air, accelerate the electrons. The electrons collide with the neutral molecules—those without electrical charges. The sum and substance of all this activity is that energy is always being increased or released.

Energy is radiant. The energy release oscillates, or vibrates, in the ultraviolet band, the visible spectrum, and on up to infrared. If it is in the visible part of the spectrum, the plasma glows in blue and red colors.

Those blues and reds are visible to the human eye. But when people see blue- or red-glowing clouds, especially clouds moving erratically, perhaps even in a long straight line, the last thing they're going to believe is that they're seeing a *cloud.* Only *objects* glow and move in that manner, and so the mental process of addition is swiftly under way. They start adding details, and the plasma cloud becomes an object. A machine. A thing. A *real* UFO. Since the UFO is beyond their understanding, they *know* it's a vehicle of some sort.

Ball lightning is another ladle stirring the UFO pot. It comes in about every shape, color, and size one could imagine, from a few inches to more than thirty feet in diameter. It appears most often in orange and red, but it can skip along the spectrum to higher electromagnetic energies and flash into being in violet, blue, and green.

Sometimes the edges of ball lightning are fuzzy, like the edges of a cloud. But it's just as liable to show up with edges as sharply defined as an airplane wing. Sometimes a sharply defined discoid is surrounded by a glowing haze.

Ball lightning is close to home: it drifts low over the ground. And what really frags out people's minds is that it quite often rotates and sometimes hums, whirs, pulsates, or buzzes. It's also been known to give off a rasping sound, a smooth keening cry, and to sound like the bass treadle on an organ.

If that isn't enough it can hover over land or open water. Sometimes it will drift slowly, sometimes race at hundreds of miles an hour. It can fly straight and level or angle into the sky with tremendous speed, and it has an affinity for making right-angle turns. It can race over the ground or sea, and abruptly, faster than the eye can follow, completely reverse its direction.

And ball lightning in any one of the forms described has an affinity, an electrical appetite, so to speak, for things that have electrical systems: like automobiles, boats, and airplanes—whether they're standing still or moving. Anything with an ignition system gives off a tremendous electrical field, which is a siren call to any ball lightning in the vicinity.

Ball lightning picks up—homes in on—the electrical field, follows along like a faithful dog. Its own powerful electromagnetic field plays havoc with car (or boat or plane) engines, lights, or radios. Sometimes it knocks out these systems completely by saturating—literally drenching—them with energy.

What always aggravated such situations is that it is impossible, absolutely impossible, to create the exact conditions under which the object—the disk-shaped, gleaming, glowing, buzzing, rotating *thing*—appeared. So it ends up with the witness convinced that there's a conspiracy afoot, because what sane human being could deny what happened?

All the investigator can do is take notes on what was reported, and put it into his file. He'll try to categorize the sighting—suspected plasmoid or ball lightning, a mirage from reflectional dispersion, or, if there are even greater details that cannot be answered, he'll slide it into the folder marked "Unknown."

There just wasn't a goddamn thing you could do with a sighting after the fact. Which was why Fenton made his decision early in his investigation of the Gulfstream incident not to pay attention to any such reports.

Before the week was out, Dale Fenton was fast becoming an expert on phenomena within the Devil's Triangle. Everything he'd heard—from people who had been personally and directly involved—convinced him that most textbooks on the weather characteristics of the Triangle should be burned.

"I've learned to be suspicious of my magnetic compass anytime I'm flying in that area," Al Dickensen told him. Dickensen was a commercial pilot for an air-taxi outfit operating to the north of Miami. "North Andros seems to be the worst. I don't know how many times I've watched that mag compass spin like it was crazy. I don't know what sets it off. The thing sometimes spins to the right, sometimes to the left. There's no way of knowing. All I do know is not to trust it."

"Al, when you lose the mag compass, let's say your directional gyro hasn't been corrected. There's not too much VHF down there, especially if you're low. How do you handle it?"

The old-time pilot gave him a crooked grin. "Very carefully, Fenton, that's how. It's crazy, but you can't even trust your directional finder half the time in that area. The damn thing points everywhere but to where the station lies."

"Why?"

Dickensen shrugged. "*You* tell me, friend. All I know is that there's a bend in the beam. I know the books say that can't happen. Screw the books. It's happened time after time. And more times than I want to remember, you run into zones of radio silence. The radio just quits working."

"Component failure?"

"No way. The set works. It gets power. It works, but it just doesn't do anything."

"You've always come back, Al." He laughed as Dickensen rapped his knuckles on his desk. "Ever lose anybody in the same area?"

The man sobered. "I've known five pilots personally who ran into some sort of shit down there and . . . well, I don't know what happened to them, but they disappeared. And we never found a trace of anything or anybody."

"But you still fly down there."

"Fenton, they killed forty-seven thousand people on the highways last year. You still drive, don't you?"

Fenton made an appointment for dinner with Dick Special, a Nationial Airlines pilot who'd retired at sixty years of age, and had, in the nine years since then, been flying small jets and other aircraft all across the Devil's Triangle. "It's the weather that's knocked some of those people out of the sky," the old man said. "Oh, not the sort of thing I can sit here and prove, Dale, but the odds, circumstances, you know, the things that can hit, let's say, a hundred pilots, and you know a dozen or more aren't going to make it back home. I don't know about UFO's and electromagnetic twisters and the rest of that horse hockey, but I do know that there's weather out there you just don't run into anywhere else."

Fenton described the howling headwinds he'd run into with Gulfstream 697D, despite a real-time forecast that told him he had a tailwind. Special laughed with him. "That's happened enough times to me," he concurred. "But I've run into stuff at lower levels. Like five thousand. I was climbing out one time in a Lear. We were just going through five thousand when I ran into what seemed like a waterfall. It was like flying right into Niagara Falls. No warning. One second everything was as nice as pie, and the next thing, we were standing on the tail and going down. All this time, the airplane is shaking like . . . You ever see how they mix paint in a hardware store? The way a vise grips the can and shakes it like hell? That's what was happening to us. Before I ever knew what was happening, we were down to less than a thousand feet. Then I heard this terrific bang, and we were going the other way."

Any sign of humor was gone from his face; his eyes were dead serious. "I didn't think we'd make it. We were being shaken like a terrier killing a rat. I had no control; absolutely none. The airplane was . . . well, 'gyrating' would be a good word for it. We got spit out of whatever had hold of us at fifteen thousand feet. Baggage was thrown around. I had four passengers, and the seatbelts broke on three of them. They all had broken bones."

He finished his drink in a long and meaningful swallow. "Now, you take some of these people in another type of plane when they hit something like that. Maybe only a thousand feet up, or even ten. First of all, many aircraft couldn't take even that initial shock. The structural loads would be great enough to tear the wings or the tail off, and they're just . . . gone. Even if a ship held together, I imagine more than one of them has been dragged right into the water, and that's the end of *that.*"

Arthur von Thron, a commercial-air-taxi pilot operating out of the Bahamas, described what he feared most of all. Waterspouts, like nowhere else in the world. "And I've flown over most places on this little old clay pot," he emphasized. "But I've never seen 'em come up so fast or act so mean or there be so damned many of them, and all at the same time." He gave Fenton a lopsided grin. "Sort of gets you right here, don't it?" he asked, holding his hand over his heart. "Like flutter, whop, wheeze, when you see *them* mothers."

"You don't look very upset," Fenton tossed back at him.

"Man, I should of been dead three dozen times out there!" Von Thron exclaimed. "A dozen times between Miami and Grand Bahama—what the hell is it, ninety or a hundred miles or so, right? In just that distance, I've seen as many as seven or eight of those damned waterspouts. Very few of them are white. They're dark gray, and almost all of them are cone-shaped, you know, like a tornado. Which is what they are, of course. But these mothers suck up millions of gallons of water, maybe billions of gallons, for all I know; they suck it up from the sea, and they drag it upstairs like nothing you ever saw. And you know what happens to the stuff? Eight or ten thousand feet high, it gets spit out as hailstones big as baseballs. You know what that feels like? Like getting hit right in the ass with shit from a gun as big as a goddamned locomotive. Happened to me once. Tore out the windshield, turned the leading edge of the wings into what looked like the guts of a cat turned inside out. I managed to ditch before I passed out. My two passengers dragged me out onto a raft."

Fenton asked, "What about those waterspouts? Ever get hit with one of those?"

Von Thron stared at him, then shook his head in disbelief. "If I had, Fenton, you wouldn't be talking to me right now. Man, they're each a full-blown *tornado.* You got winds doing maybe three to five hundred miles an hour, and water is moving through it like a hose. Water at five hundred miles an hour, man! No airplane would *ever* survive a thing like that."

It went like that. Pilot after pilot, the finest and most skilled of men in the air, related their experiences with weather that was unpredictable, impossible, lethal. They spoke of lightning streaking from skies greenish in hue, with swirling bands of yellow and orange, leaving the air metallic-tasting, even thousands of feet above the water.

"I was flying about fifteen hundred feet up," one

pilot told Fenton, "when we hit one of those goddamned lightning sectors. That's as good a name for them as any, I suppose. But what scared the hell out of us was what happened to the lightning *after* it hit the water. It didn't just disappear. It flickered over the surface. Ever see a tube of mercury drop on a table? The way it splatters and runs in all directions? The whole damn ocean was spattered with fireballs of every size and color and—"

"Ball lightning," Fenton broke in.

"Damned if I know. But this stuff was everywhere, and we saw one big concentration of it, and it was burning in the center. I flew that way, because it just didn't seem possible. Know what was burning? A ship. A goddamned ship that was being hit by wave after wave of lightning running along the surface of the water. The burning we saw was the ship itself. There wasn't an inch of it that wasn't on fire. We called the Coast Guard, and we circled the area until they got a flying boat out there. It was too late. Even the ashes were gone."

Dr. Fred Atkins. a weather scientist working at the University of Miami, rattled Fenton's cage. "We're issuing regular warnings now, whenever we can, of course, on neutercanes. We—"

Fenton echoed the word "Neutercanes?"

Atkins smiled. "It's still pretty much of a new term," he explained, "but it's real enough. A neutercane is . . . well, call it a freak storm of great intensity, covering a small area. It doesn't show on weather maps, because it brews up too fast and disappears even faster. The Gulf Stream has something to do with it, of course. The storms are only a few miles in diameter. Some last less than a minute, others as long as an hour. But when they come up . . . well, it's every man for himself. They just tear apart the ocean surface. In no time at all the waves are twenty to thirty feet high. Small boats can't survive that kind of storm, and anything caught flying directly through the neutercane would be lucky to get out.

So the Devil's Triangle had to be the single most vicious area in the world for unpredictable, violent, lethal weather. He was almost ready to let it go at that when he met with Jeff Hawke, a British pilot who'd flown fighters with the Royal Air Force, and for the last ten years had run his own international ferry service for anything from single-engine crop dusters to four-engine jetliners. Fighter pilot, stunt pilot, air-show specialist, airplane pilot—name it, and Jeff Hawke had done it: "He doesn't fly an airplane. He straps the damn thing on like a pair of wings. . . ."

Jeff Hawke had flown across the world's different oceans a total of four hundred and seventy-two times and had never yet lost one of his airplanes. That was a record one could label only as extraordinary.

"I've heard you've run into some unusual things on a few of your crossings," Fenton opened carefully.

"I know of at least six other pilots who've had something of the same sort happen to them. If I hadn't spoken with them personally, I'd never be telling *you* a thing right now, because you wouldn't believe a word of it. . . ."

Jeff Hawke told Fenton that many of his flights were through the Devil's Triangle. "I'd never paid much attention to the stories one hears about the Triangle. The weird ones, we call them. I mean I've run into nasties all over the world, right? Then *it* happened. . . ."

Hawke had been flying a Piper Aztec with long-range tanks from Fort Lauderdale Executive Airport direct to Bermuda. Right along whatever invisible line made the northwest boundary of the Triangle. The weather was excellent for that sort of flight—fair-weather cumulus, thick white cotton puffs covering the ocean between four and eight thousand feet. A neat tailwind at eleven thousand, where Hawke would be cruising. In the jargon of the former RAF pilot, "a piece of cake."

"Then," Hawke said quietly, "it happened. Not what you'd expect when things start going to hell. Nothing with a bang. I was on autopilot, everything was neat as a pin. Nice flying. Then, I began to get dizzy. Now, that sort of thing doesn't happen to *me*. Thought it might be some food, you know? But no queasy feelings in the belly. I shook my head a couple of times, put the air flow right on my face. Didn't help. I looked at the panel. Everything where it belonged, you know? The horizon perfect, autopilot perfect, all the engine things in the green, where they belonged. Then I looked at the mag compass. As the people say, a bummer.

"I couldn't see it. Not the compass, but the card. It was spinning *that* fast. Blur. That's all it was. Just a bloody blur. Going so fast, couldn't see a thing. Just that blur. And I felt like I was going. Passing out, you know? First thing I did was push the seat way back. If I was going to slop around that machine like a sack of grain, I didn't want to fall on the yoke. Right into the water, that way. Ruins the flight, right? So I go back with the seat, and I think I really ought to do up the trim. Change of CG, of course. But I couldn't do it. Tried, really. But no strength. Weak as a kitten. Couldn't even mew if I wanted to.

"Time to give in, old fellow, I tell myself. Put my head back against the rest, and then I get a good look at the sky. *It isn't there.* I mean, the ruddy sky ought to be where it's always been. But, no sky. Just a cream, like a creamy yellow. No clouds, no water, no horizon. And I'm slipping. Can hardly keep my eyes open. Last thing I did before I went down the tube was to look at my watch. My arm felt like lead. Barely got it high enough to see my watch. Fixed the numbers in my head, I did. And that was it."

Fenton stared at Jeff Hawke. "What in the devil happened after that?"

Hawke scratched his chin. "I came back to things just one hour later. Fifty-nine minutes, to be exact. Didn't have the foggiest where I was. Still flying to the northeast, if I could trust the gauges. Which I'd have been a fool to do. But I could see the sun, I knew the time. Northeast it was, all right. The problem was, like I say, I didn't know where I was. Not dizzy anymore. Felt . . . well, drained. Shouldn't have been, because I certainly had a beautiful rest for an hour. Felt, though, like all the strength was sucked or drained from me.

"Looked up, and there it was. Beautiful. Lovely contrail. Boeing or Douglas, from the looks of it. Got on the horn right off, gave them a call. They came back, I told them I was under them, and asked where the devil was I. They sounded sort of strange when they answered. It isn't the question one usually hears in the middle of the ocean.

"I didn't believe them when they told me. I'll spare you the details, Mr. Fenton, but I was seven hundred miles from where I'd been an hour before. You figure it out. I can't. I'm in a bloody machine cut back to economical cruise, true air speed about one-eighty or so. And in that hour the bird covers a distance of seven hundred miles? It's impossible, of course. No way about it. But it was true. I turned back and landed after flying due west. I landed, by the way, in Virginia.

"Absolutely impossible."

Dr. Rudy Wells watched the sleek Baron come

around smartly from the taxiway, dipping gently on the nose gear as Dale Fenton parked before the main hangar of Space Coast Aviation on Merritt Island Airport. The doctor waited until the blur of propellers had become lifeless blades to greet his friend. Fenton stepped down from the airplane, then walked toward Wells.

"Well, it's the midwife to the cyborg in person." Fenton grinned as they clasped hands. "How does it feel to be even more famous than Marcus Welby?"

Wells bared his teeth. "Any more remarks like that from you, Dale, and you'll be the first man in history to have a six-million-dollar dork."

"I value it a bit higher than that." Fenton laughed. He slapped the doctor on the shoulder as they walked to Wells's car. "Still poking and stitching day and night, Rudy?"

"In somewhat less crude terms than that, yes," Wells told him. He drove slowly from the airport. "Let's not keep the old country doctor in suspense," he admonished Fenton. "Speak, or I'll commit a medical disaster upon your person. Are you going to admit you came here to pick my brains about the Devil's Triangle?"

Fenton's eyebrows rose a bit. "How did you know?"

Wells chuckled. "Super Sleuth is in the middle of the hottest case in years, and he shows up *here*? You're looking for a way out of the quicksand."

"That," Fenton growled, "is as good a term as any." He studied the 520 Causeway before them as Wells drove toward Cocoa Beach. "Where to for dinner?"

"The Mousetrap. I'd have arranged a sukiyaki special at home, but Jackie is off to the White House for several days. And I don't think you'd care to sample my gastronomical bumbling."

They turned left on A1A and drove north to the

restaurant. As they entered, a beautiful waitress moved before them with a tray of drinks. Fenton stared at legs that just wouldn't quit. "That's new since I was last here," he murmured.

"That's Linda," Wells told him. "Admire from a distance, but don't touch. She belongs to—"

"Never mind. I can guess. He's—"

"The six-million-dollar bastard," Wells finished for him. "The original article."

They followed the hostess to a booth and settled in. Linda took Wells's order for drinks. "I've ordered margaritas," Wells told Fenton. "Two of the drinks they serve in here, and your tongue will be loose. You'll babble, and maybe I'll learn enough of your problem to help."

The drinks came quickly, and Fenton didn't hide his admiring glance. "I understand you belong to a six-million-dollar bastard," he said.

She glanced at Wells. "Ignore him," the doctor told her. "He escaped only last week, but we still have hope."

Fenton studied the retreating legs. "Thanks a heap," he grumbled.

"Cheers," said Wells, and started on his drink.

It took three to settle Fenton down. He began slowly, explaining the case in general, adding more and more specifics. He ran through what he'd learned from other pilots, the details they had gathered personally and through the computers. He laid it out neatly, emphasizing his belief that the hysterical weather of the Triangle could probably account for most of the ships and planes that had been lost, including those that vanished without a trace.

"Yet," Wells reminded him as he put aside the menu, "you can't explain what happened to that fellow Hawke."

"No explanation," Fenton admitted.

"And you're not going to seriously, um, recommend that Hawke was blown off course by five-hundred-mile-an-hour winds, are you?"

"No. That would be a bit much."

"It also wouldn't explain a spinning compass. And it wouldn't explain at all, would it, the extreme lethargy, the unconsciousness for an hour? But there is something familiar in all that."

Fenton looked up with sudden interest. "Don't leave me at the altar, bearded one."

Wells tapped the menu. "Wouldn't think of it. Good; here comes the beautiful one." They ordered and returned to their exchange. "This ennui, so to speak. It's happened before."

"Hawke did say he knew of several other pilots who'd gone through the same thing."

"Not just pilots," Wells said. "Have you ever heard of the luminous wheels beneath the surface of the ocean?"

"Oh, shit. Not you, too? I—"

"Cool it." The beard bristled. "You've been spooked by too many UFO investigations, my boy. You've lost perspective. The luminous wheels, or glowing wheels, or spoked wheels that shine, whatever you want to call them, have been seen by mariners for hundreds of years, and in most seas of the world. Sometimes they're indistinct, sometimes they're sharp. The size varies, because we're never certain of the observers' accuracy."

"Amen," muttered Fenton.

"Be quiet, indulge yourself in your shrimp cocktail, call Linda for another round of drinks, and *listen.*" Wells finished off the drink before him and pushed aside the glass. "The glowing wheels are still being seen. I do *not* know what they are. But whatever they are, when one moves from the depths to the surface so that it's visible, two things happen.

First, a magnetic compass goes haywire. Second, either at the time of the wheel's appearance or, more usually, some time afterward, the people in the proximity of the wheel are absolutely drained of energy, exhausted."

"The spinning compass and Hawke passing out."

"Precisely."

"Any idea why?" Fenton asked.

"None. I'd venture to say something electromagnetic is involved, however. And an electromagnetic field can leave a person utterly exhausted. There's reaction to body chemicals, that sort of thing. Also, there's a direct relationship between brain activity and an electromagnetic field, especially if the field is localized and strong enough."

"You're suggesting, then, that Hawke was involved in some sort of electromagnetic field?"

"I suggest nothing. I point out that what happened to him is similar in a number of ways to what's happened to men at sea when they've encountered this glowing-object phenomenon."

Fenton toyed with his fork. "Think I can establish a relationship between these glowing wheels and what happened with Jeff Hawke, and tie it in to the airplane we're looking for?"

"Not even by some extraordinary long shot," Wells responded. "Look, the needle in the haystack is a lark compared to what you're trying to discover. An airplane that *appears* to have violated a whole slew of natural laws. Perhaps even unnatural laws. None of us knows. How do you look for something you can't see and can't find and that doesn't show when you've examined just about every possible aspect?"

Fenton jabbed his fork in the air. "I'm not trying to solve the mysteries of the Devil's Triangle, unless . . ."

"Unless," Wells finished for him, "it has a pertinent, direct, meaningful, and useful bearing on your investigation."

"Neatly said, medical wizard," Fenton said with a bow.

"There's more to it than that. If you *could* solve certain mysteries of the Triangle, it really wouldn't do you a bloody bit of good."

"Hah! You're so right."

"So what you've got to do is crack open a few mysteries that bear directly on your ghost machine."

Fenton winced. "Is that your best choice of words?"

"It'll do for the moment. I wish I knew how I could help you directly."

Fenton studied his friend. "You flew a lot with the Air Force, Rudy."

"Fifth Air Force, to be exact. Spent a lot of time in Japan and Korea with that outfit."

"You still flying much?"

"Depends," Wells said, speaking over a mouthful of food. "Much more than I ever thought I would, but not as much as I'd like."

Fenton spoke carefully. "You were pretty uptight about the big blue for a while, Rudy."

"You mean scared shitless, don't you?"

"That's about as eloquent, I guess."

Wells sat up straight, a bit testy of a sudden. "Let me explain it, if I can. This fellow who goes with Linda—"

"Not him again."

"Him again. We were in the Air Force together. He's a complete lunatic with an airplane. Nothing is sacred to him. He flew, among other things, as a stunt pilot. A drunk act."

"*That* figures."

"You miss the point. I'm absolutely comfortable in the air with him. I've watched him perform. He has about as much precision as a water buffalo skating on thin ice. He's all over the sky, he's mad . . . and he has a perfect safety record. I learned a lot from him. He enjoys the sky. He's friends with it. He goes up in an airplane, and he fairly chortles with glee. Every flight is like his first, and he's been flying for twenty-six years. He's . . . well, like a kid. The airplane seems to know it. The sky knows it. And you just get the feeling that there's no use worrying about anything with this man. I know that he whipped my problem for me because he never busted his ass trying to cure me. He just invited me along, and everything happened of its own accord."

Fenton smiled. "I'd like to meet him."

He's in Hollywood right now, shouting at producers and rattling cages. It's one of his great pleasures in life. But I said all that for a purpose, Dale. The only way you're going to get anywhere in this Triangle business, at least tonight with me, is to be as reckless as I felt I was being when I climbed into an airplane with that lunatic friend of mine. You've got to let loose, listen with an open mind to anything I might say to you."

Dr. Rudy Wells leaned back in his chair and smiled at the man before him. "You see, I *do* have an idea about what happened to Hawke and what may have happened to that airplane you're trying so hard to find."

"For Christ's sake, tell me!"

Wells shook his head. "Not yet. First, I want to eat my dinner, and I recommend you do the same. And don't eat too quickly, because—"

"I understand, Mother."

"And watch those half-words," Rudy snapped, digging into his steak.

"Have you run any correlations with the Devil's Sea?" Rudy Wells sipped coffee and stared across his cup at Fenton.

"Not that much," Fenton said. "No, don't start spouting off at me. We've established the relationship. It's real. There are two places on earth where the magnetic compass hangs true north. Anywhere else in the world, there's normal variation involved, as much as twenty degrees. But if you work with the eightieth meridian—"

"That's longitude, isn't it?"

"Uh-uh. It's the degree of longitude that runs south from Hudson Bay through the, um . . . well, the Cleveland area in Ohio, and continues on south into this area. In fact, the eightieth meridian runs just a couple of miles to the east of Miami. It's a no-variation line."

"So anytime you're along this meridian, true north and magnetic north are exactly the same?"

"Right. And that line of no magnetic variation runs right through the area known as the Devil's Sea."

"Give me some landmarks."

"The meridian slices a part of the Pacific Ocean to the east of Japan. It runs between Iwo Jima and Marcus Island. The Japanese and the Filipinos hate the place. It seems to be worse for ships than the Devil's Triangle. There's all sorts of talk about seaquakes, tidal waves, cyclones that leap up out of nowhere, waterspouts, terrible magnetic storms—the works. Let me back up a moment. I was talking about the eightieth meridian right off the Florida coast. But that line of no magnetic variation on the other side of the world, is better described as longitude one-forty east."

"Take Honshu, the main island of Japan. How far south of there?"

"About two hundred fifty miles."

Wells nodded. "Now I've got a fix on it. Wait a moment . . . I remember. There were ships lost there during the war, with no explanation. Just attributed to combat action no one reported. We used to send planes south to Guam from Japan, and we had some pretty wild losses there. We really didn't have any choice, so we figured it was weather. Christ, we lost fourteen fighters one day—"

"*Fourteen?*"

"Fourteen. P-51's on a ferry flight. There was some weather in that area—they were flying to Guam—but the weather planes sent out ahead said it looked pretty good, and the pilots had full oxygen, so they could have topped just about anything in that ship. They had enough fuel for about sixteen hundred miles. We never heard from them again."

"No distress—"

"Nothing, Dale. Look, I don't want to get into a word hassle about the *possibilities* of what might have happened. I *can* tell you this, though, and it's based on military experience. Not on private pilots. Not even on commercial pilots involved. But on extensive military records. We had hundreds of incidents of planes flying through there, off the Bonin Island, through what you call the Devil's Sea, where crazy things used to happen."

"Like what?"

"Radios wouldn't work. Magnetic compasses went crazy. Direction finders were useless. Sometimes even the flight instruments wouldn't operate. Airspeed needles would wander, even rate-of-climb indicators. They'd show tremendous changes in altitude, and the plane was flying along as smooth as silk."

Fenton's expression was sour. "That's just the kind of encouragement I need."

"You're too close to the forest to see the trees," Wells said critically.

"Perhaps you'd better tell me what the trees are supposed to look like," Fenton retorted.

"You're still debating the existence of such effects," Wells tossed at him. "There's your error, Dale. Stop trying to prove or disprove what hundreds, maybe thousands of pilots have encountered. It's a road to nowhere. *Accept* that these things are real. That's terribly important."

Fenton leaned back in his seat. He didn't answer for a while, but clenched a cigar between his teeth and lit up. "All right, Nostradamus. Why is it so important?"

Wells flashed a look of triumph. "Because then you won't be chasing the wrong ghosts."

Fenton studied Wells through a cloud of smoke, starting to comment, but checking his own words. "You'd better run that by me again," he said after a while.

"You're convinced the missing airplane, the . . . what was it?"

"Grumman Gulfstream II. Twin-engine executive jet, but the size of a small airliner."

"Reliable?"

"The best, Rudy."

"You're convinced it wasn't lost from natural causes, I assume?"

Fenton shifted in his seat. "You've got to have a baseline from which to work," he said carefully. "Everything involved in this case supports that line of thinking. No, I just do not believe natural causes are involved. There were no storm areas before, during, or even after that flight. Other aircraft in fairly large numbers were in the area. There were God knows how many boats and ships. Because of the shot that day—"

"I remember. I was at the Cape when the Titan went. I even saw that airplane. We watched it circle before liftoff, and I remember some people talking about it."

"Well, because of the shot, the electronic surveillance was extreme. The only thing out of line, Rudy, was that ARIA being hit by lightning."

"And they made it back."

"Sure."

"So now," Wells said, "you've got to increase your definition of natural causes. Would effects such as a spinning magnetic compass be considered as contributing to the loss of the airplane?"

"No. Airplanes like that Grumman don't hang life or death because of a mag compass. They could lose just about *all* their instruments and make it back fine. It takes more than that. Jesus, remember what some of those bombers looked like when they came back from raids over Germany? They were shot to pieces, torn apart. Flying wrecks. And yet they flew hundreds of miles to make it back home. So forget a spinning compass, or radios that go out, or combinations of them. It's *not* enough."

"What if they lost both engines at the same time?"

"It could happen, but it never has. *Never* with those engines," Fenton emphasized. "But for the sake of argument, we'll say it did. They're up at thirty-three thousand feet. They can glide a long way. They've got plenty of time to restart the engines. They've got islands all over the place. If they can't reach an island, they can ditch. The sea condition was perfect for that. They've got radios, emergency beacons that operate in the air and on or in the water. Nothing was ever found in the way of debris or wreckage. The odds are so wild that—"

"Okay, okay, I get your point. Look, what's the safety record for the Gulfstream II?"

Fenton had a pained expression on his face. "It's *perfect*. And I mean perfect. In all the years all those airplanes have been flying, only one was ever lost. And that was on a test flight when the crew was beating hell out of the airplane. In terms of operations in the field, they've never scraped a knee with that bird."

Wells stubbed out a cigarette butt, lit another immediately.

When he didn't speak for several moments, Fenton leaned forward, looking steadily at the doctor. "It's time to quit playing your little game, Rudy. You've been building up to something."

Wells nodded. "I wanted the air cleared of everything else first," he admitted.

"Do you *know* something I should?"

"I think so."

"Goddamnit, *give*."

Wells let out his breath. "All right. Consider the possibility that the airplane was lost because of something beyond our experience. By that I mean this X factor has been experienced before, but we have no proof, we can't reproduce the situation on demand, and we're not even sure what's involved. But we do know there's an effect. And the craziest possibility becomes real if we have some indication in the form of proof, even though it may not be directly involved."

Fenton stared at the doctor. "Okay. You've set me up. Let's have the rest of it."

"There seems to be growing proof," Wells said slowly, "that what happened to that fellow in the Aztec—"

"Jeff Hawke."

"What happened to Hawke, and a number of other pilots, may also have happened to the Gulfstream you're looking for."

"Hawke came back," Fenton reminded him.

"But many planes haven't," Wells said with a touch of scorn. "Including your precious Grumman."

"Admitted."

"Dale, please understand, I'm dead serious about

this. I think the evidence points to there being a time anomaly as the cause of those disappearances."

"A *what*?"

"A time anomaly."

"What the hell is that?"

"A tear, a rip, a bend, a distortion, a twist—whatever—in time."

"Mother of God. I don't believe you said all that."

But to his surprise, Wells showed no anger. He leaned back and folded his arms. "Let me know when you're ready to talk sensibly," he told Fenton.

"*Me* talk *sensibly*?" Fenton's voice rose. "And to think I've put myself under the knife in your hands! You're a lunatic." He watched the doctor remove an envelope from his inside jacket pocket. "What's that?"

"Proof."

"Huh?"

"You'll catch flies if you leave your mouth open like that."

"Proof of *what?*"

"A time jump."

Fenton groaned.

"I didn't say theory, man. I said *proof.*"

"That's impossible."

The envelope disappeared back into the pocket. "Forget it, then."

"Rudy, I'll—"

"No sweat. Just forget I ever brought it up."

Fenton rubbed his cheek. "Let's hear it. I'm crazy to listen to another word, but let's hear it."

"Dale, what some people suspected for years has finally been *proved.* The best description for it is 'time jump.' "

"How'd they find out about it?" Fenton couldn't keep the sarcasm from his voice.

"Cesium clock variations."

"Who?"

"Cesium clocks. That's a layman's term for it. Nuclear-decay systems. The most accurate timekeeping and measuring systems in existence. Accurate down to a tenth of a millionth of a second per year."*

Whatever trace of sarcasm had appeared in Fenton's voice was gone. He began to look hungrily at the envelope, still unopened, in Wells' hand. "Who, uh, uses these things?" Fenton asked.

"National Bureau of Standards, United States Naval Observatory, Strategic Air Command, and the National Aeronautics and Space Administration."

"I'm listening. Carefully. Open that damned envelope."

The rustle of paper held him with cobra fascination. "How'd that stuff come to you, Rudy?"

Wells shook his head. "No go on that, Dale. You'll have to respect my promise of confidence to the, uh, source."

Fenton nodded and gestured him on.

"The conclusion drawn from what happened," Wells spoke slowly, "is that the earth—the entire surface of the planet—has some unknown number of times in the past gone through what the . . . what the person involved calls a time jump. That's his phrase, not mine." He glanced up at Fenton and then returned to the paper as he continued. "This time anomaly was first detected with a . . . let's see, yes, here it is—a Hewlett Packard 5061A Cesium on Kwajalein Island in the Pacific. It's used for measuring satellite-passage time, incoming ICBM warheads during reentry tests; that sort of activity.

"What they call a time jump, Dale, is a difference in the cesium time standards between one set of equipment in one part of the world and the findings

*Author's note: The time jump information on these pages is *not* fiction.

or readings made from an identical set of equipment in another part of the world. Such as a difference noticed in cesium timekeeping between equipment on Kwajalein and another set in Maryland. Cesium equipment is always identical, no matter where the equipment is located. Or it *should* be. We're dealing with radioactive decay for material measurable down to atomic-disintegration levels. Let's just say it's the most accurate system in existence." He tapped the paper. "But not too long ago, the impossible happened. They found variations."

Wells sipped coffee. "Um, here. The first time there was a time shift, a jump in time, literally, was during the period from November 23, 1973, to January 10, 1974. Measurements were both by Cesium decay and satellite track. What the scientists discovered was that on November 23, 1973, the cesium equipment on Kwajalein was lagging the Naval Observatory cesium equipment by three-tenths of a microsecond. This lag, which had not happened for more than twenty years before this, lasted, um, until December 21. That's just about a month.

"On December 21 the lag disappeared. The Cesium readout suddenly matched its time readings between Kwajalein and Maryland. According to what my friend explained, the scientists at first figured something was wrong with their equipment. They couldn't find a thing. To be absolutely certain, they kept round-the-clock comparative records with another cesium system buried deep underground. It seemed to have some shielding effect against what was happening on the surface."

Wells looked up. "They made a major point of that. Time on the earth's surface was suddenly different from time deep beneath the surface. *There were actually two different times.* People on the surface of the earth were living in one time frame, but anyone who was down deep, and heavily shielded, existed in another time universe. They wouldn't notice the effect, because the difference was in microseconds. But let me go on.

"For three days, time again was normal. Then, it happened again on the, uh, the twenty-fourth of December, in 1973. Now the lag jumped to one-point-one useconds—useconds are microseconds. Two days later, on December 26, the recorded time lag was one-point-two microseconds; the next day, it was still one-point-two microseconds. On January 4—this is now 1974—the lag was measured at one-point-one microseconds. Six days later, the lag decreased to zero-point-four, and stayed that way for the rest of the month. Since then it has never jumped again." Wells folded the paper. "Then again, maybe it has and they're just not saying anything."

A long silence followed. Fenton finally relit the cigar that had turned cold. He studied the smoke before him.

"Jesus Christ."

"Amen."

"It's real, then."

"It is."

"Did they get any other effects?"

"You're not going to believe it."

"Let's have it."

"They did time-relation correlations with a Minuteman ICBM launch from Vandenberg Air Force Base in California. Dale, before I say any more, I've checked this out thoroughly, and I want to emphasize that it's true."

"What *happened*?"

"The warhead disappeared."

Fenton hesitated, then shrugged. "That sort of thing happens."

"No, it doesn't. They track those things every inch

of the way. They had a nominal launch, all three stages burned perfectly, the warhead separated. On the downslide of its trajectory, it vanished from all tracking scopes."

"Losing something is one thing. Insisting it vanished because you lose your radar is something else."

Wells had a strange expression on his face. "I'm glad you're sitting down."

Fenton looked at him with suspicion.

"The warhead showed up again. *Three days later.*"

Fenton stared.

"It showed up again three days later in the exact same point in space that it had disappeared from."

"It couldn't have."

"It did. They recovered the warhead. Identification down to the serial numbers of equipment inside."

"But that's *impossible*!"

"I know. They did their time checks. At the instant the warhead disappeared, there had been a time jump, as recorded with the cesium-decay equipment."

Fenton felt as if his head was splitting wide open. But the reference, and the possible link, was there. "What all this comes to, then, is that when a time jump takes place, whatever gets caught where the . . . the . . ." He groped unsuccessfully for the words.

"They consider it, at least for purposes of semantic identification, a tear in time. Use any word you want. Tear, rip, break, twist. They're all the same. Something happens to space-time, like a shift into a different dimension. They're convinced this happened with the warhead. They have absolutely no idea how or why it reappeared. In one dimension it had vanished for a period of seventy-two hours. Whatever happened through that time bend or jump, it was shifted or phased in the same instant, only three days later, in space-time back here on the world we know."

"Rudy, this is all true?" Fenton was almost pleading that it wasn't.

"It's true, Dale."

Fenton sighed. "Then you're telling me this could, this *might* have happened with the Gulfstream."

"I can't possibly say it did. But *could? Might?*" Wells shrugged. "Who knows? It might be gone forever. Wherever that may be.

"It may never come back. *If* this is what happened to it." His smile was thin, humorless.

"But then again, it just might come back. Someday. Someplace. Sometime."

Chapter 11

Herbert Carruthers was waiting for him when he reached his office the morning after his skull-bending meeting with Dr. Rudy Wells. Fenton had spent half the night wrestling with what he'd learned in that astonishing exchange, but he still wasn't prepared to move based on what Wells had said. His instinct urged him to follow his professional approach to the case, and any doubts he'd entertained about staying true to instinct were banished by what Carruthers reported.

"I could have called," Herb explained, "but I'm sick and tired of that telephone on my desk. I needed to talk with you directly."

Fenton understood. Being somewhere out in the boondocks with the action far removed was a great contributing factor to ulcers. He eased into the chair behind his desk and lifted his feet. Dottie brought them coffee and slipped from the room.

"It's been three weeks," Herb said, the unnecessary words betraying his nervousness. "It feels like three months, and it's not getting any better. The heat's on us, Dale."

"Three weeks is hardly enough time for warming up in a case like this," Fenton said, annoyed with even a suggestion of defending what he'd been doing. "The Pentagon on us again?"

Herb shook his head. "I only wish it were that simple." Then he dropped his little bomb. "It's Positronics, Dale. They've filed in court for payment on their policy. Make that plural," he added with distaste. "Policies."

Fenton came upright. "I don't get it. No one can go to court this fast on a claim like this, Herb. It'll never hold up. You know that."

"I've got news for you," Carruthers said testily, and as quickly as he showed his temper, he apologized for his words. "But, damnit," he went on, his inner heat unabated, "what's happened in the past doesn't seem to hold water right now. I tried pushing it off, and it's not working. Look, you're deep into research on the Devil's Triangle, and—"

Fenton was halfway out of his seat with those words. "Hold it right there, Herb," he said quickly. "I am *not* doing research on the Devil's Triangle. For Christ's sake, man, I'm after the reasons, the cause or causes, behind the loss of an airplane and the people it was carrying. If it had disappeared in the Amazon jungle, I'd be researching that. The Devil's Triangle, or whatever they call that patch of water, is incidental."

His words had little or no effect upon Carruthers. "That may be your story," he said with a glum expression, "but it's got teeth for Positronics. Their legal department hired a scientific-research organization. They've done one hell of a job on documenting aircraft losses in the Triangle—or within the boundaries of what's commonly accepted as the Triangle. It doesn't matter if you or I feel it's an arbitrary measurement, Dale. You see, their interest in the Triangle has nothing to do with the mechanics of what happens there. I'll admit it's a fine line, it's even razor-thin, *but it stands up legally.*" He was out of his seat, pacing nervously. "They've presented to the court a list as long as your arm of aircraft disappearances in the past, going back to that fare-thee-well with those five torpedo bombers in December 1945. They made a lot of brownie points with the DC-3 in 1948, the Convair that just happened. The individual flights are important—"

"To whom, damnit!"

Carruthers stopped in mid-stride and looked steadily at Fenton. "To the *court.*"

"But precedence in an aircraft loss isn't enough," Fenton protested, "even—or especially—when there isn't a trace of wreckage, a body, not so much as the first sign of what happened to the machine!"

Carruthers shook his head slowly. "You're missing the point, Dale. Or maybe I'm not making myself clear. Their counsel has argued in the petition that there is more than simply substantial proof that the Devil's Triangle, from unusual weather conditions, from forces and elements physical but still not yet understood fully by us, is the direct and sole cause of the loss of aircraft and people in the past, *and*, much more to the point, that Gulfstream Triple-Six Delta falls into that same category."

Carruthers held up his hand. "No, wait one, Dale. It's more than claims about spooks or weather. They presented to the court, to argue precedence, a list of insurance-claim payoffs that have been made—*without a shred of physical evidence being necessary.*"

Fenton felt the sinking in his gut. He could almost spell out what he was going to hear.

"Now, that's a powerful argument on their behalf. For example, the case of the five torpedo bombers and that Mariner flying boat in 1945. Full insurance payments were made to the surviving kin by the government. Right there they have a beauty of an argument. The United States government in that action has recognized that elements and forces unknown were considered so bona fide that payments were not only justified but mandatory. In effect, the government, then, has sanctioned the unusual and startling nature of the geographical area known as the Devil's Tringle. Want more? The commercial carriers, like that DC-3 and Convair 440, were paid."

"The Convair? This quickly?" Fenton's words echoed in his own head.

"Three policies have been met," Carruthers replied. "What Positronics is doing on the basis of these precedents is establishing a pattern. Call it what you will." He rubbed his forehead, as if the rubbing might push back the headache hammering him. "Positronics says that our actions are unfair. They claim that by our insistence upon a long investigation we are trying deliberately to violate their contract of payment upon proof of loss. The Triangle, and everything I've just said—and that's only a part of it, I'm sure you understand—establishes the loss. Prior payments on coverage is a second precedent. They also cite the sea and air search with the finest and most advanced equipment in the world used to find the airplane and the whereabouts of Harold Mazurski. They say, and they're backed up by the government calling off the search, that absolute proof—as established by precedent—exists beyond any and all question."

Carruthers was hating every word, but it had to come out. "Their further argument, and it's one the court is damned well considering, is that Positronics should not be denied immediate payment of coverage. They stress the loss to their firm of the services of Dr. Mazurski, and that the main reason the insurance was taken in the first place was to protect their investment and their work program in the event the services of Mazurski were denied them. And now that this loss has been demonstrated . . . well" —Carruthers gave a monumental shrug of defeat— "they want their due, and they want it fast."

Fenton's eyes had narrowed as he listened to the recitation. "I assume they're going for the whole bundle?"

"All sixty-two million," Carruthers said, the gloom about him deepening.

"Jesus," Fenton swore quietly. For the next several minutes he ignored Herb. He was trying to get the pattern in his head, trying to link the inexplicable with the legal. Finally he looked up. "Did you bring the case file, Herb?"

"I brought every goddamned last scrap of paper," Carruthers told him. "A copy of what you already have. Every page of the legal brief. The petition, the records, the precedents—in short, the works. It's all with your secretary. She's laying it out for you."

Fenton nodded. "I had a pretty . . . well, a strange meeting last night, and this has hit me without warning. I want some time. I'll read the background material later."

Fenton was violating one of his cardinal rules, which was never to carry out your investigation without always examining every shred of evidence that might bear on a case. He was tired; he was still angry over what he'd learned from Dr. Rudy Wells. He was fed to the teeth with mysteries and phantoms. No matter; not one bit of it. He should have sent Herb off to occupy himself with something, anything. Alone, undisturbed, he should have at least scanned the material for anything unusual to crawl off the pages for his attention. He'd always worked like that before.

But it would be some time before he would study the files brought to him by Carruthers.

* * *

"I didn't get the name."

"It's Colee. Linda Colee. She says it's not important—it's urgent."

Fenton scowled at the intercom speaker on his desk. Christ, Herb hadn't been gone even twenty minutes, and . . . "Dot, who's she with?"

"Transmarine Underwriters."

Abruptly he recognized her name. Now that it had a tag on it. Transmarine was an outfit he'd dealt with many times in the past. With all the boats carrying their policies in the Miami and Bahamas areas. . . . He pushed aside his thoughts. "All right, Dottie, send her on in."

"You won't be sorry, boss. This one's a lady."

"What the hell is that supposed to mean?"

Click. He swore at the speaker. One day he'd stuff— He broke off a mental picture of his secretary eating her damned telephone as the office door opened. Fenton came to his feet, judging the woman who approached. Colee was an investigator with Transmarine, and they'd crossed paths before. Attractive, neat as a pin, and smart as a whip. He judged her at between twenty-nine and thirty-four years old; with this type of woman, it was difficult to make it any closer. That didn't really matter. What she could do and how she did it was everything in this business. And she'd already made a minor name for herself culling out frauds and charlatans in the ever-popular game of sinking ships for inflated insurance values.

"Thank you for seeing me, Mr. Fenton," she said graciously. He nodded to a chair by his desk. "I'm well aware you're extremely busy on the Positronics case."

He smiled at her. He liked her style. "You just saved me a long explanation."

"Shall I get right to it? I don't think I'll need too much of your time."

"Good. I haven't got it to give." He sat back, waiting.

"Transmarine, Mr. Fenton, holds a policy on a hydrographic-research vessel. It's privately owned, and almost brand-new. In fact, this was its first deep-ocean shakedown cruise."

"Past tense?"

"Very good, Mr. Fenton. My slip there," she said quickly. Lord, a woman without excuses. His interest rose. "The ship—they christened it the *Seeker*—was making a full-effort shakedown voyage. It had fifteen people aboard—yes, past tense. When it last reported in, it was about ninety-five miles off the coast at Saint Augustine. Everything was fine."

She looked at him soberly. "No one's heard from the ship or her crew since. Do you want to ask me the inevitable questions, or would you rather I just capsulized the information?"

Linda Colee was a pro. He gestured for her to go on.

"It's a familiar routine, Mr. Fenton. The weather was excellent. Sea state calm. Winds ten knots from the northeast. Visibility as far as you could see. A high-pressure condition in the area. Communications perfect. They even had the new low-frequency Omega system aboard for navigation anywhere in the world. And the *Seeker* was virtually unsinkable. It was designed to remain afloat even if it turned turtle or simply lay on its side. It could be tossed about like a cork and remain afloat. It had every known type of emergency-broadcast and survival equipment aboard. Four days ago it vanished."

She sighed. Obviously she'd come to know the information by heart. "The vessel was even designed, in the event of a disaster, to release several satellite-communicating emergency location transmitters. They *can't* sink unless they're crushed, and the spheres were tested to ninety tons per square inch without damage. A floating mine, a torpedo, an explosion, a fire, even the *Queen Mary* running right over it couldn't turn off those transmitters. Two more were built into the hull. It's an experimental program they were working on with the Navy and with NASA. Those things could go through a volcano, and they'd still function for several days on internal power."

Her brow furrowed with some inside pain. "Mr. Fenton, everything stopped transmitting at the same instant."

Time jump. . . .

The words leaped unbidden to his mind. *God-damnit, shut up!* he snapped at that irresponsible voice within his head. Jesus, was he going to be haunted by his conversation with Rudy Wells? He forced his attention back to the woman.

"Miss Colee, let's keep it tight. What do you expect from me?"

"For purposes of my own investigation, Mr. Fenton, I want to fly the search pattern in the area where the *Seeker* was last reported."

"You don't need me for that."

"I want more than a highly qualified pilot, Mr. Fenton. I want . . . well, whatever feelings or conclusions, or anything, from the best in the business." She was making no attempt to butter him up. They both knew he was the best. "When that flight is made," she said, shrugging, "I can send in my report and be done with it. There's still the chauvinist problem, Mr. Fenton. I intend to have my report backed by your presence."

He started to speak, broke out laughing instead. "You don't come in without confidence; I'll say that." He rose to his feet and came around the desk by her.

"Miss Colee, I admire your attitude, your approach, and many other things about you. But I'm afraid you rang the wrong bell. Any other time, I'd do it just because of that beautiful brass you threw at me." He shook his head. "But not now. I'm locked into my own case."

"I didn't come begging, Mr. Fenton."

"Oh?"

She smiled at him. "I have something to trade. It involves Positronics. And I think you want *very* much to know what it's about."

"Don't stop now, lady," he said quietly.

Like the best in any other field, the best investigators in the insurance field function on the basis of their being a very special breed, a group closely knit so they may keep tabs on what's happening with their opposition. The opposition, essentially, is really on the same team. Cross-correlation was often the key to success in trying to weave sense through a web of distortion, and no investigator worth his or her salt ever closed his mind to the problems or the successes of his peers. There were different ways and means. To Fenton it was a matter of different strokes for different folks, but they could all read their mutual body language. So it was, this same moment, as he studied the woman sitting across his desk.

Linda Colee laid out her cards on the table. "We're involved heavily in the coverage of a large cruiser. Or," she corrected quickly, "I'm investigating a policy he may write. The vessel is almost in the category of a small yacht, really. The price tag is one hundred and ten thousand. All that is prologue, Mr. Fenton." She shifted in her seat, judging Fenton, as she knew she was being appraised.

"When I was going through my checklist on the buyer, there was *something*—I wasn't sure just what."

She smiled. "You know how it is. There's nothing wrong, nothing on which you can put your finger, but things simply aren't right. The buyer . . . the man himself, his life-style, his background and record, his income, the pattern of that income, his circle of friends, his taste in furniture; whatever. *None* of it fit with a boat that carried a price tag of over a hundred thou. Well, people *do* come into money, of course, but even those that do, find it difficult to shake old patterns that quickly. Drastic changes without unquestioned background always bother me."

Fenton nodded, agreeing, listening patiently. Linda Colee was doing fine, painting her canvas as she saw necessary. This was one business in which you didn't gloss over details.

"Well, when we initiated our investigation, the man came up with the story; oh, his name, by the way, is Walter Ferguson. Anyway, he offered the story, and by now I could have predicted it myself, that he was coming into family money. He was somewhat secretive about it. He hinted about a family inheritance he was playing close to the vest so that the scavengers—as he called his relatives—wouldn't try to horn into his act. It just did *not* fit," she stressed anew. "Even the way he explained things smelled wrong. *I* may be wrong," she said slowly, shaking her head to dismiss that possibility, "but my intuition tells me I'm not. Ferguson may be everything he claims to be, but all my antennae are up and quivering madly and insisting that all the vibes are bad news. I mean he even had the down payment on the policy. He's going through every step except actually coming up with what he needs to purchase that ship outright. The insurance hold he's bought is returnable. Our company insists on that."

She shook her head. "Sorry. I'm confusing the issue. The gist of it all, Mr. Fenton . . ."

He smiled at her. "It's the same family tree, Linda. The name is Dale."

"Dale it is, then." She smiled back. "Anyway, I was sort of chewing on whatever was bothering me, when finally the bell in the back of my mind started ringing. That's where you come in."

"With this Ferguson?"

"Uh-huh. Ferguson. It's the company he works for."

"Lady, you have a knack for dramatic pauses."

She laughed. "Sorry about that." The laugh and smile went away. "The company. Positronics."

Bingo!

He was half out of his seat with just the one word. There it was; the first crack in the door. A sliver, a tidbit, but Fenton had built mountains with less of a start than that. He felt a quiet jubilation. There's nothing like vindication for what's crawling around in the back of your mind and nagging away at you. He sank slowly back into his seat, the thoughts already racing through his head.

Money; a hell of a *lot* of money for a man named Walt Ferguson. A man who worked for Positronics. The company that stood to pick up an enormous payoff on insurance coverage. By itself that could bring on hard-nosed suspicion, but not much else. But this *one* item, this Ferguson, coming into enough cash to push for a yacht, for Christ's sake. The fool, Fenton swore, gratefully, to himself. Fenton turned from his sudden introspection to Linda Colee. "What else can you give me on Ferguson?"

"He works in the avionics shop. The one the company runs for its aircraft. I want to be sure I have that right."

"Avionics? It implies electronic equipment for aircraft."

"I thought so." She tossed her head to move long hair from the side of her face.

He gestured for her to hold her words for a moment and buzzed his secretary. "Dottie, do a fast check for us on a Walter Ferguson. He's in Positronics' avionics shop, probably at Herndon Field right here in Orlando. And, Dottie, keep it low profile. I don't want Ferguson or anyone else to know we're looking. . . . Right. Good girl."

He turned back to Linda Colee. "I won't try to hide it, Linda," he told her frankly. "You may have opened a door I haven't even been able to find."

"I'm pleased," she said, and her expression left no question of her feelings.

"You know how these things go," he said, yielding a measure of confidence with his words. "You form small links, and then you try to twist them into a chain. Avionics is a critical item here. If my hunch is correct—and you've given me the basis for it—then Ferguson had something to do with that missing Gulfstream. And if he did, we could just be getting a grip on a domino situation. One starts, and the others . . ." His shrug was eloquence enough.

Five minutes later Dottie Johnson was standing before his desk to hand him a terse information memo. He scanned it quickly, and Linda Colee could read from his expression that he had found paydirt. He gestured with the paper. "It looks like we're in," he said. "He's in the avionics shop that works directly with the company aircraft, all right. Aircraft support and maintenance, to pin it down just a bit more. And *that* means," he stressed, the touch of elation clear in his voice, "that he would be one of the men who could have worked on Triple-Six Delta.

Well, I can find out easily enough." He dropped the paper back to his desk.

Walter Ferguson was a technician. Overnight he'd come into a bundle of money. His story of family inheritance was of the substance one finds in tissue paper. *Wet* tissue paper, at that. You put it all together. Ferguson was one of the men in a position to set up the missing Gulfstream for destruction. No way to know yet if he had, but the finger of suspicion pointing in his direction was monumental in girth and expanding with every passing minute.

Positronics had already put in for the full insurance payoff of sixty-two million. So, whoever within Positronics stood to benefit by the payoff had already dropped the promised bundle on one Walter Ferguson, to keep him out of the way. And Ferguson, greedy enough to purchase a whacking, great expensive boat, had drawn attention to himself and could be the one to lead Fenton to the real power behind the scenes.

There was immediate work to be done. He gave Dottie a list of instructions, and called his second team, in effect turning them loose on Ferguson and everything connected with *anything* he'd done in the past several months.

"You know I'm grateful," he said finally to the woman who'd cracked the ice wide open. "I'd be delighted to make that flight with you. Do you have an aircraft, or would you like us to provide one?" He grinned. "On the house, of course."

"If you wouldn't mind, I'd prefer to use our Aztec. It's got special marine-survey equipment aboard. It's a good airplane."

"Time and place?"

"Boca Raton. Would eight in the morning be too early? We could have time for coffee at the field that way."

He stood and clasped her hand. "Eight it is, Linda. Thank you again."

That night he kept his thinking lamp at full burner. He had no doubts he would nail Ferguson to the nearest cross. But the man had far greater value for where he'd lead Fenton.

Was Dr. Harold Mazurski directly involved? Or was he, as Fenton had considered before, simply an innocent passenger? Or was Ferguson working for someone who wore two faces? Was the intent to get rid of Mazurski for reasons that had nothing to do with money? Was there a vendetta involving Rena Kim Maynard herself? The girl was stunning, but also the kind of woman who'd left a bloody trail of castrated swains in her path. That was less likely than the other possibilities, but not so remote that it could be ignored. His team would have to follow every possible lead with each and every policy written on the aircraft, the crew, and the passengers. Fenton checked his own thoughts as Wilfredo Pérez came to mind. The man had been high in the Castro hierarchy. Had there been an attempt on *his* life? That would take gumshoe work of a different kind, but just as important as pursuing phantoms hiding in the leaves of insurance policies.

He was startled when he realized how swiftly the evening had raced. Three in the morning. He cursed to himself. He arranged his working notes for Dottie to type in the morning, told her where he'd be during the day, and stretched out on his office couch rather than losing time in driving to his apartment. He needed sleep.

He didn't do well. Something kept nagging at a corner of his mind. He couldn't shake the feeling that he'd left a few vital pieces out of their proper slots. He clawed his way once from a nightmarish dream sequence of the missing Gulfstream slamming into the side of a mountain, to disappear in a shattering explosion. But that was crazy, because there were no mountains where that airplane had been flying. Yet the fiery blast had been carved brutally into his mind. A hunch? Some warning sense trickling down from his subconscious? He stumbled to his desk and scrawled details of the dream onto a pad before it left his mind completely. Back on the couch, he sank into a leaden stupor, hating himself for not being able to turn off the thinking switch inside his skull.

Chapter 12

Fenton eased the Transmarine Aztec into the air from the Boca Raton runway and into a left climbing turn to follow the coastline on up to Saint Augustine, where he landed to top off the tanks and do a final weather check. He figured that once they reached the area for the pattern of search, he'd hold the power to sixty-five percent. That would give him four hours' endurance, with more than ample reserves to make it back to the coast.

In the weather office he hesitated over the reports. The forecast promised scattered clouds at four thousand feet, with light winds out of the northeast, about what could be expected for that time of year, but the charts showed signs of a low-pressure trough. He studied the charts and the satellite photos. There didn't seem to be any reason for that trough unless some indication of changing weather went along with it.

The weather specialist shrugged at his query about the pressure readings. "That's not strange for up here," he said diffidently. "The Gulf Stream does that a lot. Heat patterns in the water, that sort of thing. I wouldn't even think twice about it."

"Good enough. Thanks." He went to the Aztec, where Linda Colee waited with a Thermos and sandwiches. He fired up and was cleared for immediate takeoff from the quiet field. He confirmed flying through the Air Defense Identification Zone, received a "Good day, sir," from Air Traffic Control, and pointed the nose out to sea. Linda released her seatbelt and turned to a master control panel behind her. Four of the six seats in the plane had been removed to make room for the extensive electronic aerial-survey equipment the Aztec carried.

"I'm tuned in to just about every possible frequency that ship would use," she said in reference to the vanished vessel. "And this goodie"—she pointed as he glanced at the panel—"makes a continuous slow-band sweep. If they happen to be broadcasting on some oddball frequency, this receiver will pick it up and sound an alarm for me."

When they reached three thousand feet, she opened a small flap detent in the belly of the Aztec and released three hundred feet of antenna wire. "We developed this from the Navy's magnetic anomaly detectors for antisub warfare," she explained. "The ship we're looking for was built to give off a special magnetic signature, completely separate from any broadcast system. If it's afloat, this will pick it up. If it's at the bottom of the sea, at least down to about a thousand feet—or approximately one hundred and eighty fathoms—we'll get some indication of its presence."

"What about other ships?" he queried. "There's enough of them at the bottom in these waters. Stuff that went down in the war, for example."

She shook her head. "We're on a discrete pickup. Only that equipment intended for use with this gear will produce a signal."

It went about as quietly as one would expect from such a flight. When he reached the search grid area, he followed the course indicated on the chart she held in her lap. The air was calm, disturbed only by occasional light slaps of turbulence. Scattered clouds a thousand feet above them etched irregular shadows across the ocean surface. Several times they saw large vessels passing in the distance; once they flew over a huge tanker.

"You don't really expect to find that ship," he said by way of half-statement and half-question.

She pressed her lips together before answering. "I wish I had more hope," she sighed finally. "It's so frustrating, Dale. *Something* should have been left. Especially those automatic floats with the emergency transmitters in them. Those things were so strong," she emphasized with sudden heat, "that they survived tests in which they were fired against concrete walls from steam ejectors. They worked perfectly every time. They were even lowered to a six-thousand-foot depth. The pressure didn't bother them. They came up to the surface, just popped up every time, and broadcast like crazy." She shook her head again. "It's just damned impossible. And frustrating," she added unnecessarily.

"Ever have this sort of thing before?"

"A complete disappearance? Oh, sure. But that's to be expected. Good grief, Dale, every year at least fifteen major ships—and this is Lloyds of London speaking—disappear without a trace." She gestured casually. "A big ocean out there. Then, you figure how many small boats go out where they shouldn't and get swallowed up by the sea. We lose some every year to hijackers and—"

"Come back to that," he said.

"Drug runners, for one," she explained. "We know they hijack fast cruisers. They hail them at sea and just take over. They're dealing in really big money, and they don't mind disposing of a few bodies every now and then. No witnesses. They use the boat for a fast delivery, for which they can make a few hundred thousand dollars, sometimes over a million. Then they take the boat back to sea and sink it. Some of them take the boats to South America, where the serial numbers are changed, the boats modified enough so they can't be recognized and can 'disappear' into somebody's private or fishing fleet. But all those things I can understand. Not this oceanographic ship, though."

"Linda, I've heard stories about ships being found at sea, in perfect condition, but with everyone who was aboard"—he hesitated over the word—"vanished." He started to laugh at the idea of entertaining what was to him errant nonsense, but the look on Linda Colee's face stopped the first sign of that amusement.

"The stories are true."

He checked his immediate rejection of that simple statement. "That from direct observation?"

She nodded. "Look, Dale, I'm not going to waste your time or mine with a list of all the so-called disappearances of ships in the Devil's Triangle. There are so *many* reasons why they can go down. Explosions, fire, sudden storms like the neutercanes we're learning about, shifting cargo in heavy seas; there are dozens of valid reasons why vessels disappear without a trace, and why we can't find a sign of wreckage later." She smiled suddenly. "And there are enough stories about ghost ships and flying dutchmen to fill a library. But those other cases? Oh, they're true enough, and I know, because I was involved with several of them." She shuddered with memories. "It was the summer of 1969, the last two weeks of July, to be more specific. The weather through the whole area of Florida, through the Bahamas, was perfect. We had a high-pressure area that was a Chamber of Commerce dream. The satellite pictures—we went back to study those later—confirmed everything we had from direct observation. Planes, ships, everything."

He saw her stiffen slightly. "And in those two weeks, we found four ships—all of them within a hundred miles of the Florida coast—drifting. Without a soul on board."

"You mean abandoned?"

"I do *not* mean abandoned," she said with anger. "I mean that we found the ships—I personally boarded two of them—and not a single living thing was aboard. Not a human being, not a dog or a cat or a bird. Nothing that was alive. And there had been no weather at any time. . . ."

"How can you be so sure of that?" he asked, and his tone implied open disbelief.

"Because of the condition in which we found those ships," she answered. "The instruments were working. We had one ship, at least, with dishes still on the table, with the coffeecups half-full and personal articles lying about which would have been thrown about in every direction had there been weather. Lifeboats, rafts, vests—*everything* was aboard every ship. The radios worked perfectly on every one of them. The logs that three ships kept were in perfect order. Not a sign or a hint of anything wrong. Except," she added, "that nothing alive was on those ships."

He couldn't answer her. "Any ideas?" he asked finally.

She shook her head. "None. And we never let go. We've kept surveillance of all people who were related or involved. In their daily lives, I mean. Families, friends, business associates. Dale, they just *vanished.*"

"What's your guess as to what happened to them?"

Linda Colee shrugged. "There are strange things

between heaven and earth," she said quietly, "about which this one woman understands . . . nothing."

She dropped the subject, turning to the thermos jug instead. He put the airplane on autopilot and accepted a coffeecup and sandwich. They remained silent. She smoked a cigarette, then put away the thermos. She drew an X on the search grid marked across her chart. "One last run," she murmured.

And so it was. They were about to turn to make the final line across the grid. Fenton stretched and looked about them. A merchant ship was a faint silhouette on the far horizon, and high overhead, a thin vapor trail etched its passage across the sky. They made the last leg of the search pattern, and Fenton eased the Aztec into a wide turn that would start them back toward the Florida coast.

They were about seventy miles out when visibility started going to hell. One moment they were flying beneath a mottled pattern of scattered clouds with the slowly increasing haze of early afternoon. Then, with shocking swiftness, as if they'd flown into a huge pall of smog, the faint haze thickened into a putrid creamy yellow. It was like flying into a cloud that hung in the air between them and the coastline.

He'd had his senses come alert quickly before—as when he had run into that impossible headwind while flying that Gulfstream. But now fear came screaming to life. For what happened was not of an instant, but a swift and flickering succession of events, as if before his eyes there flashed a motion-picture screen gone mad with an erratic but constantly speed-increasing projector.

He was on a heading of 060, rushing into the northeast, before starting that final leg home, when he saw what he'd heard about from so many pilots. The compass. That goddamned magnetic compass spinning before him, whirling crazily, so fast he couldn't see numbers familiar to him most of his life. It was a blur invisible to his senses. As the compass thumbed its nose at sanity, the Aztec shuddered its length from a sudden blow of turbulence. The world out there was chewing on itself, like a mad dog chewing upon its own entrails only moments before savaging its belly. The sky, even as he stared, lost the characteristics of air so common to him. His limbs reacted without deliberate volition, for he was, after all, a man of skill and experience, but his nostrils had flared with some instinctive smell of fear.

Linda Colee was staring at his face. She turned her gaze from the sudden highlighting of his skin to tendons drawn skull-tight and looked where his own eyes had stared, to the compass whirling in a blur. Then back again to his face. Then she turned, her body twisting half-around, held by the tension of the seatbelt she had subconsciously tightened, and he left the control of the Aztec to habit and instinct, and turned to look with her. The magnetic monitor, flashing red, a malevolent cyclops winking obscenely at them, and below that single-orbed message, the needle pegged all the way over to the right.

"That's impossible!" she gasped. "The magnetic flux . . . it *can't* be that high!" He showed the question in his face. "It's as if we were flying over a huge magnet, Dale . . . a mountain made of magnetic ore . . . but it's impossible . . . there's nothing in this area, not even at the sea bottom, *nothing*, that could affect this instrument like this!"

He didn't answer. The thought hit him with a grisly feeling in his stomach. Even as he punched in different numbers and frequencies on the VHF radio, he knew it would do no good. Static blasted from the cabin speakers like an electrical storm. The DME was worthless. Nothing worked.

He winced as Linda grasped his arm. Before the

Aztec was an eerie flickering halo. A purple glow enveloped the whirling propellers. Linda exclaimed in sudden fright, and her teeth clasped the back of her hand to hold down her shout; little tongues of transparent flame flashed between the propellers and the fuselage.

"Saint Elmo's fire," he grunted, just coming aware of how hard he was working to control the plane in the pummeling turbulence. "It's the electricity in the air we're picking up. The plane is soaking it up and trying to get rid of it at the same time. It's trying to get rid of us." He paused. "There'll be more of it," he said grimly.

They smelled the stink of danger. Invisible and visibly glowing forces charged the air, irritated their skin, and brought their clothes clinging to them. They tasted the electricity, and the flat metallic taste clung to their mouths. Linda's hair lifted from her head, literally alive with electricity, and a small cry of fear escaped her when tiny blue flames crackled about her face. She brushed madly at an apparition that was horribly real.

The sky was filled with a mass both dark and white, a wall of something *churning* madly within itself. The base of the *thing* was barely a thousand feet above their altitude. The Aztec was plunging madly, and Fenton had come back on power, slowing their air speed, bringing the airplane within the speed envelope that guaranteed its structural validity, no matter how it might be thrown wildly through the air.

He glanced back at the wing, at the small wicks trailing behind the metal. Wicks that would normally drain off the static electricity always present in the air. But they were so supercharged that even as he watched, the wicks grew to many times their normal length, each extending into a single streamer of pale-blue flame. New electrical fire appeared. Flaming sparks danced about the plexiglas of the cabin.

Linda stared in horror at the miniature tongues of forked lightning playing off the nose, growing in brightness and size.

"Just hang on!" Fenton shouted to her, for he knew what was coming. And it came in those next seconds. The small fingers of flame had become a huge serpent's tongue of dazzling fire. Fenton knew those signs, all right. The Aztec was soaking up electrical charges many times faster than the Saint Elmo's fire could release it from the machine. Sparks spattered from the propellers and the wings. He recognized the signs that the serpent's lash of flame was about to discharge—violently—from the airplane.

It came with a dazzling flash and a roaring explosion that crashed through the cabin. Linda screamed, then clapped her hand over her mouth.

"My God . . . lightning! We were hit by—"

"No!" he told her quickly. "We did that. Discharged the bolt. It came *from* us, and . . ." He cursed as a vicious gust hurled the nose up, at the same time slamming it wickedly to the left. He let the plane wallow as much as he dared, but he had to force the Aztec back to a semblance of control.

And the electrical saturation of the air became worse. It was everywhere, the flat taste in their mouths something they could touch. The Aztec suffered from a steady vibration punctuated with sharp blows of increasing frequency. Beads of moisture appeared on the curving windscreen.

The churning wall before them was closer. There was no place to turn and run. A pale glow illuminated the cabin. At the same instant, the world, miles before them to each side, began to glow. Fenton stared in total disbelief at lightning leaping vertically through the air like a wall of living bars. The sky was literally burning with electrical fire that seemed like golden liquid, so fierce and repetitive was its existence. Suddenly there appeared a great thick shaft of golden light, the gasp of a sun about to die forever, the single mighty, slanting pillar preceding the ultimate fury. The air was white and black and gray, golden fire, and yellow and blue and green spraying across metal. The electrical fire was about them again, snaring them in a snarled web of naked energy.

Then everything that had happened was as nothing against what came suddenly before his eyes. From the cleaver-edged bottom of the dark mass enveloping them, he saw the dagger points. Wedge shapes, utterly black, extending from the belly of the thick cloud form. He had seen them before, the terrible *mammato,* the beginning of tornado funnels. One time he had seen two of them together, dipping from clouds, but now, impossibly, as far as he could see to his left and to his right, the mammato extended from the cloud and began to writhe. He clawed about into the start of a turn, but behind them there was only blinding white.

Snow! By all the gods, how could there be . . . ? But then he threw the questions from his mind. It was impossible, but it was there, snow all the way down to the water, and even as he looked at the seething white in that direction, he was scanning his instruments, and they had gone mad. Magnetic flux? Whatever the hell it was, he couldn't trust them anymore. The air speed needle was swinging wildly, the rate of climb was a thing berserk, and . . .

He turned back. If they had to go into the water, he had to be able to *see* what the hell was happening. Into the water? My God. He looked down to see what had *been* an ocean. Now there was a hellish white fury, the surface whipped and lashed into spray. *Forget the goddamned water!* he shouted to himself, for far greater danger was ahead. He knew he had to fly toward those growing tornadic shapes, because those he could at least see with his eyes. In the blinding snow in the other direction they could fly into a tornado funnel without ever seeing the final fury that would shred the airplane like paper.

The dagger points were deep now, individually extended, and they formed into enormous vacuum-cleaner hoses, snaking and undulating until they speared into that wind-whipped ocean and turned white as they became waterspouts sucking up billions of gallons of water. They had to fly toward them, between them, dodging if they could . . .

The worst was just about to *begin.*

Dale Fenton had flown through thunderstorms with all their hellish violence. He knew the spine-jarring smack of clear-air turbulence, the effects of lightning strikes, the tumbling air fall of great currents sweeping down moutains. He had experienced lightning, hail, sleet and ice, rain so thick it became a sluggish porridge in the air, dust, and sand—all of it.

But he had never known *this.* Even the crashing thuds of turbulence he had believed to be the peak of this impossible storm were only the gentle prelude to what hit them now. It was as if they had crashed into a living wall of turbulent, seething air.

The Aztec leaped wildly, hurled by an invisible blow to one side and hammered downward all at the same time. So stunned was Fenton by the shrieking hammer that smashed into the airplane that the control yoke was ripped from his hands. He had no time for fear as he fought to regain control. He tasted blood in his mouth and knew the hammer blow had jerked his body so wildly that he had bitten through a lip. Then came the fear, for the horizon tilted wildly and then slowly rotated all the way around a circle before his eyes, *no matter what he did with the controls.*

The airplane no longer obeyed his commands. It ignored his movements with the yoke and the rudder pedals and the throttles and the propellers. It was a maniacal dervish dancing to the tune of invisible forces, and Linda and Dale were being punished cruelly for their simple error of being here, at this moment, when all was terror in the sky.

Nothing Fenton did with the yoke, moving it forward and back to control the stabilator, affected their altitude. The rolling motions were so severe at times that full aileron-control movements, moving the yoke from side to side, were as ineffectual as waving at a boulder falling down a mountainside to deflect its path. The rudder was a joke, as if there were no connection between the pedals beneath his feet and the tall vertical-control surface of the tail. Yet there were rare moments when the machine responded to his frantic movements. He flew now, because he had to, with the throttles and the propeller controls.

Flight had become a blurred orchestration of body and mind. His feet were moving constantly on the rudder pedals, his left hand from side to side and forward and backward in attempts to coordinate the berserk machine, and his right hand played its symphony between twin throttles and twin propeller controls. He had slowed their speed to prevent the high air speeds from tearing them up. He rammed the prop controls full forward to get the greatest speed of rotation of the propeller blades. The speeding props gave him more meaningful response from the engines when he worked the throttles, and at the same time, added some measure of gyroscopic stability.

Not for a second was there surcease from the violence hammering at them. The airplane shook and banged and rattled. It was not just thrown about, hurled from side to side, rolled wildly, or tossed up and down; all these things happened simultaneously, and there was yet another effect. The airplane was shaken and battered with swift and severe movements, as if they were caught in the jaws of some huge terrier.

Time had no meaning except that every moment lasted forever. He fought to keep control, knowing even as he did that most of his efforts were worthless; he was fighting for those instants the savage air released its grip long enough for him to right the airplane, to claw for some altitude before the downdrafts slapped them contemptuously into the boiling water below.

He was gasping for air. The physical punishment was so severe that his breath was hurled from his lungs, and he had to fight, literally, to suck air into his tortured system. Every hammer blow banged the air from his system, yet instinct warned him that he was gasping, breathing *too* swiftly, that he was hyperventilating, saturating himself with oxygen—which meant dizziness and blackout. But how in the name of God was he supposed to control his breathing like this! Every minute was a lifetime of trying to stay conscious, of fighting to keep this insane machine under control.

Almost at once the muscles knotted within his arms and his legs, in the packed ridges at the sides of his back, in his neck, under his legs just beneath his knees. He felt his feet dancing on the rudder pedals, and he did not know if the stuttering movement was muscle tension or the fear spilling from his system down through his legs, making a mockery of his twitching feet. His fingers were white and cramped, and his forearms felt like blocks of wood as every muscle and tendon and nerve was abused to the point of involuntary cramp.

He feared for the airplane. He could hear and feel and sense the machine being twisted from one end to the other. The metal forming the cone of the afterfuselage was flexing madly, and he heard the sharp cracking and banging sounds of metal twisting and buffeting; it was as if a child were bending a sheet of thin aluminum back and forth, back and forth.

What filled his mouth and mind and body with the stink of fear, drenched him in adrenaline-whipped perspiration, were the sudden blows when he totally lost control. The seatbelt dug wickedly into his abdomen when the Aztec shot skyward, impelled as if by a great slingshot, and then, just as quickly, stopped the upward motion and hurled them downward. He no longer expected the machine to remain whole. He was flying and fighting because life was nothing more than flying and fighting. When the storm gave him a moment, he could right the wings, measure them level with the wind-torn horizon. But only for a moment, and then the laughter of the storm boomed as control was ripped from his hands and he sat, as helpless as an armless and legless infant, while the Aztec whirled.

Then whatever shreds of sanity remained fled from them, as the airplane tumbled—literally—nose over tail, the wings rolling, all of it whirling and spinning and tumbling, tossed and pummeled without control, like a leaf within a squall.

The twisters danced their insane cakewalk across the boiling froth of the ocean, and several times they stared wide-eyed as shotguns blasted in their faces, great hailstones hurled from the tops of the twisters and sprayed down upon them, the vomitus of wind and rain and whirling frenzy in the form of the waterspouts.

He had made it though the line, that fearful string of killing vortices extending from the sea into the black that swallowed them up high overhead—made it knowing that if a wingtip, any part of the machine, touched a waterspout, they would be crushed and ground to splinters mixed of metal and human flesh. Only once did they come close, only once did the capricious movement of a waterspout threaten them directly. It was a sight neither would ever forget, the undulating rope of the column swelling in size, Fenton struggling frantically to maneuver away from that killer. Tongues of lightning spit from every surface of the twister; it was a living column writhing within itself, wind and fury and lightning and God knew what else. Fenton seemed to throw the airplane to the side as the monster thundered by, its locomotivelike roar louder than his own engines and the shrieking of the wind.

But when they tumbled past and away from the twister, the surcease from one hell was replaced with the other—the maddened air.

The woman by his side screamed suddenly, a short, piercing cry cut off almost as quickly as it began. He saw that her head had slammed against the upper door lock, that blood had spattered onto the window. Her head tossed crazily from side to side, but he dared not, even for an instant, take his hands from the controls to help her. Help for the woman could mean death for them both.

The blow that had ripped Linda Colee's head had hurled them wildly down. Fenton felt himself pinned like a fly against his seatbelt, his head slamming into the overhead. He was looking through a film of red. He tried to make sense of the instruments, but could not trust them, could barely trust his own eyes, so severe was the physical punishment being inflicted upon him. But they were going down, falling, plunging, and the warnings screamed in his mind, and his right hand pushed against the throttles, all the way forward, full power, the propellers howling. *And still they descended,* until there was that moment when Fenton gave up all hope.

For suddenly they stabilized. The airplane thrummed and vibrated through every inch of its skin, but the violent shaking was gone. The nose was pointed up at a steep angle, and rate of the climb indicator showed a sixteen-hundred-feet-per-minute rate of climb, *but they weren't moving.* They were suspended, frozen where they had stopped their descent. The airplane was flying, the wind sped past the wings, but all they could do was to hold their position. And before them, towering like a massive black-green wall, reared a monstrous wave—how high, he had no way of telling, but the wind-lashed froth at the crest of the wave was *higher than they were in the air, and tumbling down upon them.* And there was no escape. He stared in horror as the moutain of water came crashing down upon them, and he waited; there was nothing to do but wait, with his right ,hand hammering at the throttles, the yoke sucked back in his gut, the Aztec pinned on some invisible wind board, just hanging there and waiting for the falling water to bring with it the final blackness. He had yielded all hope when his body slammed down into the seat, his right hand fell helplessly from the throttles, as the wind spat the Aztec upward, hurled it as from a catapult, threw it back into the skies, while the storm played its cat-and-mouse game of granting a brief respite of survival before another genie leaped without warning upon them to complete their destruction.

A blow to the back of his head told him that the

electronic gear had ripped loose and was being tossed about wildly. He knew that if one of those heavy containers ever came forward it would crush his skull like a thin eggshell. A heavy monitor did come loose and tore into the side window; instantly the roar at the broken window assailed him—the sound, and the freezing rain, and the airplane shuddering from an internally destructive force.

He stared in disbelief as cracking sounds, barely audible against the greater sonic fury, showed him instrument glass breaking up before his eyes. He looked at the engine gauges, and the RPM needles were fluctuating madly. Was it simply the gauges, or were the engines going, drowning in the water poured into their innards? He had thought of lowering the gear for greater drag and stability, but now, unable to trust the readings of engine instruments, he dared not, for he might suddenly be flying with only one engine, and the drag of the gear could throw away their last chance.

The lightning came anew. He saw it at the same instant a white heat speared his side, and he knew that in the violent twisting of his body one way, and the motion of the airplane another, he had torn tendons or broken some ribs. The pain was a sensation of wet hell along his side, but he gritted his teeth anew, and he flew the airplane because that was all he could do.

They were being slammed with the same punishment he had felt when first they were assailed by this impossible storm, the Aztec jerking up and down in a staccato frenzy. Through it all, he smelled that acrid, ozone stink of the lightning. Searing bolts smashed into the ocean, and others crashed upward from the boiling Atlantic, to disappear somewhere over him. Lightning, liquid gold, blinding white, pale electric blue, bolt after bolt after bolt, a cannonade of furious gods, energy rampaging on every side.

He had a glimpse of ropes of pure energy twisting within the greater bolt, when he went temporarily blind. The explosive roar shook them like an antitank shell blasting into the airplane. The energy of each lightning bolt cracked its whip of forty-five thousand degrees and sent out its superheated air. Shock waves sledgehammered the airplane. Electric eels miles long pulsated and twisted and writhed within their being. And from the eye-distorting shadowy lines where there had been lightning, the shock waves slashed outward and pummeled thunder against them.

It was never-ending, this pitching, rolling, sliding, tumbling, hammering world. The Aztec was wearying of the struggle: it was spilling away its own structural energy, protesting in every metal fiber, through every skin panel, groaning and creaking and banging through the wings and the fuselage and the engine mounts and the tail.

There was no world, only pain and tears on his cheeks, and that wet fire along his side, the woman helpless and bloody next to him, the wallowing an unspeakable fury in total control of their lives, the roar of wind and engines raging only scant feet above the waves, the huge swells so close beneath them, the spray standing forth like long gray knives.

Sweat ran into Fenton's eyes, half-blinding him, and he could only try to blink it away. Not a second to spare his hands from the controls, his fingers cramped and swollen and white at the knuckles. It could not last much longer. His body was screaming its collapse. And the Aztec had lasted far beyond the limits of its builders.

The sweat soaked him from his hair down, stabbing salt into his eyes, pooling in the hollows along the base of his neck, collecting at his waist, soaking his trousers, squishing into his boots. He ached and he pained, and he wanted just to quit, to let go, for his gut was a mess inside and his ribs were on fire and his mind was so goddamned tired.

The sky lightened its darkness, and there, impossibly, off the right wing, was a shoreline! A surf chewing along a beach; a road; and immediately beyond, angling away, a broad and long runway of some airport, wet grass to each side. He felt amazement at the clarity of his own instincts that warned him not to land on the concrete or macadam or whatever the hell that surface might be, but to try to get to the grass so that if the still-thundering wind caught them and blew them sideways, the wheels would slide instead of digging in and tumbling them end-over-end. He didn't really care how he landed; he only wanted the solid earth beneath his feet, and he would gladly slam this machine into the ground, wrecking it if necessary. *Anything* to get out of this boiling, stinking, hellish sky.

Chapter 13

He came over the runway trying to turn into the wind, but the Aztec, wings vertically to the ground, refused to answer to its controls. They were indicating 160 miles an hour, but the airplane was stalling, shuddering through its length, the wings shaking. The controls were useless mush. In desperation, he yanked power on the bottom engine and rammed forward the throttle for the higher engine. The shift in power brought down the nose, and he evened the throttles beneath his cramped, pained fingers. He went forward on the yoke, and the Aztec dived like a thing berserk. He let her drop, coming back easily. There . . . a dozen feet to go, and suddenly they were swooping wildly into the air again, four hundred feet high, helpless, every movement with the yoke producing a ghastly vacuum of response. Then they were plunging again, and he aimed to get into the shelter of a grove of trees, hoping the wind would crown beyond those trees, and he knew it was working when suddenly the vibrating hammers ceased, he was in a pocket of calm, and he thanked all the gods he knew and slammed the airplane to the wet surface, turning closer to the trees to use them as the only safety there was. He kept high power to the engines and pushed full forward on the yoke, working the brakes as best his quivering feet would permit, and he knew that so long as he stayed within this shelter, and the wind did not shift madly, they would survive.

Through salt-blinded eyes he saw the crash trucks rushing at them, the flashing red lights a sight of absolute beauty, and there was a man standing in the wind before him, safely out of the way of the propellers, moving his hand back and forth before his throat in a signal to cut power. Fenton hesitated only a moment, and he chopped the throttles and yanked back on the mixture controls, and his now badly shaking hands managed to hit the master switch and turn this incredible, wonderful machine off. He saw bodies rushing at the Aztec from all sides, men throwing themselves to the wings, hanging on to the tail behind him. Ropes appeared suddenly, and men were hanging to them, and heavy equipment was suddenly all about them, and he knew it was all right now, as the Aztec, buffeted by the ground winds but snared safely by men and ropes and heavy weights, was moved closer to the trees, and lashed to the trunks.

Dale Fenton sat with shoulders hunched, his head on the vibrating control yoke, the tears streaming down his face, every muscle in his body screaming. He shook, a palsied movement that threatened to snap muscles and tendons, and he ground his teeth together in the supreme effort to lift his head as hands outside the airplane opened the door, and he heard the wind anew, and someone was helping to remove Linda Colee from the cabin, and voices were shouting at him, imploring him to do something, but his fingers were lifeless, twisted things, and he held them up in mute supplication to the men who stared, and then understood, and someone eased into the cabin and removed his seatbelt and rolled back the seat, and half-pulled and half-dragged him from the machine.

He let go then, just let it all go, his eyes clenched shut, the tears squeezing through, and he remembered, but only dimly, being walked and supported and moved within a vehicle, and faces staring at him, voices exclaiming in wonder, and he heard the shrill cry of a siren and the lurching movement of a vehicle, and that was all he knew until he came slowly conscious again lying on white sheets and staring up into the face of a doctor.

The doctor smiled at him. "Don't try to move yet, Mr. Fenton." He didn't want to move. Easy enough to listen. A nurse slipped a pillow beneath his head, and the movement sent pain lancing through his side. He looked back to the doctor, who nodded in response to the unspoken query.

"Two ribs. Very neat job, Mr. Fenton. How you managed to break two ribs in that airplane is a mystery. How you managed to survive that storm is a greater mystery."

"How's Linda?"

"She'll be all right. She's been sedated. She suffered a mild concussion; there's a nasty wound in the side of her scalp. Thirty stitches. Some shock, but that seems to be more emotional in origin." The doctor shook his head. "I saw your airplane. Incredible. Someone tried to land a four-engine Boeing just before you came down. They didn't make it. Oh, the crew got away all right, but they tore the gear off and messed up the machine. When I think of you in that light twin, I . . ." He let his voice trail away.

Beyond the doctor Fenton saw a captain waiting to talk with him. He . . .

A *captain?* He looked again. A captain in Air Force uniform. He moved his head slowly from side to side. My God, he was in a military hospital! It came back to him suddenly. Trying to land in the Aztec . . . the crash wagons, fire trucks. They were Air Force. He had . . .

"I know this is trite," he managed to say, "but where the hell am I?"

The captain came forward. "Captain Bill Thompson, sir. You're in the base hospital at Patrick Air Force Base."

Patrick! That was 170 miles *south* of St. Augustine! How the devil could they have . . . ?

"I've spoken to General Scott in the Pentagon, Mr. Fenton. We've been directed to offer you all assistance and cooperation. We've notified Miss Colee's office, as well as your own, as to where you are. We've been authorized to keep Miss Colee here as long as it's necessary before we transfer her to a civilian hospital. You can stay here yourself as long as you'd—"

Fenton shook his head. He struggled to one elbow, and the captain leaned forward to assist him. Fenton winced, then gritted his teeth. He came to a sitting position on the bed, ran his fingers over the heavy bandages wrapped tightly about him. He held up his hands and studied them. "For a while there," he said quietly, "I didn't think these would ever work again." He flexed his fingers, and the pain was still there, but at least he could use them. He looked up at the doctor. "All right if I leave?"

The doctor nodded. "Walk lightly, Mr. Fenton. You've got bruises all over you."

"I appreciate everything you've done."

The doctor laughed. "A pleasure, Mr. Fenton. You know you should be a dead man, don't you?"

Fenton looked from the doctor to Captain Thompson. "Was it that bad?"

"Worse," Thompson said. "Let's get you dressed

and get some coffee into you. I'll tell you all about it."

Fenton hesitated. "I should see Li . . . Miss Colee."

"She won't wake up for at least twelve hours, Mr. Fenton. Her office has someone on the way right now to be with her."

"Okay." He eased to his feet, and Thompson helped him dress. He smiled to himself. His boots were still damp from the perspiration that had poured into them. Thompson walked slowly alongside him as Fenton worked his way carefully along the hospital corridor to the commissary. He passed up the coffee for a bowl of soup, sipping slowly. He was stunned when he looked through the windows to see scattered clouds moving gently before a mild breeze. Sunlight washed the world with late-afternoon warmth. Fenton stared. "I can't believe it," he said finally.

Thompson laughed. "It's a beautiful day, all right."

Fenton snorted. "What the hell happened to that storm? Not too long ago, Captain, my world was coming to an end."

"Fifteen minutes after you landed, just after we were getting your clothes off to work on X rays," the captain explained, "that storm was gone. Like someone throwing a switch. I never saw anything like it. One moment that wind was doing better than a hundred knots—*you* were in it, so you know—and seconds later"—he gestured suddenly—"sunshine and roses all over the place."

"Let me ask you something," Fenton said. "How much warning did you get of this thing?"

"The big blow? That's another odd thing about it, Mr. Fenton. None. And I do mean none. We're still trying to figure out what happened."

"But you people have about the best weather system there could be. I mean, you run the range, you're tied in to every weather survey there is, you're real time, with civilian and military metsats, and—"

Thompson held up a hand, laughing. "Sure, we're on direct readout from the satellites, and we *did* get a warning. One of the ATS satellites gave us what was happening. Fenton—" and Thompson's voice sobered—"the time it took that storm to build was less than three minutes."

"That's impossible, you know."

"I know."

Fenton chewed on that a few moments. "I saw at least fourteen waterspouts at one time. I had to get between a couple of them to make it back."

"*That's* impossible," Thompson said. He let out a low whistle. "Mister, I'm glad you didn't have me along for company out there."

Fenton gave him a crooked grin. "I could have used some help," he said.

"I'll bet. We had some fun and games here. Three funnels touched down. We lost a few airplanes here at Patrick, but generally we did pretty good. The civilian area took a beating. Up in Cape Canaveral they had two apartment buildings torn to pieces. Just tore the roofs off and chewed up what was inside. A trailer park looks like it was hit with a saturation strike. Over on Merritt Island the airport was . . . well, it looks like it went through a meat grinder. Fifty or more planes wiped out, from what we hear, and most of the hangars gone. We've got damage reports coming in from everywhere. There must have been one, maybe two hundred boats lost. No one had time to do a thing, and—"

Thompson broke into his own conversation as a master sergeant in fatigues approached the table. He drew up a chair and looked at Fenton. "Sir, you the pilot of that civilian aircraft that came in here during the big blow?"

Fenton nodded.

"I hope you're not planning to go anywhere in that thing, sir."

"Sergeant," Fenton sighed, "at this moment, flying is the *last* way I want to go anywhere."

"That's good, sir, because you've got more prayer than you have airplane." He shook his head. "We just went over your bird. Professional interest, you might say. And we're all convinced you pray pretty good."

The sergeant chuckled. "You came in more on prayer than you did on metal. Every antenna and aerial is gone. The wind that came in through that broken window buckled all the skin in the aft fuselage.

"The fuselage is so far out of line you wouldn't believe. You hit some hail, I guess. The leading edges of your wings make it impossible for that ship to fly. If you weren't in the air when that happened, you could never have gotten off the ground." He rubbed his chin as he ran the other data through his mind. "Most of your instruments are busted. The props took a beating. One blade on your left prop . . . well, the edges were chewed up so bad it would have gone in about an hour or less of just normal flying. One aileron is about to go; it's hanging on by the safety wire only. One attachment point on the right-front seat, to the floorboards, broke clean off. I don't know what you were doing with those throttles, but the linkage is shot to hell. Half the screws on that airplane are gone. And you lost the plastic shell from your left wingtip. Just gone, like that," and he snapped his fingers for emphasis.

"Sergeant, don't tell me any more."

"I don't have to, Mr. Fenton. I'll put it in a nutshell for you. That thing can't, repeat, can *not* fly. It's a candidate for the junk pile."

Fenton grimaced. "Thanks, Sergeant."

The other man stood up. "Think nothing of it, sir. But if you have any more four-leaf clovers like the kind you carry, I'd sure like to have one of them for luck."

Thompson stared at him when they were alone. "Great day in the morning," he said quietly.

Fenton laughed, and winced from the stab along his ribs.

Thompson studied him carefully. "Bad?"

"As they used to say in vaudeville, Captain, it only hurts when I laugh."

Chapter 14

"We . . . we th-thought you were d-dead!" she wailed, throwing her arms about Fenton. He gritted his teeth against the feeling in his ribs and tried gently to disengage a near-hysterical Dottie Johnson from about his neck.

He held her at arm's length, perplexed by her crying. "But why?" he asked. "You couldn't have known we were in that storm. All you knew was that I was flying off Saint Augustine, and Patrick is nearly two hundred miles away. *We* didn't even know where we were."

"Y-you don't understand," she cried.

She wiped tears from her cheeks. "Don't you r-remember? You were supposed to fly your Baron to Nassau today. It was on the schedule. You had that interview with the people who said they saw an airplane disappear. When I got your note this morning that you would be flying with Linda Colee, I figured Mike Stevens could handle the interview."

She moved back from Fenton, to half-collapse in a chair.

"Go on, Dottie," he told her quietly.

"I told Mike to do the interview for you. But he and I were the only ones who knew about the change. I mean, your name was still on the manifest here in the office, and also at Herndon Airport. You know, they had the slip to have the airplane ready for you. So when Mike took off early this morning, I suppose everyone assumed it was you in the airplane."

Fenton made an effort to keep from shouting at her. "Dottie, what the hell are you trying to tell me?"

"Of course, when Mike went down . . ."

When Mike went down . . .

"Dottie, get a grip on yourself. Tell it to me calm, and tell it straight."

"Mike's in the hospital. We thought it was *you*." She sniffled away a fresh onslaught of tears. "He flew from Herndon," she went on, "direct to West Palm and—"

He broke in. "And I usually fly over Vero Beach on that run," he said quietly.

"I know. That meant he was over land just a little longer than you'd normally be. He crossed over West Palm and started for Nassau. He was going through the ADIZ; in fact, he was talking to Air Control when it happened."

The rest of it came out in fits and starts. Mike Stevens had been flying through the Air Defense Identification Zone, had gone through the final air-traffic control line in a routine flight, when he suddenly lost both engines. *Both*. The odds against that with a ship as well maintained as Fenton's personal airplane were outlandish. The key to all this, and Fenton saw it at once, was that Mike was still fairly close to the coastline when he lost all power. Had Fenton been flying, and following his usual Orlando-to-Nassau route, he would have been fifty miles or more out to sea when the engines quit. Quit? Correct that, he told himself. Those engines didn't quit. They'd been rigged to fail.

Without power, but with plenty of altitude, Mike

turned immediately back toward land. Since he was talking with the traffic center, they had his Mayday immediately and started help on its way. And Mike did everything he could to get a restart in the air with even one engine. Fenton could picture what went on in the airplane. Mike switching tanks, working the fuel pumps, whatever might work. Nothing did. The engines turned over but choked and missed badly. Still, he had plenty of room and a calm sea, and he set up the Baron for a ditching in the water. Center told him a chopper was on its way, and that's always comforting news to a guy who has the ocean rushing up to meet him.

Mike Stevens set her down in textbook fashion. But after he ditched in the water, the airplane exploded.

"You mean it blew when he hit?" Fenton asked Dottie.

She shook her head. "No, not that. Apparently Mike made a perfect landing in the water. Some people in a boat nearby watched the whole thing. The airplane bounced, they said, then settled smoothly. They saw the door open and Mike come out on the wing, dragging a life raft with him. He was standing on the wing to inflate the raft . . . *that's* when it exploded."

Fenton took the explanation in silence. "It can't happen that way," he said quietly.

He got on the phone. First to the hospital at Palm Beach. Mike was doing as well as could be expected. Then to the Federal Aviation Administration people at West Palm who'd monitored radio with Mike. Then the Coast Guard at Jupiter and the pilot of the chopper. When he finished all his calls, the pieces were falling into place, and Fenton did not like what he had put together.

There'd been no fire or other problem in the air, because that would have been evident in Mike's conversation with traffic center while he was gliding down. He did a great job in ditching, and he was out on the wing, inflating the life raft, when the airplane exploded. The blast hurled Mike high into the air; the people in the boat had seen that, as did the helicopter pilot. Mike received serious burns, and the blast broke his shoulder and one leg. He was going down, unconscious, when the people in the boat got to him and hauled him from the water.

And, the Coast Guard people were quick to say, if that chopper hadn't been there right after the boat grabbed Mike, and if the chopper hadn't had a paramedic aboard, and if they hadn't got him to that hospital within scant minutes . . . well, their discussion about Mike Stevens would be funereal.

And I was the one who was supposed to be in that airplane. The only reason I'm not in the hospital, or dead, is because of that insane flight in that storm. . . .

He started rushing along multiple thought streams. It was all tied in with what Linda Colee had brought to him. The first splinter in that solid door facing him. Now it was yawning ever wider, and new and murderous peril was reaching out to him as quickly as he tried to move through the doorway. He wanted urgently to plunge deeper into what had happened, but he recognized he was still too hurt, too dazed from everything that had happened to him, to attempt any clear thinking.

He called Mick Satterly into his office and started his rundown on what had happened.

The muscled, hairy tree trunk sprawled in the chair before him held up a thick hand. "I know the story," he said with his half-growl of a voice.

Fenton nodded. "Conclusions?"

"You're marked," Satterly told him, characteristically blunt about his answer. "The way I see it, they've assigned a contract on you."

Fenton didn't answer for several moments. He had already approached the same thinking on his own. "They wouldn't have needed anyone else if things had gone their way today."

The beefy man shrugged. "You're talking prologue, man. By now they know. They've also tipped their hand. Most people might not have tumbled to what happened. You're a pro. They've got to figure you know. Your guard comes up, so they've got to bring in a soldier who's good and also fast." Satterly shifted position, and with a groan the chair beneath him threatened to collapse. "From here on in, Dale, I start earning my keep full time."

"Which means?"

The man smiled. "It's baby-sitting time, boss."

"Yes, I suppose it is. Although I usually take good care of—"

"Stop it," Satterly said, brusque. "You got to sleep, you got to take a shower, you got to take a crap. You need eyes in the back of your head. That, even you ain't got, man. So"—he shrugged again—"now you got a new shadow."

"All right." Fenton sighed.

"You got hardware with you, boss man?"

Fenton showed a thin smile. "I didn't think I'd need it over the Atlantic, Mick."

"You're back in jungle-time. You carry heat, I carry heat. *All* the time."

"I thought I was the boss around here."

"Only so long as you're still breathing." Satterly. had said his piece. He moved about some more in the chair. He had the "waiting" look on his face that Fenton knew so well.

Fenton buzzed for Dottie. He had her send flowers to the base hospital at Patrick, and made arrangements to speak personally with Mike Stevens at Palm Beach the next morning. Suddenly he was exhausted, his eyelids so heavy he had to make a conscious effort to keep them from closing.

Satterly drove him to his apartment. It gave Fenton the chance to lean back in the car and close his eyes. But he was still too wrapped in turmoil to stop thinking.

His first order of business was to find out who the hell was after him, and find out *fast*. Because whoever had the finger on Dale Fenton *had* to be the man who had destroyed the missing Gulfstream. And now, more than ever before, he was convinced that the Gulfstream had been done in by an expert.

Of course, he lacked proof, but there were more things in life and in this business than proof. He was, especially after today, acutely aware that a storm could destroy any airplane without leaving even a trace or hint as to what might have happened. But one item dismissed that possibility from his mind where Triple-Six Delta was concerned. The government had rerun the film from weather and military reconnaissance satellites starting hours before and continuing to a full day after the disappearance of the Gulfstream. Any storm would have left its signature with those systems. But that deck had been dealt, and it was clean.

There *could* have been a catastrophic equipment failure. It had happened with other airplanes. Anything could have happened. The damned airplane could have been hit in a billion-to-one impact with a meteor, for Christ's sake. Bullshit, he told himself. When the pointer on the wheel of probability flips over and starts spinning on the wheel of possibility, the "could-have-happened" clause gets thinner.

Because there was that new fly in the ointment. If there was a natural cause to the loss of Gulfstream

666D, then no one would have to bother with a very sophisticated attempt at murder set up to look like an accident. There would be no need to get Dale Fenton out of the way. But someone knew Fenton's skills. And knew he was a last item standing between the killer and his payoff.

And they would try again. Unless he came out winner first.

Chapter 15

The Sunshine State Parkway stretched before him with only light morning traffic. It was one of those great Florida mornings, a strong breeze from the east keeping the air pleasantly cool. Fenton kept his window down to enjoy the pleasure of grass-scented air. The drive was delightful, but the future wasn't. Whoever was working so hard to erase Dale Fenton wouldn't be satisfied with anything less than full success. Someone meant to guarantee Fenton his own private space in the obit column.

No one from his office would move alone anymore. Everything at work, or to and from, would be done in pairs. There were round-the-clock guard shifts for the office and for the home of anyone working closely on the Positronics case. After all, snatching a secretary and holding a knife at her throat could mess up the investigative process.

Fenton had no doubts that Walt Ferguson was their man, but Ferguson was only a worker for the opposition; he sure as hell wasn't initiating any moves. Mark one pawn and hold for later pickup. The man for who Ferguson worked was the man Fenton needed to identify—before Fenton himself was creamed.

Fenton figured they'd be coming after him "with insurance"; there could be another try by an amateur, which meant setting up an airplane. That could be Ferguson. But the second squad would be the most dangerous. The odds were they would be pros. Whoever was masterminding this caper wouldn't hesitate to buy some hired guns. Mick Satterly was convinced this was the way it would be done.

Fenton ran the details through his mind again. Ferguson had to be the one who'd set up Triple-Six Delta to be destroyed in the air. But was Ferguson also the one who set up the Baron in which Mike Stevens came so close to buying the farm? The way it looked, Ferguson *had* to be involved.

But there was a towering question mark in there. How could Ferguson have gotten to the Baron? How could he get to the company airplane, in the company hangar, without being spotted? Whatever he did to the Baron would have taken time. Heracles maintained good security with its aircraft. So where the Baron was concerned, he could be dead wrong about Ferguson. Dale Fenton cursed to himself.

Fenton took the Palm Beach exit from the parkway and drove directly east to the hospital to see Mike Stevens. He eased into a parking slot but remained within his car. He opened his attaché case, checked out the equipment within, closed the case, and let his eyes move slowly through the parking lot. Everything seemed quiet. He pressed a hearing aid a bit closer to his left ear, and then heard the words for which he'd been waiting.

"Clear one." He nodded to himself. Moments later he heard, "Clear two."

He left the car and went up the main steps of the hospital entrance. His name had been left at the reception desk, and he was waved through. He took the elevator to the fourth floor to Stevens' room, where a surly guard demanded identification and then blocked the door until he checked with the guard inside the room. There was a double team of armed guards baby-sitting Stevens around the clock. The surliness pleased Fenton. The guards weren't being paid to win popularity contests.

Mike was doing fine. He had enough bandages on to qualify for an Egyptian tomb, but he still managed a go-to-hell grin when Fenton made some smart-ass remarks about Stevens' losing a good airplane. Then they settled down to business.

An hour later Fenton was almost certain as to the method Walter Ferguson had used to get to the Baron. There were still some holes in his conclusions, but they could be wrapped up within a day or two. Right now he wanted to concentrate on how the engines had been rigged.

Both engines had bombed out at approximately the same moment. Would someone have messed with them directly? The odds were against that; it took too long and was obvious. From Stevens' description of how the engines failed and of his inability to get a restart, Fenton was convinced that someone had poured a chemical directly into the fuel tanks, a chemical powerful enough to do its job despite being mixed with a great quantity of high-octane fuel, a chemical poured into all four tanks. Whoever did the job knew something about flying, knew that many pilots take off and climb out on the main tanks, switch to the auxiliary tanks for level flight cruise, and back to the main for landing. So the chemical had to be in all four tanks to be *certain* the altered fuel would get to the engines in flight.

Everything was timed for the engines to quit *after* the airplane had crossed the coastline and was well over the Atlantic. But Mike Stevens told Fenton his ground speed had been reduced by headwinds. So the airplane was much closer to land than had been anticipated by whoever fixed the engines.

What happened *after* the ditching was the key to everything. The explosion.

Fenton took his leave, checked out with the guards, and took the elevator back to the main floor. Outside the entrance he paused, listening to the little gizmo by his ear. Everything was clean. He went to his car and drove off back to the parkway, heading north.

The move came twenty minutes later. His rear-view mirror showed a truck in the left lane, coming up fast to pass. Then suddenly the tiny voice in his ear was shouting: "*Brakes! Hit the brakes! Hard!*"

Fenton's reflexes were working before he gave the move conscious thought. His left foot slammed against the brake pedal; he went flat on the seat and pulled the wheel slightly to the right. The tires squealed, and the Corvette slowed from the panic brake action.

A coughing blast roared at him from his left, and something crashed into the windshield. He felt the spray of glass against the back of his neck and his head.

He kept on the brake pressure, and the Corvette came to a stop in a wild skid across grass. Fenton hit the handle of the right-front door and rolled out, cursing the sudden pain in his ribs as he hit grass. He threw himself behind the car and edged up slowly with a gun in his right hand.

The truck that had been passing him raced away.

He pulled the small microphone from his jacket lapel on the reel wire. "Jill, you copy?"

The voice in his ear came in clearly. "Copy. You okay, Dale?"

"Yeah, I'm fine. You got that truck in sight? It's going away from me, moving fast."

"I've got it," came the answer.

"Just lay back behind them. Call in to the State Highway Patrol. Make sure they understand those people are armed to the teeth."

"Got it, boss. See you later."

Fenton smiled. No one would ever suspect that pretty black girl in the sports car of being a member of Fenton's team. But then, Jill Peck wasn't supposed to be "discovered" by anyone.

A powerful car pulled onto the grass behind him. The door opened, ad Mick Satterly's hulking form approached. "Good. You're alive." Satterly examined the windshield. "Shit. They meant business. A riot gun did this. Bad news, that stuff."

Fenton nodded, taking a long breath. "If you hadn't made your move when you did . . ." He let the rest of that sentence hang. "What tipped you, Mick?"

The big man shrugged. "That was a U-Haul rental. Nobody rents one of those things and barrels along the way they were moving. Meat on the table for the cops. I moved up behind them in the right lane. When I saw the muzzle start coming out of the right window, I figured it was time to start yelling."

A car with flashing blue lights came boiling to a stop alongside them. A state trooper came out of the door fast, relaxed when he recognized Satterly. He'd also heard the call-in from radio dispatch. He told Fenton he'd arrange to have his car towed in after he got some pictures of the windshield, and Fenton promised a full report to headquarters.

They climbed into Satterly's car and started rolling. "You got an agenda, boss man?" Satterly asked.

Fenton nodded. "Herndon Airport, Mick baby. And we go in quietly."

Satterly drove slowly to the large hangar where Southern Avionics handled most of the electronics work for the field, as well as for the aircraft owned or used by Sierra Insurance.

They bypassed the front office and went unannounced to the main workshop in the rear of the hangar. One long wall held an impressive display of electronic equipment, fronted by workbenches filled with testing equipment and tools. Another wall showed boxed instruments, antennae, and parts. The workshop was fully equipped with small side chambers to perform just about any work for all the aircraft that came into Herndon Airport, from small private ships to executive jets.

As Fenton approached, a man turned from an ELT workbench. Mick Satterly drifted behind, to where he could keep Fenton and anyone else in sight.

"Hey, mister, you can't come in here," the man said, as though trying to protect the bench on which the emergency locator transmitters were tested before being shipped out for aircraft installation. "All customers are supposed to stay in the front office."

Fenton ignored the reprimand and read the nameplate on the man's jumpsuit. "Dickinson," he said aloud. "Ted Dickinson. That your name?"

"Hell, no, it's Shirley Temple. Didn't you hear what I said? You gotta go through the front office. You—"

"The ELT equipment your responsibility?"

Eyes narrowed at the question. Fenton smiled. "You didn't answer me."

Dickinson flicked a glance from Fenton to Satterly and back to Fenton. Then, before Fenton could anticipate the move, Dickinson pressed a call buzzer by his side. "We'll let the boss handle you, mister." There was a smirk on his face. "You'll see what happens when—" He looked up as another man came through a side door.

"Mr. Harris, I don't know who these people are," called Dickinson, "but they won't leave like I told them to and—"

"I'll handle it," the other man broke in. He looked at Fenton. "I'm sorry, but whatever business you have, we can handle in my office. Would you mind?"

Fenton shook his head slowly. "My business is in here." He nodded at Dickinson. "With him."

"You a bill collector or something?" Harris demanded.

"Or something," Fenton replied.

"Look, I don't want to get nasty or anything, but if you and your friend don't leave here immediately, I'll have to call the police."

Fenton looked at Mick Satterly and shook his head. Harris saw the exchange and shrugged. "Okay, if that's the way you people want—" He stopped as Satterly blocked his return to his office.

"Just listen," Satterly advised. "Just stay right where you are and listen."

"Who are you? What do—?"

"Just *listen*, will you? It's easier all the way around."

Harris judged the heft of the man before him. "All right, but when this is over I'll—"

"Sure you will," Satterly said soothingly. "Later."

Fenton moved closer to the technician. Body language had a semantics all its own.

"You're in charge of servicing the ELT equipment." Fenton made the words a statement, not a question.

"Well, yeah, of course, I mean, that's my job here."

"And you run them through a bench check before sending them out for aircraft installation, right?"

"Look, mister, if you got a complaint, all you got to do is—"

"Where do you keep the ELT's you've checked?"

Dickinson glared at Fenton. "That ain't none of your damn business."

Fenton nodded slowly. It was time to put on the squeeze. There'd be hell to pay if he was wrong. But he was ready to give monumental odds he wasn't. Slowly, with all the drama he could bring into the move, he withdrew the automatic from his shoulder holster. Light gleamed on the weapon as he injected a shell into the chamber. "Mick, lock the doors." His eyes flicked from Dickinson to Harris. "No noise. No sudden moves. Everybody play it *very* cool."

Harris shook his head in disbelief. "Look, if it's money you guys are after, I'll open the damn safe. You can—"

Fenton gestured with the gun. "Please. Just keep it quiet."

He locked his eyes on Dickinson. "Now. Once again, Dickinson, where do you keep the ELT's?"

Dickinson pointed with a shaking hand. "That wall. Third row. We got about nine of them in there."

ELT's could be tested electronically, but all that proved was that the systems were operating. What was wanted was to check the transmission on 121.5, the emergency transmission frequency. But in order not to have the test picked up for the real thing, it was done in a heavily shielded room.

"Where's your test room?"

"To your left. Over there."

"You said you had nine ELT's here."

"Sure. That's right."

The gun came around slightly. "Where are the others? The ones even your boss doesn't know about." Fenton knew Harris was staring at him, but he didn't take his eyes from Dickinson.

"What other ones? We ain't got no other—" The gun came up, pointed unwaveringly at his heart.

Dickinson paled. "They're . . . over there." He pointed. "That locker."

"How many?"

Dickinson's voice shook. "Three."

"Get them. *Slowly.*"

He stayed behind Dickinson, keeping enough distance to make any sudden move of the other man a useless effort. The last thing he wanted was to see this man dead. Fenton needed Dickinson's memory and vocal cords in excellent shape.

Dickinson used a key to open the locker, came out with three of the emergency transmitters.

"All right," Fenton said. "The test transmission room. Bring them with you."

"Look, mister, I—"

The gun moved. Dickinson nodded and went to the room, carrying the three transmitters. Fenton motioned to Satterly. "Bring Harris over here."

The ELT was required on any aircraft used for flying any appreciable cross-country distances. The compact transmitter was usually affixed to a part of the airplane most likely to escape total destruction in the event of a crash, and so most installations were made somewhere in the tail assembly. Deceleration, immersion in water, the heat from a fire, or manual control—any one of these could set the ELT to howling its distress call on the Mayday frequency.

Transmission could also be initiated by radio signal, but to Fenton the automatic initiation was the key for the moment.

In the ELT test transmission room Dickinson waited with the transmitters in his hands. Harris watched without a sound. Fenton gestured with the gun. "The ELT's. Hook 'em up. No conversation."

Dickinson had the look of a cornered animal as he placed the transmitters on the test rack, plugged in a test line, and set the switch to manual transmit. Perspiration beaded his face.

There was no audible sound in the room, but Fenton checked the test panel himself. All three sets generated a full-strength signal.

With that slight distraction Dickinson made his move. With a hoarse shout he shoved Fenton violently to one side and bolted for the door. But he got only as far as Satterly's right fist, which landed with a dull thud in Dickinson's stomach. He collapsed to the floor.

"Quick!" Fenton shouted. "Get him out of here!" Satterly shoved Harris behind him, out of the test room, and dragged the unconscious Dickinson from the room. "Get around that wall," Fenton warned. They moved across the main room, behind a row of equipment racks.

Harris looked at Fenton as he put away the gun. "Look, will you *please* tell me what the hell is going on here?"

"Just hang in. You'll find out in a moment. And keep your head *down*."

Fenton glanced at his watch. "It should happen just about—" He never finished the sentence. A dazzling light flared from the doorway of the ELT test room, followed instantly by an explosion. The blast cracked whip-hard against them, and they were on the floor, staying low, as smoke boiled through the room. A wall from the ELT testing cell buckled and sent heavy cinderblocks tumbling by them.

They climbed slowly to their feet, Satterly holding the now conscious Dickinson in a brutal armlock.

Fenton turned to Harris. "I'm sorry we had to do it this way."

"Jesus." Harris looked from Fenton to Dickinson, then stepped around the equipment rack and stared at the shattered test room. When he turned back to Fenton, he didn't seem at all confused anymore.

"I'll call the police," Harris said.

They sat in Harris' office. The police had come and gone, but not before Fenton had talked on the phone with Orlando Chief of Police Mel Roberts. "They'll put out a cover story," Fenton explained. "A fire and explosion of unknown origin in Southern Avionics. The story will say that Ted Dickinson was killed. They'll keep him on ice under a John Doe until we let them know it's okay to indict him for attempted murder."

Harris' face was grim. "Now I know what happened to that Baron," he said slowly. "The one you were supposed to be flying."

Fenton nodded. "Right. There were two separate shipments of ELT's to your shop. The nine on the storage racks were perfectly normal. But there were those four others, three of which Dickinson kept here, under lock and key."

"He installed the other one in your Baron?"

"He sure did. An ELT containing about a pound of explosives, probably RDX, and a timing device set for about two minutes after activation. They were accustomed to seeing Dickinson work in the hangar, so no one questioned his installing a new ELT in the airplane. And he needed only a few moments to dump a chemical into the fuel tanks."

What Fenton didn't tell Harris was that he knew where those gimmicked ELT's had come from—a man named Walt Ferguson, who was in a perfect position to rig the ELT's in his own shop at Positronics and then get them to Ted Dickinson at Southern Avionics.

And there was something else. The rigged ELT's could be set to transmit, and then explode, by radio signal. All that was needed was for another jet to fly within a few miles of Triple-Six Delta, transmit the signal, and fly away: the explosion would follow two minutes later. And there *were* two ELT's installed in the big Grumman.

With the police issuing the cover story that Dickinson had been killed, Walt Ferguson would start to relax. And Fenton was counting on a relaxed Ferguson to lead him to the man who had ordered Triple-Six Delta destroyed.

Chapter 16

Fenton returned to his office and put in a call to Irving Schechter at the National Security Agency using a code scrambler: only their two phones would be intelligible; any tap on the line would produce nothing more than audio gibberish.

Fenton laid it out quick and neat, and Schechter agreed that Ferguson was the man to tail. They worked out a fast arrangement for splitting their surveillance: Fenton's team would keep visual watch over Ferguson; the electronic surveillance would be left to the NSA specialists, who'd place bugs and radio-transmitting devices in everything but Ferguson's jockey shorts.

They also agreed on not squeezing Ferguson, for they knew that the first move against Ferguson would be waving the red flag to the man they still couldn't identify. So they had to bide their time.

A week later they hadn't learned a thing. Yet Fenton was satisfied. He was convinced that sooner or later there'd be a flaw in Ferguson's finely prepared armor.

No one else, it seemed, shared Fenton's patience. Schechter certainly didn't, and a call from Herbie Carruthers showed that the man in Colorado was close to playing his old ulcers game. "General Scott's been on my ass all morning, Dale. Didn't Schechter give the Army the details of what happened with your airplane? And the scene at Southern Avionics with those ELT's?"

"How do I know what Schechter did or didn't say to the Army?"

"Well, damnit, they're supposed to keep each other informed."

Fenton almost choked. "Herb, what are you trying to get from me? An apology for what the NSA does or doesn't do within government? For Christ's sake, I—"

"Hold it, hold it," Carruthers said, his own irritation soaring. "I'm setting up a special meeting, first thing tomorrow morning, in your office. I'll be there, and so will General Scott and several people of his staff. All right with you?"

"No."

"No?"

"You asked, I answered."

"How the hell can you say no?"

Because I don't work for the goddamned Army!" Fenton yelled. "And I didn't think it was necessary to remind you that *you* don't work for them, either."

"Damnit, all they want to do is ask some questions."

"The Army never just wants to ask some questions, Herb. They want to find some way of using us for a patsy to get them off their own hot seat."

"I told the general it was okay."

"You're a dumb shit. But all right. Tomorrow morning." He couldn't find the patience in himself even to say good-bye.

"And you're convinced that Ferguson, or whoever he works for, was successful in destoying the Gulfstream in the air?" General William Scott leaned forward, his forearms resting on the conference table in Heracles' office.

"General." Fenton took a deep breath. "Let me get something straight. I am not a district attorney. That isn't my business. I cannot *prove*, not in any court of law in this land, that Walter Ferguson specifically and deliberately destroyed Triple-Six Delta. But I *am* convinced that—"

"Convinced isn't enough, Mr. Fenton."

Fenton would gladly have thrown the tin-starred, irascible son-of-a-bitch from his office. But the look on Herb Carruthers' face stayed both his words and his hands. Fenton sighed and gave it another shot.

"There are two kinds of conviction, General, and you're just going to have to go with mine. I'm convinced that what I've been telling you is the way it happened."

"Then why the devil don't you have the authorities pick up this Ferguson fellow?" Scott demanded. "They could hit him with some drugs and get the truth out of him in a couple of hours, and we'd be through with all this nonsense."

Fenton took a *very* deep breath. "Because this isn't the Dark Ages, General Scott, that's why. Because it's against the law. Because *we* must work within the law so that whatever we discover will be acceptable in a court of law. Otherwise, that information is useless to us."

"I know, I know, it has to be acceptable to some idiot with black robes in a courtroom." Scott slammed his hand against the table. "And in the meantime, we have nothing definite on Dr. Harold Mazurski, the computer program is in dire trouble, our whole national security is at stake, and you quote me platitudes about the damned law!"

Fenton shook his head. His smile lacked humor. "I was always under the impression, General, that you swore an oath to uphold and to protect the laws of this country."

"You are insulting me, Fenton."

Herb Carruthers came galloping into the breach. "Look, Dale, I understand how the general feels. There's no *proof* involving this Ferguson. It will be Dickinson's word against Ferguson's, and that's all."

Fenton looked at Carruthers. "We don't have proof yet, but we will. You see, we know that Ferguson *did* work on Triple-Six Delta. It all ties in. More to the point, Herb, we also know that Ferguson personally installed at least one or two new ELT's on that Gulfstream. The shop records show that. Ferguson didn't hide what he did, because he never expected to have the bloodhounds on his tail.

"But when they came after me, Ferguson personally couldn't get to the Baron. So he had to find an accomplice. Someone he knew. Someone he could buy. He knew Ted Dickinson. Not surprising, because they're both in the same business, and as it turns out, some years back they used to work together. Anyway, Ferguson went to whoever was supplying the funds for this whole operation and got enough cash to offer Dickinson a payment he just couldn't turn down."

General Scott broke in. "Why are you so sure Ferguson went to someone else for the money?"

"He didn't have enough himself. He made the move to buy that boat of his, but he still doesn't have the bread to close the deal. He got paid something in front, and he gets the rest later when Sierra Insurance pays off—or is supposed to pay off. But in the meantime, Mr. Big, whoever he may be, latches on to the fact that we're closing in on him. I'm the source of his problems, the cause of the insurance-payment holdup. So they come after me. And I'm glad they did, because they opened a can of worms they just can't close anymore.

"Anyway, there's more to an operation like the one they were setting up than just having the airplane blow apart in the air," Fenton said. "It's my guess that something went wrong with their plans. I think they wanted the Gulfstream to crash in full view of witnesses so there'd be no question that the airplane blew up or crashed."

General Scott shook his head. "Fenton, that's the craziest thing I ever heard of."

"In this business, *General*, you're an amateur. Do you want to hear the rest of it? If you do, shut up and listen. I'll answer your questions. But I really don't give a shit for your inept comments."

Scott's face went hard. He brought his lips together as the two men locked eyes but finally Scott nodded.

"The best thing for them to do," Fenton continued, "was to wait for the moment they considered best suited to their needs. The airplane, let's say, is coming in for a landing. It's been making a descent from high altitude. Every airplane that does that flies with a potential bomb in each wing. You've got pressure buildup from fuel vapors. You—"

The general broke in again, but this time his question was genuine. "What about venting?" he demanded.

"It can go wrong. It's happened before. Sometimes the vapor discharge just stops. Any sort of electrical buildup can set off the tank like it's a giant bomb. That's the point. It's happened before, we know how it can happen, and they could operate on the basis that it happened again. Hell, it's not that difficult for them to pay off an accident team to get in there first and make sure there were no signs left of any explosives being involved. They're out of the continental United States, free of American jurisdiction. They could rig that report without any trouble. And we'd be stuck with that accident report, because there wouldn't be any ties we could establish between Positronics and that investigating team."

Fenton leaned back in his chair, toying with a pencil. "Once that report comes in, nothing we did would change the facts. They'd have removed the bodies, shifted around the wreckage. We couldn't undo what was done. And it's payoff time on the insurance. As far as Dr. Mazurski is concerned, General, I'm convinced he just happened to be along in that airplane at the wrong time. I don't think he figures anywhere in this."

General Scott still held his poker face. "If they set things up the way you just described, Fenton, what went wrong?"

"Many things can mess up a deal like that, General. The most likely is a spurious radio signal."

"Seems unlikely," Scott snapped.

To his surprise, Fenton agreed with him. "Ordinarily it would be most unlikely. But the air was filled with radio traffic that day. The shot from the Cape, remember? With that kind of activity . . . well, anything could have set it off. A ground signal. Something from a ship. I don't know, and the odds are I won't ever *know* beyond all question, and neither will anyone else. It happened prematurely, and that airplane went down somewhere. It disappeared from the scopes. It was at thirty-three thousand feet. It could have gone into deep water where we'll never find it. Things on the bottom in that part of the ocean get covered by sand so fast you wouldn't believe it. About a year ago a Cherokee went into the drink a half-mile offshore by Melbourne, right here in Florida. Six hours later, when divers went down, they couldn't find a trace of it. That's happened too many times to be ignored by us as a contributing factor to a so-called disappearance."

The general shook his head slowly. "Fenton, it all comes in a pretty blue ribbon, but I don't buy it."

Carruthers was openly surprised. "Why not, General? It fits." He shook his head. "I wish it didn't, but it *all* fits."

"Not necessarily, Mr. Carruthers. Mr. Fenton has amassed a mountain of circumstantial evidence and some gilt-edged theory. All neatly done. You have someone you say you can prove tried to kill Fenton in that Baron. That's clear-cut, and I'll buy that. I'll accept that this Ferguson who works for Positronics is being managed by someone who's free and easy with his money, and who wanted that airplane destroyed. But your reasoning is wrong. The single most compelling motive was, and remains, Dr. Harold Mazurski."

"You're forgetting," Carruthers said quickly, "the attempt by two professionals to kill Fenton. We told you what happened on the highway."

"I'm not forgetting a damned thing," Scott threw back at him. "Because the only people who say they were professionals are you two. You have no identification. *None*. Everything turned out to be a blind lead. You've got a state trooper in the hospital, barely alive from all the lead he took from the people in that truck when he caught up with them. Pros? Who can't shoot straight? *Both* times? No sale, Mr. Carruthers."

Scott looked at Fenton. "You keep talking about your Mr. Big. I won't say no to that. But *we* have got to have something more than your circumstantial threads when what's at stake here is national security."

The general stood up slowly, pushing his chair away from the table. "What you have, Mr. Fenton, is a great case with which to go into a courtroom to fight against your company having to pay off on a disastrous insurance policy. But you'll excuse me if I fail to offer congratulations. Because whether or not you win your case doesn't do us—your country—a damned bit of good."

The general walked to the door, trailed by his aides. He stopped suddenly and turned back to Fenton and Carruthers. "You have no idea to what extent this meeting has been a disappointment," he said in a final touch of acid. "I hate to admit it, but we were counting on you. It appears as if we were wrong. Your interest in this whole affair seems to end in your accounting department."

And he was gone.

"That insufferable, self-serving, stiff-backed son-of-a-bitch!" Herb Carruthers swore with a fine heat in the wake of General Scott's departure.

To his surprise, Fenton only grinned at him.

"What the hell are you so pleased about?" Carruthers snapped at him, glowering.

Fenton chuckled. "Jesus, the static he must be getting from Schechter. To say nothing of Conway over at CIA. He's been in the dark, and he came down here huffing and puffing, and all the time he was putting on a show."

"He came on damn strong," Carruthers argued.

"Didn't mean a thing. He figured we're working hand in glove with Schechter. He's on the outs, and his ass is on the griddle, and he got so hot under the collar he forgot we weren't in the Army taking his orders. He was really hoping we'd come up with answers that would suit *his* needs. One day he might remember that his and ours don't necessarily match."

Herb stared out the window, then turned back to Fenton. "Speaking of needs, what about ours? Can you pull off everything you said? The proof, I mean."

"Oh, we'll get it. But I told you, it's not Ferguson I want. He's easy, Herb. I want Mr. Big."

"Any ideas? Besides what you told the Army?"

Fenton shook his head. "Right now it's still somewhat hazy," he admitted. "Lots of ideas, but nothing I can bring to ground yet. It's back—figuratively, at least—to pounding the pavement. It would be nice if Ferguson slips up. He's our guarantee. But I wouldn't count on him to make any stupid mistakes. Not any more, anyway."

Carruthers slid into a chair. He pulled off his shoes and began to knead his feet. "I wonder, Dale, if we shouldn't break some of this stuff. You know, leak it through the papers. It might just force them—your Mr. Big, for example—to tip their hand."

Fenton looked at him sharply. "That's strange to hear from you."

"Not so strange, when you think of it," Carruthers told him. "Look, you know that Positronics has its petition before the court. We're in a bind. *I* believe everything I've heard from you. And you're probably right about the general. He was on a fishing expedition, so it stands to reason we probably know more about this whole affair than the Army or NSA or CIA." He shook his head in a sign of regretting the pressures on him. "But can we go to court with what we have?"

"No," Fenton said flatly. "We'd lose. There's no question about proof, with what happened to the Baron—"

"But the opposition could show," Carruthers broke in, "that there are easily fifty people who'd like nothing better than to see you at the bottom of the ocean. You've done in some big ones, Dale. Don't forget that."

"You've got me there, counselor," Fenton conceded. "So the only thing we can do is stall. And we'll do it. But it's obvious that we're stalling, and Positronics can take steps to force the issue. And if they get us into that courtroom right now, you're right, we'll lose."

Fenton shrugged. "So it's appeal time, then."

"No other way," Carruthers agreed quickly. "But I want you to be sure just how much time is against us. If only we had a single piece of wreckage, *anything*. . . . The lack of any physical evidence works so damned hard against us. At least, as far as the court is concerned." Carruthers shook his head and grimaced. "The government played right into Positronics' hands. The search they carried out, with every sophisticated system known, hasn't turned up a thing. It all adds to their case. And in the meantime, old man Maynard is really raising hell about getting those policies paid off, and—"

"What did you say?"

Carruthers stared at Fenton, who had bolted from his chair, and stood, almost menacing in his posture. "Jesus Christ, Herb, tell me that again."

"What . . . ?" Carrathers looked puzzled. "All I said was that Charles Maynard was raising hell about the delays we've been feeding into this case."

Fenton smacked his forehead so loudly it startled Carruthers. "Good Lord," Fenton groaned. "It's been right in front of my eyes all this time! And I was too stupid to see it! *Dottie!*" He didn't bother with the intercom. He shouted her name so loudly they heard him in a dozen offices. The door burst in, and a wide-eyed secretary stood waiting.

"Get me the Positronics file," he ordered. "No; wait. Not the background stuff. You brought me a file when the first claim came in, remember? I want that one." He paced the room with a sudden animal intensity.

Carruthers watched him, held back his questions.

Dottie brought in the file, and Fenton spread papers across his desk, reading swiftly, scrawling notes. Finally he had what he wanted and pushed aside the papers. He looked up. "I haven't got the proof yet," he said by way of preamble, "but I'll get it." He held up a clenched fist. "Oh, that son-of-a-bitch. That rotten . . . Jesus, I've known some sewer-minds in my time, but this filthy bastard has absolutely got to be the worst of them all. I'll get him. Jesus, I swear I'll hang his ass from—"

"Who?" Carruthers fairly screamed the question at him.

Fenton tapped the papers on his desk. "It's all here. The one man behind it all. Mr. Big. He's been covered so beautifully, but he made one mistake, one lousy little mistake, and it was so small I didn't even see it. He—"

"Dale," Carruthers choked, "if you don't tell me, I'll . . ."

Fenton ignored him. He turned to Dottie again. "Give me the interviews with the people who knew Rena Kim best. It's got to be in there."

"Dale!" Carruthers' voice cracked with anger.

"It's *Maynard*, goddamnit! Charles Maynard."

Disbelief and shock met his words. "You're crazy! The man is . . . he's the president of the goddamned company!"

Fenton nodded. "I know that," he said grimly.

Dottie Johnson came back, her hand movements showing her agitation. "Dale, Maynard knew Rena Kim was on that plane. What father would kill his own daughter?"

But Fenton was engrossed in the file. "Here it is: not one word of closeness here. These reports all talk of Rena Kim's having a mind of her own . . . going her own way . . . attached to no one. And she was known as a man-eater. She followed only those orders that pleased her. She obviously took Maynard's assignment on that plane simply because it was convenient for her vacation plans—not because she wanted to help out Daddy. Do you think an egocentric like Maynard would be happy with that independent a daughter? Wouldn't kill her, you say?" Fenton laughed harshly. "I'm convinced he not only would, lady, but *did.* Just as she'd probably have killed him if it fit her purpose. But Maynard didn't stop there. He killed a whole crowd of people—including Dr. Mazurski. And he almost killed Mike Stevens, and he's tried a couple of times to kill me, and he's wrecked his own computer project, and . . . Oh, shit, wait'll Schechter hears *this!*" He shook his head suddenly. "No, he can wait."

Dottie Johnson and Carruthers looked at each other, disbelief mirrored in their faces. Finally Herb found his voice again. "But why should he . . . ? I mean, Maynard himself, why would *he* be the one to . . . ?"

"I don't know yet. But I'll damned well find out, and I'll bet you a plugged nickel that Mr. Maynard for some time has been trying to make himself the kingpin in this business. In heuristics computers. You know, tying up supply and demand, controlling the flow, the peripheral industries, all so that he could crack his own whip. If this heuristics program with Mazurski is even half as great as the government's made it out to be, and Maynard could get full control, then he'd have limitless political capabilities. Potential beyond anyone's wildest dream. Want to bet he's been manipulating stock behind the scenes?

"Damnit, Herb, you know how these things work. He buys, pledges, borrows, steals, manipulates; he does anything he can to get controlling stock not only in Positronics but also in the critical peripheral industries. Its walking a razor's edge. He can fall at any time, but if he pulls it off, by God, he has made it.

He could become the most powerful political figure in the country, maybe even the world. He'd have full control over the heuristics system, and that. would let him control everyone about him. He didn't give a damn about Mazurski or that Pentagon project. The man was mad with lust to become some new electronically programmed messiah."

Fenton slammed his fist against his desk, winced from the feeling in his ribs. He took a sharp breath. "I'll dig it out. I know what we'll find. He overextended himself. The stock market had the bottom drop out of it. And Maynard went overboard by millions of dollars, and unless he could cover his manipulating, he'd lose everything. The one thing he needs more than anything else in the world is money. Big money, and . . ."

Dottie's face was white. "So he killed his own child."

"He did. Because her death would point the finger *away* from him."

Carruthers shook his head. "Where was the weak point?"

"The first claim for the insurance," Fenton pointed out. "That sort of thing is *always* handled by legal counsel. But I missed it when Dottie first brought me the file. Even you had talked about it to me, Herb, but you never spelled out *who* was pushing the claim. Dottie had it in those papers she gave to me, but I missed it. It was so damned innocuous."

He rose to his feet, pressing a hand against his side. "Maynard putting in the claim personally, instead of leaving things to his attorney, is the sign I've been looking for all this time. He was too anxious, sweating too hard. Time must be running short for him. You know the routine better than I do. We would *never* get anything more than a notification that the airplane was missing and presumed lost. And that notice would come by registered letter.

But don't you remember? *Now* it's clear. We had a *phone call* from Maynard's office to tell us, right after it happened, that the Gulfstream was missing.

"Jesus, Herb, the search was still under way then! There had to be something more than that, you'd think, before that outfit would start screaming for its blood money. Evidence of some kind, a clear indication that there really wasn't any hope anymore, and then, *even* then, we'd receive notification by registered letter, if only to keep things legal.

"But by then Maynard knew the plane wouldn't be found. Not in one piece, anyway."

Chapter 17

The rest of it was detective work. Old-fashioned, gumshoe, and unglamorous. But effective. Weaving the net from hints and nuances and innuendos and circumstantial evidence. Working on the basis of intuition born of experience. Using semantics and psychology and patience and more of the same.

They discovered early in their gumshoe campaign that their telephone taps were useless. Nothing was picked up in phone conversations between Maynard and Ferguson that could have convicted a moth of blind passion for a flaming candle. That in itself told them something. The two men had to communicate, and would never risk doing so in writing or through an intermediary, so there *had* to be another way. The answer stared them in the face. Electronics. The two men used radio. Easy enough, given the facilities of the company, and safe enough with careful wording. The avionics shop had test frequencies, and transceiver equipment could be justified in the Maynard house or workshop—what better than a home hobby workshop?—and their messages were neatly cryptic. But Fenton and his team were on the prowl. The conversations they might pick up would be worthless in any courtroom. But Fenton was after threads of circumstance that would in the near future solidify into the bars that make cages.

Meanwhile, the financial power machinations of Charles Maynard came under covert investigation by the SEC. Fenton's office provided the government team with the information they needed for their search for illegal manipulation of stock. Once that was started, Fenton dismissed it from his mind. The SEC boys were smart, and they were tough, and they knew just what to do.

They kept the pressure off Ferguson, just nudged and controlled the man as if he were a puppet. Linda mending nicely and back at work, cooperated to the full. She put through the Transmarine insurance for the ship Ferguson intended to buy, with just enough hesitation to let Ferguson know they wanted to know more about his dollar source, but were willing to accept his "private conversations" of family funds.

Fenton put his best agent in charge of collecting the growing dossier on Ferguson's private life. Jill Peck was set up with a local radio station near the Positronics facilities where Ferguson worked; as a roving broadcaster she had every reason to be anywhere and everywhere. She used several professional friends to keep the surveillance going around the clock.

Harry McManus of Fenton's staff got the assignment for Charles Maynard. The dour Scot, with his long record in accounting, experience with IRS, and bloodhound instinct, was perfect for the assignment. But McManus—and this wasn't unexpected—never found so much as a button out of line. It was almost as if Maynard had come to recognize the flaw in his activities and had committed to low profile his every move since he had demanded the payoff.

Fenton kept building the case and planning the wheeling and dealing that would get Sierra Insurance off the hook. For several policies would be ruled void if Fenton could prove homicide: long ago Herbie Carruthers had had his fill of airplanes being blown up for various and sundry reasons, and so his policies were written with well-defined conditions under which payment might be invoked. If Fenton kept on piling up the evidence, then the losses sustained by Sierra Insurance could be cut from eighty to ninety percent. And there's a lot of drastic in that sort of cut.

He knew they'd get Ferguson, when the time was right, to turn state's evidence. Ted Dickinson, in the cooler in Orlando, was already singing like a frenetic bird. Once Ferguson saw the net prepared so methodically and understood he had a choice of singing or spending twenty to life behind bars, he'd apply for warbler competition in nothing flat.

And that would lock up the case against one Charles Maynard.

And then it all fell apart, like trying to squeeze and at the same time hold onto sand flowing through clenched fingers.

Jill Peck gave him the first of the one-two-punch combination. She came into his office early one morning carefully closed the door behind her. One look at the beautiful dark face and he knew something was coming unglued, and fast.

"Maynard's beat us to the punch," she told Fenton, wasting neither time nor words. "His organization is better than we expected. He found out we were laying it on him, and he moved to get his weak point out of the way."

Fenton knew what it was going to be.

It was.

"Ferguson's dead."

"How? Damnit, you and Harry were . . ." He let his voice trail away. "Sorry, Jill. Go ahead."

"I was tailing Ferguson when it happened. I was a couple of car lengths behind. He was just going through an intersection. Another car came sailing through a red light and plowed full tilt into the driver's side of Ferguson's wheels. It killed him like *that.*" She snapped her fingers.

"What about the other man?"

"He was a hophead. Man, the worst kind. He was really strung out on speed. Wild, really wild. Whoever set up that dude really knew what he was doing."

"Spell that out, Jill."

"Like I say, he was strung out on speed. You know, they lace that stuff with strychnine. It gives a cat a wild rush, a real sexual high that's way out of sight. The million-mile orgasm." She shrugged. "You can figure the rest."

"Let's hear it," he prompted.

"Well, as I see it, they tell this dude he does what they want and he owns the world. Heaven and earth all wrapped up in whatever goodies he wants, with no limit on the payoff. For good measure they give him a taste of what tomorrow brings. Then they spell out how they want him to come through the red light and cream this car, and after he's flying, they put him in their car. By now he believes anything, including that he's got a charmed life and can't be hurt. Someone with a walkie-talkie calls in Ferguson's car, and this dude is sitting there, tromping brake and gas pedal to the floor, and by the time he hits Ferguson's car, he's doing fifty, maybe sixty per. That also takes care of witnesses."

"He was killed?"

"No, but his system is glowing with speed, probably IT-290, and a lot of strychnine, and the crash gives him a hell of a shock, see? He had enough stuff in him to squeeze his heart like it's rotten grapefruit. He wipes himself off the board. The police have him on the blotter as a junkie who OD'd. They don't give a shit. Can't blame them. Why should they?"

He sat back, the news weighing on him like a ton of wet cardboard. Good Jesus Triple-Damned Christ. . . . He had no doubt Maynard set it all up, but there wasn't any way to connect him with the death of Ferguson because some freaked-out speedhead had run a red light.

Oh, it was neat, all right. But, Fenton swore, he'd make sure it wasn't good enough. Mr. Charles Maynard just wasn't going to get out from under that easily or that quickly. They still had Ted Dickinson in protective custody, neatly bundled up, and Fenton would see to it his security was tripled. In the meantime, Maynard was in a financial trap of his own making, and he wouldn't be making any long trips. He'd be around. He was wiping out all the fingers that could point to him. He was winning, he was convinced. Well, let the son-of-a-bitch keep thinking that, Fenton grumbled to himself, because . . .

Jill sat patiently, waiting for him to say something. "Hey, I'm sorry," he told her with a crooked grin. "I forgot you were there."

"Thanks a heap. Got any more compliments?"

"Sorry." He laughed.

"You got good reason to be, I suppose."

"Well, they say bad news comes in bunches."

"You sound as though you're waiting for the other shoe to drop."

The telephone rang. The sound startled them both. "Could be the other shoe, boss." Jill smirked.

"Could be," he said, reaching for the phone.

Dottie was waiting for him. "Long distance," she

told him. "From Puerto Rico. Do you know a Dick Lowen?"

"Lowen? Sure, he runs an air-taxi operation in the islands. Old friend of mine. Put him on."

He listened to the voice on the telephone. It was the only time Jill Peck had ever seen Dale Fenton's face drain completely of blood. "Hang on," he said. He cupped his hand over the speaker and turned to Jill.

"Dick Lowen just talked to a pilot who landed at his strip in Puerto Rico. The other man had been on a long flight to an island off Brazil. He told Dick he'd seen Gulfstream Triple-Six Delta."

"Where?" she snapped.

"In the air."

Jill gaped. "But that's impossible!"

"I know it is."

"Can . . . can this pilot give us any proof?"

"No."

Fenton was acting strangely. "Why not?" she demanded.

"He said . . . he said the Gulfstream disappeared."

"*Where?*"

"While he was looking at it."

Chapter 18

Fenton made the flight to Puerto Rico in a Lear jet with Neil Walker by his side. But he met with the pilot, Ira Lyons, personally at the small field he used for his charter operations. It was a neat and profitable business, and it spoke well for the attitude of the man behind the work. For that matter, Ira Lyons checked out as about the most perfect man you could want for a witness to some event in flight. He was fifty-two years old, beefy and solid, in perfect health, and a man of extraordinary flying experience.

Lyons had been flying a turboprop Merlin on a private charter from Puerto Rico to some ungodly island called Fernando de Noronha, a possession of Brazil, stuck in the middle of ocean about 250 miles northeast of the South American coastline. The island served as Station Nine along the Eastern Test Range of tracking sites for missile and space shots. Otherwise there wasn't much to it, since the total real estate involved was five miles in length and less than two miles wide. It had an old wartime airstrip, the tracking station, and a population of a thousand people, who must have spent most of their waking time wondering what the hell they were even doing there.

Fenton could understand a charter flight for military or business purposes to the island, but there wasn't even a remote reason for Gulfstream 666D to have been anywhere near that forsaken chunk of island rock.

Could the Gulfstream have set down on some island, anywhere, a remote chunk of rock, without anyone knowing a thing about it? Hell, the alarms for Triple-Six Delta, including the awards for any real information, were hefty enough to have flushed a dinosaur from a cave.

"I knew that Gulfstream had been missing for a long time," Lyons explained to Fenton. "All the pilots working the islands keep up with those bulletins, and we always keep an eye out for a ship that's listed as missing. That's why, when I saw this Gulfstream, I was sort of primed in the back of my head to look for details. You know, type, color, numbers, the rest." He reached into his wallet and withdrew a sheet of paper on which he'd jotted down just what he was talking about. "There it is," Lyons offered. "Time, position, altitude, speed, course, even my instrument readings at the time."

"It's all there," Fenton offered by way of appreciation. And it was, exactly as Fenton himself would have done under the same conditions. But there was something missing, something strange, and even the old pro Ira Lyons was hard-put to explain it.

"It's not in those notes," he said, "but you sure ought to know about it. I was talking with Center at the time—when I saw the Gulfstream, I mean—and we were on radar in the Merlin. Confirmed pickup and traffic; you know how it goes. But when I talked with the radar people, after reporting the Gulfstream, they had never had a second target on their scopes. That's sort of crazy, you understand?"

Fenton felt a chill coming on. "Look, Mr. Lyons, I

hope you'll understand my position. Questioning what you're saying and all that. I—"

"Hell, man, fire away."

"It seems incredible you could have seen those numbers so definitely," Fenton said. "Couldn't it have been another Gulfstream?"

Lyons nodded. "I'd ask the same question if I was in your seat," he said pleasantly. "The Gulfstream came at us from, oh, about four o'clock and slightly higher. In fact, I don't think whoever was flying it ever saw us. He couldn't have been more than a hundred feet over us. In fact, I had to put that bird I was flying into a pretty violent maneuver to be sure we didn't have a midair. You know what it's like at such a moment. Everything is crystal-clear. And I saw those numbers. Three sixes and the letter D, and there just ain't no mistake about it."

"One more thing?"

"Shoot."

"You told Dick Lowen that the airplane sort of flickered in your vision. Could you explain that a little more?"

Honest confusion showed on Lyons' face. "Fenton, I've flown all over this world in just anything that's got wings on it. I flew Navy off carriers in World War II and I flew with the Navy again off Korea, and I *never* saw anything like this. When that thing passed over us, I was so damned mad that without thinking I hauled the Merlin around in a tight turn to the left, just to get a better look at the airplane. It was there, going away, but it seemed to be flickering, as if . . . well, hell, I can't really describe it. Like it was glowing and flickering at the same time. And then, just like that, it was gone."

Fenton thought over what he'd heard. "That pretty well describes what you'd see if a plane were moving away from you through thin stratus. Sun angles could provide the glow effect, that sort of thing."

Ira Lyons laughed at him. "You go ahead and believe what you want, Fenton. Call it stratus clouds or sun angle or poor vision on my part or whatever. I know what happened, and I know what I saw, and I've got to tell you right out, I really don't care what you believe or don't believe. I'm not trying to prove a thing, mister. I just wanted to be courteous to you as a favor to a mutual friend."

Fenton let Walker fly the bird back to Florida. He spent the trip walking the chasm between thinking and brooding.

Well, could the damned thing have been hijacked? That had always been a live possibility. *If* Triple-Six Delta *was* seen in the air, then the hijacking theory took on enormous substance. Fenton groaned to himself. *If* the rabbit hadn't stopped to take a crap and *wasn't* caught in the act, then the hound would never have caught him. *If*, *if* . . . But the Gulfstream could have been involved in a hijacking. The crew could have been bought by Maynard, with orders *not* to harm the passengers, but to fly them to some remote island and keep them on ice until told to bring them home. Maybe Maynard *didn't* have the stomach to kill his own daughter and was running some wild-assed plot to collect insurance by hiding airplane, crew, and passengers by harping on the Devil's Triangle. Maybe, maybe, maybe.

But the hijacking possibility was riddled with weakness. If nothing else, the eventual return of the crew and passengers meant an immediate return of the insurance payment, and anything of that ilk would tear open the power machinations of Charles Maynard. When a man played for world stakes, he didn't set limitations with a sign reading DO NOT PASS.

He went as far as it was necessary for him to go and the rest of it was dewy-eyed nonsense.

Fenton came into his office the next morning with the disposition of a grizzly bear shot with a 30-30. Dottie recognized the signs, moved about him quietly, had his coffee before he had a chance to ask. She was so efficient in anticipating his moods that he finally threw her out of his office.

Then he sat and thought until his head ached. He hated what he was going to do next. He punched in direct-dial call to Cocoa Beach to the office of Dr. Rudy Wells. Three minutes of insisting that he didn't want a goddamned appointment with the doctor finally got him Wells on the phone. "I'm about to perform a vasectomy," Rudy told him. "If you hurry, I can let you have one for half-price."

"Never mind the horseshit, Superstitch. Look, I *need* you. I want to talk some more about that, ah, that subject we discussed some time back at dinner."

"Oh, ho," Wells chuckled. "Didn't you have enough?"

"Damnit, I haven't time for fun and games," Fenton snapped. "I said I needed your *help*."

"All right, Dale. What is it?"

"Do you have an engineer or scientist from the Cape who could answer some questions on what some satellites or Skylab may have found, relevant to what we were talking about? I mean, the sort of information that's not made the press yet."

"Man, you don't want much, do you?" Wells said in a low voice touched with disbelief.

"Rudy, it's important as hell."

"There's one man. He goes all the way back to the thirties and NACA. And he's worked on every manned space program since Mercury."

"Who is he?"

"He's semiretired now. His name is Shoaf. Harry Shoaf."

"Can you two have dinner with me tonight?"

"Your bed or ours?

Fenton shook his head. "I can meet anywhere you'd like," he told the doctor. "But I'd like it quiet."

"I'll arrange for a private room, upstairs at Ramón's. On the 520, right near—"

"I know where it is. What time?"

"Make it nine. I've got hospital rounds."

"See you then."

"Watch your joint." Wells chuckled. "You don't want it slipping out of time." He hung up.

Harry Shoaf could have flown with the Wright Brothers, to judge from his knowledge of aerodynamics and astronautics. He'd worked with more of the greats in the business than Fenton could even remember. He was also cool and collected. Decades of emergencies and wars had taught him to keep his cool no matter what. He was also sincere in his desire to help.

In the private dining room above Ramón's main restaurant, the best prime rib he'd ever had steaming on his plate, they went into that insane conversation he'd had before with Rudy Wells. That matter of a time jump, as Rudy had called it.

"Do you want a long explanation," Shoaf asked, his eyes twinkling, "or a simple statement that everything Rudy told you was true?"

"Keep it simple and I'll be grateful forever."

Shoaf smiled. "Shakespeare used to have a saying about 'time being out of joint,' and it turns out the old boy knew more than he realized. This business with the cesium time systems is the real thing, Fenton. No doubt about it."

"And this cockamamie story from Superstitch here about the Minuteman warbead? That's also true?"

Shoaf didn't answer for a moment. Instead he leaned back in his chair and looked long and hard at Wells.

The doctor shifted uncomfortably. "Well, goddamnit, Harry," he blurted, "he goes back a long way with me."

"Longer and deeper than I realized," Shoaf finally said. "You're not supposed to know that."

"Outside of this conversation, I don't know it."

"All right."

"I wish I'd never heard it."

"It's true," Shoaf said. "It's also not the only case."

"Jesus." He shook his head. "How the hell do you accept something like that?"

Shoaf laughed. "Don't fight it. Trying to understand, at this stage of the game, is beyond your means or mine. Or anyone else's, for that matter. Look, Fenton, in the last ten years we've destroyed almost every concept on which hard astronomy was built. What we've learned in this last decade has raped and violated the standards by which we understood the world and the universe. If you think a time jump—call it phase, warp, distortion, whatever—is hard to accept, you ought to study the nature of black holes. You start out with a sun several times the mass of our own star. You go through a supernova like nothing you can imagine. A single star putting out more energy in an instant than our whole galaxy of billions of stars burns in a year. The damned thing explodes outward, and it also implodes, and it does it simultaneously. Know what this is? It's a gravity explosion. Pure, naked gravity. A few years ago we couldn't even think in those terms. The end result of this explosion-implosion is a white dwarf. But some of them keep collapsing until they become neutron stars. And beyond *that* is the black hole."

Shoaf dabbed with his napkin at his lips. "You can't even begin to comprehend a neutron star, Fenton. Think of the atom. Only one part in a hundred thousand is matter. The rest is empty. A collapsing star squeezes together the electrons orbiting about the atomic nucleus. Matter becomes impossibly compressed. Know how big a neutron star is? It has the same mass as our sun, but it's only six miles in diameter. Good God, man, *think* of that! See this sugar cube? On a neutron star it would weigh over a trillion tons. If you had it here on earth, it would whip to the core of this planet faster than you could think about it. The gravity pressures of a neutron star are so fantastic that the electrons have been squeezed down from their orbits and rammed into the protons of the atomic nucleus. It changes protons to neutrons. The whole damned star is made up of neutrons packed together.

"When you get gravitational stresses of this sort, it twists time and space like I can twist this napkin. The surface gravity on a neutron star is about one hundred thousand million times greater than on this world. Do you know the escape velocity of earth, the speed we need to reach another world? About twenty-five thousand miles an hour. To get off a neutron star, Fenton, you'd need a speed of two hundred and twenty million miles an hour. On that kind of world the mass is so incredible that time dilation is a fact of life. Clocks run about ten percent slower there than they do here. That's a time bend, a curvature of time, *and it's not theory.*"

Shoaf leaned forward. "And, Fenton, that's just a transition stage to the black hole. The black hole makes a neutron star seem as light and airy as a Ping-Pong ball. The black hole is a gravity-time vortex so impossibly dense that nothing can ever escape its grasp. Try to understand that. Nothing, including light, can escape a black hole. Since the gravitational field is infinite, acceleration is infinite. And if you've got infinite acceleration, you destroy time. Know what *that* means? Infinite acceleration means exceeding light velocity. If you do that, you have infinite mass. You're beyond the Einsteinian universe. Just think on it a moment, Fenton. Infinite acceleration, infinite mass. Space and time share the same fabric of weaving. You've utterly destroyed that fabric, so *time* is destroyed along with it. Under the infinite acceleration of a black hole, a trillionth of a second is quite the same thing as the lifetime of this entire universe. Which we've measured back to some fifteen billion years. Beyond that," Shoaf said dryly, "we're myopic and can't see."

Fenton stared at Shoaf, looked at Rudy Wells, then turned back to Shoaf. "Quite a theory."

"You miss the point, old man!" Shoaf told him with unexpected delight. "It's *not* theory. We know time is twisted so violently out of its own being that it doesn't even exist anymore. Now, why should you find it so strange that what we've *confirmed* on this enormously vast scale in deep space, this twisting of time and space, should exist to a much lesser degree right here on this planet? We are, after all, a world that is actually the densest of the entire solar system. It's like radioactivity. The sun is radioactive, and to a lesser degree, so is this planet, and to a far lesser degree, so are the three of us sitting here at this table. I daresay, Fenton, that if you had made these remarks about radioactivity, especially that of the human body, to a group of scientists a hundred or two hundred years ago, they'd have drummed us right out of town." He leaned forward and patted Fenton on the shoulder. "Bear up, old man, the reality of life is always much more staggering than the myths behind which we've hidden for so long."

Featon toyed with his food. "You know why I wanted to speak with you?"

"Oh, old Rudy here told me the basics. You're looking for a jet machine that vanished in that area known as the Bermuda Triangle, or Devil's Triangle."

"Not quite, Mr. Shoaf. It disappeared, but I'm using the term 'disappeared' in the context that we can't find it. It doesn't mean that it vanished in the sense that one instant it's here and the next instant it's gone."

Shoaf nodded affably. "I don't see why not. As good a reason as any other. It's happened before, you know."

"You *know* this to be so?"

"Absolutely. Not one little smidgen of doubt."

"But it's not the sort of thing," Fenton protested, "you can prove, is it?"

"Careful," Rudy Wells warned Fenton. "You're stepping right into Harry's favorite paradox. If something has vanished, you can't prove it's vanished because your only proof is negative, an absence of something. If you get it back again, then it never really vanished in the first place."

Shoaf grinned hugely at him. "Delightful, isn't it?"

"I don't find it funny at all." Fenton glowered. He shook his head. "Sorry. You were kind enough to come here at my request, and I'm being quite ungracious."

"Everybody acts the same way when facing the inexplicably explicable."

Fenton groaned inwardly. "Is there something, *anything*, on which a man can hang his hat besides this time-jump theory as determined by cesium time systems? Or even that magic warhead we've talked about?"

"Oh, certainly."

Fenton stared at him.

"At least seven different orbiting satellites," Shoaf went on with gusto, "have reported unexplainable—unexplainable by so-called normal standards—variations in their measurements of the magnetic and gravitational fields of the earth. The kind that can't be explained by mascons or subsurface rock masses; the sort of thing we found on the moon and on Mars. The robot stations the Apollo astronauts left on the moon are powered by radioactive isotopes: they have been performing splendidly, by the way, and—"

"He helped design them," Wells interjected.

"Tut-tut. Child's play. Anyway, the robot sites have also sent in reports of unexpected, um, call them surges, for want of a better term . . . unexpected surges in the gravitational constant of the moon. At first we thought it was instrument or transmission error, or even problems with the telemetry printout systems. We ran computer checks and discovered that these surges seemed to match, as closely as the instruments could tell us, the time jumps indicated by our cesium systems on Kwajalein and other sites. There were so many connecting factors, Mr. Fenton, we simply couldn't ignore them any longer. Nothing we'd ever known in the past could explain what was going on. Then we ran more checks, especially with the three Skylab crews. They came up with variations in gravitational constant represented by waves or surges. And those times corresponded with the findings of the cesium timing systems. As you know, the case of the Minuteman warhead, when we could obtain exact time measurements, matched precisely a three-day time jump as measured with the cesium systems."

Fenton gritted his teeth. "If only I could bend that sort of information to the Devil's Triangle, I—"

"Oh, but you can."

Fenton stared. Again.

"I've already done a bit of that for you. When Superstitch called and let me know generally what you were after, I decided to do some computer check-outs. This was for the period of those three days when that warhead was distorted, um, elsewhere or elsewhen or whatever. During that time, Fenton, four aircraft vanished without rhyme or reason within the area bounded by the Devil's Triangle. A Cessna 310 with a pilot of more than nineteen thousand hours' experience. A Bonanza, a Navaho, and a Heron flying out of the Bahamas. Needless to say, nothing was ever heard from these aircraft or their people, not then, and not since. So there is definitely a tie-in."

"But the warhead reappeared, you said."

"Most certainly it did. Coming down full tilt, too."

"But not the planes. Why?"

"An excellent question, Fenton. I wish I knew."

"Would you offer a theory?"

"I *have* a theory. Rather ghostly, though, and you might not like it."

"You've already wiped out my dinner. Go ahead."

Shoaf shrugged. "During the Battle of Britain in World War II, I was an observer for the Army Air Corps in England. You know, boning up on battle tactics under realistic conditions, that sort of thing. I was spending some time with a Hurricane outfit. They'd had a bit much of it, going after large formations of Heinkels, while the Spits had their fun with the German fighters. One night, at the local bar, I saw that everyone was subdued, talking in low tones. Didn't seem right, since they'd clobbered more than their share that day, and their own losses were minimal. I sort of drifted into the conversation. And I found that all the men of two flights had witnessed an incident so bizarre they refused to tell the story out of their own squadron. The long and short of it, Fenton, is that these men had seen an SE-5 in formation with them."

"An SE-5?" Fenton's voice seemed to echo.

"Precisely."

"But that's a World War I fighter! Fabric-covered, a biplane!"

"Precisely."

"It couldn't stay in the air with Hurricanes!"

"Of course not." A momentary pause. "But it *did.* It not only kept up with the Hurricanes as they climbed out to meet the Heinkels, it sped before the fighter formation, firing full blast at the enemy. It roared into their formation, directly into their midst, wrecking the tight defensive fire just before the Hurricanes hit."

"And you believed this?" Fenton was incredulous and showed it.

"I believed those men," Shoaf said quietly. "They were young, smart, courageous pilots. They knew what they were about. And this wasn't the first time they'd seen this SE-5. For that matter, it's not the only case of airplanes showing up when we *know* they couldn't have been in the air for twenty or thirty years or more."

Fenton pushed away his food. "You are telling me, in effect, if not directly, that those aircraft were involved in some sort of time jump. And that ever since, they've been slipping in and out of the reality we call *our* world."

"A good summation, I'd say."

"That's the craziest thing I've ever heard! According to what you're saying, that Gulfstream would be flying right now in some sort of limbo created by a time jump?"

"Yes."

"There's no way I could believe—"

Shoaf leaned forward. "Look, Fenton, haven't you ever heard of the *Flying Dutchman*?"

Chapter 19

That tore it for him. Dale Fenton could live with a great many things, but when he was asked to accept as factual a modern-day version of a ghost ship condemned forever to sail the foggy seas of the earth, caught in a web of time slipped a fraction of a second, that was *too* much.

This whole thing was completely out of hand now. Whatever scientists and doctors and anyone else thought, reality was something other than a peek into never-never land. Or limbo, or whatever they called the damned place. Fenton wasn't hidebound enough to close his mind to the things Harry Shoaf had told him about time distortion on neutron stars. But that was so far a cry from the reality of being here on earth that it just didn't and couldn't figure into his own work.

He shook his head and grinned to himself. The strange part of the matter was that if Harry Shoaf could *prove* what he had expounded so eloquently, it would be to the benefit of Sierra Insurance. Hell, the best possible thing Fenton could do was to drag Shoaf into a courtroom and get the court to accept as reality what Harry Shoaf expostulated. Because on that basis—and it would be a very real one—they would be proving that the Gulfstream and its passengers had suffered no damage, no injuries, and were really doing very well, thank you.

They were just elsewhen.

He called Carruthers and asked him to take up residence in Orlando for a while. It was time to crack down, to end this nonsense before the deal got so far out of hand there wouldn't be anything left for them to handle.

They met with the attorneys for Sierra Insurance, putting all their power into the move to snare Maynard. The Justice Department and the SEC investigation teams wanted another four days to wrap up their loose ends. The affair would be handled on the federal level, with the state of Florida coming in behind for charges of crimes committed within its jurisdiction.

At this point Fenton stepped down from running the show. The lawyers were now at the helm. From now on, gratefully, Fenton'd be in the backwash, involved only when called to present evidence, accumulated information.

Charles Maynard was arrested and charged with multiple counts of murder, conspiracy, aircraft destruction, illegal stock manipulation, and eighty-seven separate other counts. It took nearly an hour simply to read them all.

To Fenton's surprise, and no small pleasure, they were in trial before five weeks passed. The government was anxious to press forward, and Maynard's lawyers, insisting upon their client's complete innocence, had no reason to delay.

Ted Dickinson turned state's evidence to save himself a life behind bars. With Ferguson dead, the government agreed to drop all charges against him. Fenton bristled at that, and his reaction was mild compared to that of Mike Stevens, but they both saw the necessity for the move. Dickinson was the only witness directly involved in the physical mechanics of trying to kill another human being. Even with Ferguson dead, his testimony provided an invaluable link to the raising of high prison bars around Maynard.

The meticulous preparations of Fenton and his team did the rest. They had woven a brilliant web of circumstantial evidence. It wasn't necessary to prove the actual destruction of the aircraft. Conspiracy was enough, and the evidence in that category was damning.

They were near the end of the trial when the world fell on Dale Fenton.

It came in the form of a telephone call. Direct from Nassau to his office, transferred to the federal courthouse in Orlando. Whoever was on the other end of the line was willing to wait. Fenton finally got the call.

"Fenton? Tim Haggerty here. From the Bahamas Ministry of Tourism."

"What is it, Tim?"

"I hope you're sitting down. Someone's seen that missing Gulfstream of yours."

Jesus Christ! Not some more of this shit!

Guarding his tone: "Where, Tim?"

"On the ground, right here at Nassau Airport."

Fenton left Herb Carruthers to deal with the company attorneys and get a recess of several days. With Mick Satterly and Jill Peck he flew the Lear jet to Nassau International Airport in the Bahamas, where Tim Haggerty was to meet him at customs.

In another aircraft behind them, but delayed by several hours, were members of the legal staff for Charles Maynard. Still another group, relegated to commercial-airline schedules, was made up by members of the prosecutor's office.

They were all after the same thing. To talk with the witnesses who claimed to have seen Triple-Six Delta. On the ground, for God's sake.

Fenton found himself running through one mental false start after another, edgy with himself, trying to anticipate what he would encounter, and at the same time cursing himself for a runaway imagination. Fortunately, the Lear jet chewed up miles with satisfying speed, and before Fenton could tie his mental lines into knots, they were on the ground.

Tim Haggerty, bless his shanty Irish soul, had acted for Fenton as if following specific requests. There were three people who had seen—or who *said* they had seen—the Gulfstream II with the identification on the airplane reading 666D.

Two women and one man. Joseph Green, pilot, restaurant owner in Miami Beach. Experienced pilot, at that. Korean veteran of flying T-6 spotter planes in the front lines. Jovial, well-heeled, not a gripe in the world. In his fifties, in Nassau for a weekend of pleasure with the two women. Sarah Green, his wife. Typical. Fortyish, stout, enjoying her husband being well-heeled. Intelligent, pleasant. Her sister, Frances Goldstein. Much like Sarah Green. They'd flown together often.

Fenton needed certain baseline data about these people. What he learned disturbed him. They were as solid a section of upper-middle-class America as you could expect to find, and Joe Green was current with his commercial, multiengine, and instrument tickets.

In short, a qualified observer. Who had the number of the Gulfstream down pat. Who knew a Gulfstream I from a Gulfstream II, and a Lear jet from a Citation—in short, a man who knew his airplanes. Who had remained at the Nassau airport, in an office of Bahamian Airways that Tim Haggerty had commandeered, only because a complete stranger—Haggerty—had asked him to wait until Dale Fenton could arrive. Pleasant and gregarious was Mr. Green. Except that he took an instant dislike to Dale Fenton.

Fenton knew it and couldn't blame the man. Fenton had come on like gangbusters; instead of talking with Joseph Green, he started out by grilling him. It was Fenton's own unease and patience worn to a thin membrane, but Green couldn't know this, of course, and he damned well didn't like it. Fenton apologized, more than once, and thanked his private stars that Green seemed to understand after the third apology. Anyway, he hung in, and he took the questions.

"When did you see the airplane? The one you identified as Grumman Triple-Six Delta?"

"Early this morning."

"Can you recall the time, Mr. Green?"

"It was early. Early is when even a third cup of coffee won't wake you up, if you know what I mean."

"Yes, sir, I understand, but could you give me some time block? Before ten this morning, or . . . ?"

"Oh, no. Earlier. Sometime after seven. I like to fly early so I can get in a day at the shop. But we didn't take off for a while, I mean, like I had planned, because of the weather." Joseph Green shook his head. "I've flown in enough weather to last me the rest of my life. I'm not so much in a hurry I couldn't wait around for a while. In fact, that's how I met your Mr. Haggerty. Delightful man. I told him, he's ever in Miami Beach, to be sure and come in to see me."

"Yes, and I'm grateful for your talking with him. What type aircraft do you fly, sir?"

"Economical and safe, what else? A Twin Comanche. Without the turbocharging. That high I don't need to fly."

"Do you remember where you saw the aircraft? Triple-Six Delta?"

"It was parked at the end of the flight line. Of that I'm positive. It was the last airplane in line. It was raining at the time. And I remember I thought the whole thing was funny, you know? Not funny-funny, but funny-strange."

"I know what you mean. Please tell me what you saw."

Joseph Green scratched his balding head. "I was going out to my plane to get some charts. Like I said, we were ready to fly back to Miami, but with the rain . . ." He shrugged. "Better to sit here on the ground than sit up there doing racetrack patterns waiting to land. It's not so far that I would gain any time."

"I agree."

"Anyway, I remember going out to my Twin Comanche—you can see it from the window over there, it's red and white, with a yellow stripe—well, when I went to my airplane, I remember distinctly I didn't see any Gulfstream. An airplane like that, Mr. Fenton, it catches my attention. It's a beautiful airplane, too expensive for what I can afford, but I would love to fly it. This is important, because I was the fifth airplane from the end of the line. I remember noticing that. Four other airplanes, all twin-engine. In order, going away from me, there was an Aztec, a 310, a Queen Air, and one of them you don't see much anymore, a Twin Navion."

Goddamn, the man knew what he was seeing, and he had a memory for detail.

"So, you understand, I knew what was there. Anyway, I was in my airplane, it was starting to rain hard, and I figured I'd sit in there for a while till it let up. I was there maybe, oh, ten minutes or so, maybe a little less. *This*, Mr. Fenton, is what is important. And funny-strange, like I told you."

"Yes, sir."

"I didn't hear anything taxi by me, and any airplane to reach the end of the line would have to do that." Joseph Green looked up with a round, smiling face, but his eyes were sharp and clear. "I mean, the flight line ends there. It's all bad ground the other side of the flight line, where no pilot would taxi his airplane. It would damage it. So you understand, once again, ten minutes maybe I'm in my airplane, and nothing goes by me.

"The rain gets easier, and I climb out and stand up on the wing, and just looking, a glance, really, and there was this jet! You can't forget such a ship, it's a beauty, and besides, it was like attracting attention."

"In what way, Mr. Green?"

"The landing lights were on. *Bright*. In fact, everything was on. Landing lights, position lights, strobes top and bottom. I could even see the windows of the cabin; they were lit up also. And this surprised me, too, because those lights, they reflect, they would have reflected off my airplane, the windshield, other things, and I never saw that."

"You said the airplane would have to taxi past you to get to the end of the flight line, right?"

"Yes."

"You also said you didn't hear it, if I remember."

"That was the strangest of all. Two powerful jet engines. How could I not hear it? I had the small vent window by the pilot's seat open so it shouldn't fog up in there on me, and I could hear other things. But a jet like that I can't hear. That's crazy. I don't see it, and I don't hear it come past me, but I get up and stand on the wing of my airplane, and I *see* it. That I know for sure. It's there."

Fenton shook his head slowly. "Was it parked in line, like the other aircraft?"

"Almost. A different angle, but not much. And it was higher than the other planes, which is how I saw the numbers."

"You're absolutely sure of that, Mr. Green?"

"The glasses don't make me see worse Mr. Fenton. It's twenty-twenty I got. Commercial physical every year. Fit as a fiddle. I *know* what I'm looking at. Three sixes and the letter D. In bright gold." He held up a hand. "In fact, in bright gold with black borders on the numbers and the letter."

Those were the colors, Fenton reminded himself.

"What's so strange, Mr. Fenton, about this particular airplane?"

Fenton looked straight at Joseph Green. "It disappeared several months ago."

"So what's the fuss? It ain't disappeared no more."

"It's not out there right now, Mr. Green."

"So it came in quiet, and it went out quiet." Green looked up as his wife and sister-in-law approached and took seats by them. "That airplane we saw this morning," he told the women, "it's a wanderer. Disappears and appears, this fellow tells me."

Fenton gritted his teeth. "You, ah, Mrs. Green and . . ."

"Frances Goldstein. Nice to meet you."

"You also saw this airplane? The Gulfstream?"

"Saw it?" Mrs. Green laughed heartily. "I remember telling Frances how nice it would be if we could afford one like that. Until my husband tells me it costs more than three million dollars. A little out of our line, I'm afraid."

Fenton didn't know what else to ask these people. He'd taped the entire conversation with the unit built into his attaché case. The conversation was wild and impossible. "It came in quiet, and it went out quiet." Jesus Christ.

Fenton was building himself into a fine rage. But he had other work to do. Mick Satterly and Jill Peck were busy talking to other people even as he met with Joseph Green. When they got it all together, they left Nassau and flew back to Orlando. Fenton locked himself into a room with the federal prosecutor, with Herb Carruthers and the insurance company's legal staff.

Four days later the trial reconvened.

Maynard's defense counsel was stunned. They had expected Sierra Insurance to do everything possible to prove that the witnesses in Nassau had actually seen and beyond all question identified Gulfstream Triple-Six Delta, and that there was no insurance case. None at all. Beginning and end of story. *Period.*

But taking that tack was, to Fenton, utterly ridiculous, and Fenton convinced Carruthers and the others not to attempt that route. He did precisely the opposite. He argued that their case was to prove conspiracy to murder, to destroy the aircraft, to kill Michael Stevens and Dale Fenton. He refused to budge from this line. Carruthers went all the way with him, and together they prevailed upon a confused prosecutor to carry on the case he'd presented before this insanity from Nassau. They put Fenton on the witness stand, and he was examined by the prosecutor for three solid hours.

Fenton had no choice but to demolish the eyewitness statements of Joseph and Sarah Green and Frances Goldstein. He, Fenton, could not argue the point that Joseph Green, standing on the wing of his Twin Comanche, saw *an* airplane at the end of the flight line that he had not seen ten minutes before. But Fenton didn't care to argue the point. What he did present from the witness stand, and counsel hammered to the jury, was that the identification made by Joseph Green was absolutely and unquestionably *wrong.*

Fenton didn't know and didn't care what they saw, because it could not have been Grumman Gulfstream II 666D. He had brought the necessary records and transcripts of statements into the courtroom for the prosecution.

Fenton had all the records of Nassau Radar Approach Control. He had every record of the personnel in the tower. He had detailed transcripts of the people in Ground Control. He had sworn statements from every one of them.

No Gulfstream II was on Nassau International Airport at the time Joseph Green insisted he saw Triple-Six Delta on the flight line.

Radar Approach had worked no such aircraft or any similar type of aircraft that entire morning.

The tower had no records of a Gulfstream jet.

Nor did Ground Control.

Customs knew nothing of such a machine.

There had been no requests for fuel or other service from flight-line transient service.

No flight plan of any kind with that number existed.

No one from the airplane was seen or noticed at the airport by anyone on the ground.

Dale Fenton made it clear that he didn't give a damn what Joseph Green saw or didn't see at Nassau International Airport. Because the airplane wasn't on the field that day.

If it had been there, *it had never taken off and still had to be there.* Because not only was there no trace of Triple-Six Delta's landing at Nassau, and no record of the airplane ever having been there, there wasn't a shred of evidence on the part of Ground Control, the tower, or departure radar *of its ever having left the ground.*

There was not even a whisper of a possibility that the airplane or its occupants still existed.

The jury weighed the painstakingly accumulated evidence and the sworn testimony of Ted Dickinson, and so it ruled.

Conspiracy to commit murder. To destroy the aircraft. The reports of stock manipulations as gathered by the SEC. The financial hole into which Charles Maynard had dug himself.

Guilty.

Chapter 20

Dale Fenton felt drained of every last atom of energy. It had been the most taxing, incredible, mind-bending case of his career.

Herbert Carruthers was jubilant to the point of hysteria. Sierra Insurance paid off one million dollars on the loss of life of Rena Kim Maynard. That was all. Positronics, Inc., and Charles Maynard individually and collectively, were held responsible for the loss of the aircraft and the lives of the others.

Sierra Insurance was out from under. Dale Fenton had emerged nine feet tall and a yard wide, with the impossible now an accomplished fact. He had smoked out and run down a brilliantly planned and executed attempt to cash in on tens of millions of dollars through fraud and murder.

The night the jury came in with its verdict, Carruthers threw a staggering bash to which he invited the entire Heracles team. Every member of the teams assigned to Fenton found an envelope with a five-thousand-dollar-bonus check. Every secretary and clerk in the office found an envelope containing a check for a thousand dollars.

Fenton was almost too weary to join the revelry. He was just sick and tired of it all. He'd pulled off the best case of his career, his coffers were swollen from his share of the policies that had been saved, but he felt as if his batteries were going blank. And every person with him saw Fenton wince when, in any context, they used the word "time." An hour after the celebration was booming, he found himself a couch in the corner of the room and collapsed gratefully into its soft contours.

"Ashes in the mouth?" He looked up and smiled as Jill Peck took the seat by his side. She rested her hand on his knee and looked at him with a touch of sadness.

"The defense rests," he said, raising his glass. He took a long pull at his drink. It didn't do much for him.

"Boss, why don't you just get the hell out of here for a while? It's time for you to split. And don't let even your secretary know where."

"Just what I plan to do," he told her.

"Any ideas?"

"Where they got mountains, maybe. Where I can't even see an ocean if I look for a thousand miles in every direction. Oceans and beaches amid islands . . . Jesus, I've had them"—he held his fingers just above his eyes—"right up to here."

"Just go, baby," she said quietly. His eyes were troubled. She leaned over to kiss him lightly on the cheek. "Wish you were black, baby."

He looked at her with sudden surprise. "Thanks," he said, and the smile was relaxed. "I needed that."

Canada. That's where he'd go. It was late spring, and the weather would be perfect and the fishing even better. Way the hell up in the mountains, with thick green forests all about him, and the only water in lakes and streams. Where he could shut it all out of his aching skull. But he didn't want to go alone. He wanted a pretty face and a warm pliant body who could talk with him and share, but he sure as hell did *not* want any woman with him whose face he'd been seeing these past months.

Late that night, about three in the morning, he picked up his phone and punched in a number in Washington, D.C. Her name was Susan Ortega, and she had beautiful dark eyes and a body that wouldn't quit, and she'd always had this thing for joining her body to his.

"Eleven o'clock *this* morning? My God, Dale, that's only eight hours from now!"

"You've got things to do. Pack light. Bring your grungies. We're going into bear country."

Pause. Then a short, delighted laugh. "Damn you, you know I can't turn you down."

"Damned well you can't. Be at Dulles Airport at eleven. Wait for me in the business-aircraft terminal. We'll say it all then."

"See you, lover." The phone went dead on him.

He grinned to himself, stretching luxuriously. She was beautiful and from Madrid and she did things with her teeth . . . well, it had been a long time.

He passed out from exhaustion, and his answering service had to ring for five minutes before he groped for the phone and cursed himself awake. He stumbled into the shower, and when he came out, he reached greedily for the coffee and slowly rejoined the world of the living. He called Herndon Airport.

"Fenton here. Roll the Duke out for me, will you?"

The new airplane to replace the Baron. A beauty. Beech Aircraft had gone ape putting this twin together. Turbocharged and pressurized, a package of dynamite in sleekly compact lines.

At the airport he threw his bag into the back seat of the plane, then went to talk with the weather people. What he saw on the charts made him frown. There was a line of solid crap from New Orleans running east to Jacksonville. Most of Georgia and parts of South Carolina were solid. And the stuff was topping forty thousand feet. Too high for even the Duke.

But he wouldn't have to mess with the thunder bumpers. The line of storms extended out from the coast no more than fifty or a hundred miles. He'd take the Duke up to twenty-two thousand feet and do a wide end run over the Atlantic, skirting the edge of the front without ever getting into it. Beyond the Carolinas the sky was naked and clean and just made for flying. He'd bore a hole in the blue, letting down to Washington.

He thought of Susan Ortega and that luscious body as he walked back to the airplane. He fired up the engines, grinning with sheer pleasure as he heard their deep, throaty growl. Velvet, that sound was. The throbbing power soaked into his body, and he began to realize that it was *really* all over and he was free of it now, and he could feel the weight sliding from his shoulders.

He rolled out to the active, got his clearance, and turned onto the runway, feeding in the power smoothly, listening to the props winding up, listening to her sing. With only himself aboard, she was light in weight and especially alive, and when he brought her off the runway and tucked in the gear he held down the nose, giving the Duke her head, and at the end of the runway he hauled back on the yoke and went booming into the sky in a great and wondrous explosion of breaking free. He held the nose at a steep angle, the props clawing at air, dragging him higher and higher with their whirling talons of energy, and he kept her climbing that way, losing himself in the heady feeling of his flight.

Far ahead of him, closing swiftly with the headlong rush of speed the Duke gave him, he saw the ramparts of the great storm front. He grinned at it when the first wisps of cloud moved past him by his left. The storm had pushed farther out to sea than weather predicted, but it didn't matter, because it wasn't solid here, and the great thunderstorms reared high in loose ranks, with canyons and crevices and valleys carved between their enormous flanks. He was a mote swimming in a world of giants, but they were chained to earth and he was free, and he laughed aloud to himself as he slid close by the looming walls that stretched to more than eight miles above the surface of the world.

He glanced at the altimeter. He was climbing through seventeen thousand, and damn, it was beautiful. The sun cast its enormous light pillars from the east, and he saw his shadow flit in phantom fashion against the closer clouds. Blinding white and dark grays and deep brooding shadows, granite-cloud they were, magnificent in their power and their glory.

Oh, Jesus, how he'd needed this, too. It was marvelous, a magnificent panorama of sun-washed wonder, and then he was slipping between the cloud mountains, gently turning and twisting between the marching storms, sliding through and about the battlements, flashing by sudden rainbows, whipping through the edges of the great cumulus, feeling the Duke tremble with the unseen touches of troubled air, flashing into and out of sun and shadow, and he rolled the yoke gently beneath one hand to climb alongside a looming mountain of white and . . .

Good God!

For the first time ever in his life, Dale Fenton

could hear time grinding nearly to a halt, slowing its tumultuous rush into the future. He could feel the fabric of time tearing, breaking up, dragging itself along as if possessed suddenly with some imponderable and impossible mass. He moved with frantic desperation, and he had the yoke moving beneath both hands now, and the rudder pedal beneath one foot was hammered to the floorboard, but it was all happening with such agonizing, dragging slowness! The ultimate of slow motion, so that despite everything taking place with its terrifying speed, it all happened to him with a split-second that was an infinity of time. He had enough time to live a hundred lifespans before his eyes, and perhaps, somewhere in a corner of his mind, that may have happened, but the very fiber of his being concentrated on that beautiful swept-wing shape emerging, seeming to flicker into existence, as if by magic, from the cloud before him.

Instinct moved his arms and legs, so that the Duke screamed into the beginning of a wicked, clawing turn, punishing him with the force of the maneuver. Yet it all seemed so slow and so lazy, and he had all the time in the world to see the Gulfstream, the impossible machine expanding before his eyes on its converging course, the big gold-and-black "666D" on the side of the fuselage starkly clear, shocking, unmistakable, as the Gulfstream came around in a steepening bank, tightening its turn, turning into him.

Then there was no more time for him to move the controls, and the airplane with the gold-and-black numbers on its side expanded faster and faster until it filled the whole world before his eyes, and then he was left with but an instant, no more than that instant of total clarity and understanding, and the two machines came together in that final and terrible embrace, and a great and ultimate gout of flame speared the morning sky.

The fabric of time tore apart, and it came together.

Far, far below, people on a beach heard the thin slap of thunder. They looked up and saw shiny, fluttering tinsel in the sun as the wreckage drifted back to earth.

ABOUT THE AUTHOR

Best-known as the author of the novel *Cyborg*, which was the basis for the hit TV series "The Six Million Dollar Man," Martin Caidin is an author of many talents. His novel *Marooned* inspired not only a made-for-television movie, but also the joint Soviet-American Apollo/Soyuz mission. Caidin has written some thirty other novels under various pseudonyms, as well as ninety nonfiction books. Topics have included astronautics, oceanography, flight, military history, nuclear warfare, and cybernetics and bionics. Caidin has also written screenplays, and has served on the editorial staffs of several major aviation publications.

Unlike many writers, Martin Caidin lives what he writes, and he brings his life to his writing. In addition to being a commercial pilot, he has participated in many historic aviation and space events, including the first launch of a ballistic rocket at Cape Canaveral. In the 1950's Caidin was a member of a secret team, headed by Wernher von Braun, which initiated the earliest lunar probes. Caidin is a fellow of the British Interplanetary Society, a Command Pilot of the Confederate Air Force, and a Wing Commander of the Canadian Warplane Heritage. He founded the American Astronautical Society, and is one of the very few members, since 1950, of the Cape Canaveral Missile, Range, and Space Pioneers. Caidin's other roles include flight chaplain, deputy sheriff, undercover agent, and race car driver. Because of his extraordinary range of skills, accomplishments, and participation in world events, he is greatly in demand as a speaker and consultant, as well. He lives with his wife DeeDee—who is also his literary agent—in Florida.

Distributed by Simon & Schuster
1230 Avenue of the Americas • New York, N.Y. 10020